DERVISHES DON'T DANCE

BOOK 2 OF THE VALKYRIE BESTIARY SERIES

KIM MCDOUGALL

Published by Wrongtree Press, www.WrongTreePress.com.
Cover and book design by Castelane, www.Castelane.com.
Cover art by Pamela Francescut.

Editing by Elaine Jackson.

This is a work of fiction. Names, characters, places, and incidents either are the product of the author's imagination or are used fictitiously, and any resemblance to actual persons, living or dead, business establishments, events, or locales is entirely coincidental.

Paperback ISBN: 978-1-7772144-1-8
eBook ISBN: 978-1-7772144-2-5

Version 6

FICTION / Fantasy / Urban

FICTION / Fantasy / Paranormal

About This Book

Critter wrangler rule #5: Just because something smells dead, doesn't mean it can't kill you.

Sometimes you just need to hug your dervish.

Like when he protects you from brownies.

Or goes down into the scary basement with you because he's proud to be your apprentice.

Or when he saves the world.

Kyra Greene, pest controller to the extraordinary, is back with a new adventure!

A Guardian is dead. Fae are missing. And someone has let a golem loose in town. Ride along with Kyra Greene, the only pest controller qualified to deal with the strange and wonderful creatures that come out of the shadows when magic flares.

Books by Kim McDougall

Valkyrie Bestiary Novels
Dragons Don't Eat Meat
Dervishes Don't Dance
Hell Hounds Don't Heel
Grimalkins Don't Purr
Kelpies Don't Fly
Ghouls Don't Scamper

Valkyrie Bestiary Novellas
The Last Door to Underhill
The Girl Who Cried Banshee
Three Half Goats Gruff
Oh, Come All Ye Dragons

The Hidden Coven Series:
Inborn Magic
Soothed by Magic
Trigger Magic
Bellwether Magic
Gone Magic

Writing as Eliza Crowe

The Shifted Dreams Series:
Pick Your Monster
Lost Rogues

crowd of gawkers was gathered outside the courthouse. Pushing through them made me even later. I should have canceled all my jobs that morning. Today was verdict day and my nerves were shot, so I'd focused on work. Unfortunately, my last job was chasing a family of selkies out of the water treatment plant, and I'd had to go home and change out of my wet clothes before court.

Not used to running in kitten heels, I tripped going through the door, then skidded to a stop at the line of people waiting to get through security. The lobby was packed. Humans rubbed shoulders with elves in court dress. Imps, brownies and smaller fae were only visible by the jerking movements of others as they pushed through the crowd at waist height.

The building's air conditioner couldn't keep up with the early summer heat and the gathering of bodies. My silk blouse stuck to the small of my back, and I wished I'd put my hair up in its usual braids rather than leaving it loose around my shoulders like a heavy blanket.

Jacoby stuck close to me. Since our return from Underhill, the dervish had become my sidekick, mostly because I couldn't convince him to leave me alone. At least he'd attempted to tidy up for court. The fringe of gray fur around his face was combed, and he wore new-ish short pants. I could tell because they didn't have dumpster stains on them.

The line moved slowly and my impatience blossomed. Were they sentencing Mason right now? Would he be found guilty and sent into exile?

No, they couldn't do that. Mason had been instrumental in saving

Montreal Ward from the opji invasion last month. But for many years, he'd hidden the bloodstone, an unregistered relic of incredible magic power. That directly contravened the Black Hat Act of 2038. Certain political factions, desperate to pin blame for the opji uprising on someone, had called for an investigation that led to Mason's doorstep. The bloodstone, they reasoned, was the catalyst in the whole affair. Had Mason delivered it to authorities, the rogue faction of the fae court—led by the queen's younger brother, Alvar— would never have had the impetus to start their war.

It was thin logic, but then politics rarely has anything to do with logic. The people were scared. Not since its founding had Montreal Ward been breached in such a fantastic and bloody way. Finding a scapegoat would help them sleep better at night.

The crime of hoarding unregistered and dangerous artifacts was punishable by exile to the prison island of Grandill, some fifty kilometers west of Montreal in the Inbetween. It might as well have been a death sentence.

I imagined Mason alone on the island, with Montreal's most dangerous offenders, those murderers and psychos who couldn't be held in a regular prison. He'd have to hide every day. While in stone form, he was at his most vulnerable. It wouldn't take much for one of those murderers to smash him to pieces.

Oh, gods. This was how my thoughts had gone during the whole trial that began two weeks ago. I'd barely slept since Mason had been taken into custody. They wouldn't let me see him either, and the only glimpses I had of him were from the back of the courtroom.

The line inched forward until I stood in front of an imp holding a thaumascanner to check for magic tech and weapons.

"No, weapons in the courthouse," he said when the wand beeped at my sword. My glamor couldn't fool a thaumascanner, but I couldn't leave the sword in my truck either.

"I'll check it."

The imp pointed to another kiosk. "Over there."

I gave the sword to a second imp who registered it and then tapped his widget to mine to send me the receipt. As soon as I stepped away, the sword started to whine.

My blade suffered from acute separation anxiety, worse than a toddler on its first day of preschool. And since I had blooded it, first on Joran the dragon poacher, then on a whole army of opji vampires, the sword had become more vocal.

By the time Jacoby and I reached the top of the stairs, it was screaming in silent anguish. Silent for everyone else, except a few sensitive fae who turned their heads to look for the source of the wailing. I gritted my teeth and headed for the courtroom. As I took the last aisle seat, the blade's cry faded to a petulant whine.

This is good for us, I kept thinking. *It needs to be away from me more often. Once it realizes that I always come back to get it, things will settle.* Nice thought, but I didn't believe it.

My tapping foot was too loud in the quiet courtroom.

"Shhhh!" The man sitting next to me hissed. With a tablet poised on his knee, he took notes with a stylus. His left hand held a widget high to record the proceedings. He wasn't the only journalist in the room. Reporters and spectators filled every seat.

"Sorry," I whispered. I forced my leg down with a firm hand on my knee and tried to pay attention to the droning voice of the prosecutor. Jacoby perched in the aisle beside me, wide-eyed at the court proceedings.

"Whether through gross negligence or sheer civil defiance, Henry Mason did willfully disobey the Black Hat Act of 2038 and keep a secret and dangerous artifact, known as…" The prosecutor shuffled through his papers pretending he didn't know the name of the artifact. "Ah, yes, known as a bloodstone. We have submitted to the court, the history and findings of this rare gem…"

Yada, yada, yada.

He'd said it all before. Recapping his ridiculous arguments in his closing remarks didn't make them any more valid.

I scanned the room, trying to gauge the general mood. Three judges sat at the front of the court—all of them senators. They'd brought out the big guns because of the bloodstone's link to last spring's vampire invasion.

Senator Alice Ferguson represented the human arm of the ruling triumvirate in Montreal. She was a tiny, white woman with black hair and fierce eyes. Paddy Hosay, a ruddy-faced Sidhe, was the parliament representative for the fae. The alchemist judge had me worried. Cosmo

Toutain looked nervous. Throughout the proceedings, he shot glances at Gerard Golovin, the alchemist prime minister sitting in the front row with one ankle crossed over his knee. His suitcase sat on the bench beside him, so he took up three spaces in the packed courtroom. Black hair swept back from his prominent brow. His lips were thin but always seemed wet, and he watched the proceedings with an amused smile, like we were all unruly children that he needed to indulge.

Golovin had no love for Mason, but surely, he would side with a fellow alchemist? I hoped.

I took comfort in the fact that since Montreal Ward's inauguration, only a dozen men and women had been sentenced to Grandill Island. Conviction required a unanimous vote by three judges and rarely did a judge vote against their own kind.

And what did Mason think of all these proceedings? It was hard to tell. The prosecution had fought vehemently for a daytime trial. The defense argued that Mason's affliction required the court to accommodate his schedule. In the end, the judges sided in favor of the prosecution.

Every morning, two guards wheeled Mason into court so some pencil pusher could officially mark him present. He sat in his stone form behind the defense team's table, his expression gray and bland. It was a complete farce, and I'd already lodged a formal complaint. Little good that would do Mason now.

Dutch, his faithful manservant, sat behind him in the audience seats. When I'd arrived, he'd turned and given me a brief smile, but since then, his focus had been on the proceedings.

My foot started tapping again. I couldn't help it.

From a storage room on the other side of the building, my sword wailed. I didn't know how long I could stay away before it drove me mad.

The journalist shot me another angry look and I stilled my leg.

"To compound his crimes," continued the prosecutor, "Henry Mason did willfully bring the…ah…bloodstone within the sanctity of the city's ward, thereby endangering the citizens of Montreal."

I shot to my feet.

"That's not true!"

Judge Ferguson banged a gavel.

"Miss Greene, you have been cautioned once already about interrupting these proceedings. Sit down or I will have you removed."

"But he's lying!" Maybe my sword's agitation was infecting me. Maybe I was tired of coloring within the lines. But I couldn't look at Mason's frozen face and not speak up.

"Miss Greene, I will not warn you…"

Another journalist stood up, her widget poised to record. "The daughter of Timberfoot Greenleaf should have the right to speak in any court of this city."

A murmur went through the spectators. I stared at the elfin woman with a long pink lock of hair cascading over her face. Was she serious?

Senator Paddy Hosay leaned forward to see me better. "Is this true? Are you the daughter of Timberfoot Greenleaf?"

"I am, sir." But I'd changed my name to Greene to avoid situations like these. The fae had an odd obsession with my late father, and it made me uncomfortable.

"Then you may speak," Senator Hosay said.

A dozen widgets pointed my way, waiting to record my words for posterity. My sword cried. My dervish fidgeted at my heel. I stood straighter and calmed my nerves.

"I wish it to be known for the record, that Henry Mason did not bring the bloodstone inside the ward. I did that." The crowd murmured again. "Or rather, I brought the dragon inside the ward, and he'd eaten the bloodstone." The murmurs boiled to outrage. I raised my voice to be heard over the noise. "But I did it in order to recover the bloodstone and save the innocent dragon!"

Senator Ferguson banged her gavel and the crowd quieted.

"Thank you, Miss Greene. The court will take your confession under advisement."

I sat down. The journalist beside me now sized me up with an appraising look. My foot began its tattoo again and I glared at him. He smiled and tapped his widget against mine to send his contact info to my inbox.

"I'd love to interview you for the Sunday Gazette."

"No, thanks. I'm busy."

"How about next week?"

"I'm busy then too."

The prosecutor finished his closing statement and gave the floor over to the defense. Mason's attorney was a young human woman, dark-skinned and curvy with a winning smile. She used it to good effect, beaming at the judges and the audience as she began her closing remarks.

"Ladies and gentlemen, no crime was committed here. I think we can all agree on that. The prosecution would have you believe that this bloodstone is a deadly weapon, a nuclear bomb with the timer about to run out." She chuckled. "But that simply isn't true. They have provided no evidence that this artifact is indeed dangerous. No evidence that it should fall under the jurisdiction of the Black Hat Act. No, this trial is not about the supposedly dangerous artifact. It is about assigning blame. Vampires breached our ward for the first time in fifty years. Was that frightening? Yes. Was there treason involved? Yes. But not by my client…"

A disturbance at the back of the room made me turn. The guards had opened the doors, and Leighna, Queen of the Winter Court and Prime Minister of the Triumvirate stood in the open doorway.

The Sidhe were a tall race, and Leighna usually wore her height with grace. But closing the last door between Terra and Underhill had taken a piece of her. She was still the Winter Queen, but that sagging March winter when the snowbanks are shrunken mounds of mud and slush. Since I'd last seen her, she'd cropped off most of her gorgeous silver hair. Deep creases on her cheeks made her face seem longer and tired.

She smiled at the crowd of faces, all turned to watch her walk with a slight limp up the aisle. As she passed by, I risked dropping my wards to keen her magic. It buzzed around her like a swarm of angry bees.

She nodded to counsels on both sides and frowned at Mason, but she didn't stop until she reached the panel of judges. Then she leaned in and whispered to Judge Hosay. He nodded briskly, showing no emotion, and spoke into his microphone.

"I recuse myself from these proceedings."

Then he walked out.

Leighna took his seat, and the crowd erupted with chatter, everyone trying to speculate on this new development.

Each of Montreal's founding parties—alchemists, fae, and humans—had numerous ministers and one prime minister. Prime ministers rarely attended parliament or court, preferring to leave the day-to-day running of the city to their underlings. They had the right to sit on any tribunal, but in the forty-year history of the city, this right had never been exercised.

The fact that the fae prime minister now sat in judgment at Mason's trial meant…well, I had no idea what it meant. It was unprecedented.

Judge Ferguson banged her gavel, calling for the audience to settle.

"Prime Minister Leighna Icewolf, we were just about to pass a verdict. Shall we call a recess so you can evaluate the facts of the case?"

"No need." Leighna said. "I have been following the trial."

"Very well. This panel is ready to pronounce its judgment against Henry Mason."

Mason's lawyer rose. "I object! My client has not had the opportunity to speak on his own behalf. I demand a recess until nightfall."

The prosecutor rose too. "Your honors, this objection has already been overruled. Mr. Mason's…ah…affliction…that is…I mean gargoylism is not officially recognized by the disabilities act, and so no special provisions are in order."

I ground my teeth at the unfairness of it all.

"Objection overruled again," Judge Ferguson said. "It is my conviction that Henry Mason violated the Black Hat Act of 2038 and did willfully endanger the people of this great ward. I pronounce him guilty."

The room fell silent.

Judge Toutain flicked a glance at Gerard Golovin sitting in the front row and then said, "Guilty."

My heart sank into my shoes. Everyone had counted on the alchemist judge to side with Mason. He'd just thrown one of his own to the wolves.

Judge Ferguson called for silence again. Prime Minister Leighna leaned into her microphone. "Not guilty."

Judge Ferguson banged her gavel and said, "By the authority of the Ward of Montreal, I declare Henry Mason acquitted of all charges."

Before all hell broke loose, Gerard Golovin rose and stood before the panel of judges. His expression was unreadable as he called for silence. Judge Ferguson banged her gavel several times until the crowd quieted.

"Judges, Prime Minister." Gerard nodded, giving each judge the benefit of his full attention and slick smile. "Thank you for your service. But we have one more issue to discuss. This bloodstone is still a real threat, and it currently sits in evidence lockup in this very building. By Henry Mason's own assertion, the stone cannot be destroyed. But neither can such a dangerous artifact be kept within the ward. Therefore, I offer the services of the alchemists to store it on Perrot Island, outside the ward." He raised his voice to be heard over the sudden commentary from the crowd. "Only the alchemists have the technomancy to keep it safe. I vow to protect it until such time as its magic can be neutralized. Agreed?"

Each of the judges nodded. Leighna's lips were pinched in a frown, but she agreed.

The spectators stood, everyone talking at once. Judge Ferguson's voice was drowned out as she adjourned the court. Dozens of reporters crammed widgets under the noses of the prosecutor and defense, all trying to get their sound bite for the evening news.

In all the hubbub, no one noticed Leighna sneaking out the side door.

Eventually, the lawyers were talked out. The journalists rushed off to make their deadlines. Everyone left except Mason. He was free to go, but of course, he couldn't.

Only Dutch remained, quiet and unruffled as ever. He waited for the sun to go down so he could take his captain home. One guard stood by the closed door to the judges' chambers. He nodded when I asked to stay with Mason.

I sat in the defense counsel's chair, listening to my sword wail and gripping my hands tightly in my lap.

We waited.

An hour later, Dutch said, "I'll bring the car around."

I glanced at the window. It was near dark. My nerves were shot from the constant whine of my sword.

I poked Jacoby, who had been dozing on the chair beside me and held out my finger.

"Bite me."

He squinted one eye and shook his head.

"Please. I don't have a knife. Just bite hard enough to draw blood, then take it to my sword. Go now, while Dutch is leaving and wait for me in his car. I'll be out soon."

His sharp teeth flashed for an instant and blood welled on my fingertip.

The pain followed, but I ignored that, and smeared the blood across Jacoby's hand, then gave him my widget to show the sword's receipt.

"Go now!"

He scampered away.

A few moments later, the sword's wailing dimmed to a whine as my blood comforted it.

I watched the window darken until Mason's magic rang frantically, then settled into his usual deep bell-tolling energy. He opened and closed his fists, then tilted his head from side to side. His neck cracked and he sighed.

His hair was messed as if he'd run a hand through it just before turning to stone. It fell over his forehead in thick black curls that begged to be touched.

"You look different," he said and smiled. His silver-gray eyes flashed at me, taking in my court dress and my hair hanging loose past my shoulders.

"Different? You mean I'm not covered in dirt and blood for once."

"Yes, I don't think I've ever seen you dressed up. And are those heels?" He pointed at my shoes, and I was glad they were close-toed, so he couldn't see my ragged, unpainted toenails.

"I do remember how to be a girl, once in a while."

He leaned in. "You do it well. Always."

I let the moment linger. Then I was either going to kiss him or get back to business. I chickened out and went for business.

"Did you hear everything?" I asked.

"Yes. Bloody fools. They can't keep the bloodstone safe. No one can." *Not even me*, was the unspoken end to that sentence.

"Have you been able to prove that Golovin was working with Alvar?"

Mason shook his head. "But he knows I've been sniffing around."

"Which explains why the alchemist judge threw you over."

With only the tenuous link between Gerard Golovin and the transport company used to haul Ollie and the other abused dragons, we had no proof that Gerard was in on the attempt to breach Montreal's ward last month.

No proof, but plenty of suspicions.

"There's something else." Mason spoke quietly so the guard couldn't hear. "Something I never told you about the bloodstone."

The history of the bloodstone was personal. Mason's wife had tried to murder their daughter in some dark rite. Unable to kill her, Mason had trapped Polina's essence within the bloodstone for all eternity. But it seemed at least three factions—Golovin, the opji and Prince Alvar—had their reasons to release the mad witch. The last attempt had almost brought down the ward.

I couldn't wait to hear what other goodies Mason had in store for me.

"I lost it once, during the war." He turned his head and grinned. "That would be World War Two, not the Flood Wars."

Sometimes I could forget that Mason was over three-hundred years old.

"It was a desperate time in Europe and the stone ended up in the hands of a German army doctor. It took me three decades to track it down again. I have no idea what the Nazis used it for, but when I recovered it, the stone was…heavier. Not in weight, but in magic. Do you know what I mean?"

I did. I'd held the bloodstone, a marble-sized black rock with a shot of red chalcedony streaked through it. Something that small shouldn't feel as if it carried the weight of the world, but its magic was dense. And angry. I hadn't wanted to touch it for any longer than necessary.

"I suspect the stone gathered more souls." Mason rubbed a hand through his hair. "It has a sentience of its own now. Or maybe that's Polina. She was always strong-willed. I don't know. But it *wants* to be found. They can lock it away in a vault, but someone will break it free."

"We have to find a way to destroy it."

Mason shook his head. "Not we. Me. I have to destroy it. You have to go home and hope that Hub doesn't come after you for that ridiculous confession you made in court today. What in the hells possessed you to tell them you brought not only the stone within the ward, but a dragon too?"

"I was trying to help."

"Well, you're done helping. I don't want you involved in this mess anymore. Go home, Kyra."

I met his glare with one of my own.

"You can't tell me what to do."

"I can, and I—" Shouting from outside the courtroom cut him off. I looked at the guard, who shrugged. Then came the sound of running footsteps and more shouts.

The courtroom doors opened and Dutch poked his head through.

"There's been a cave-in at the new railroad excavation site. Several workers are dead or trapped. The whole place is on fire and…" He glanced at me.

"Some kind of beast manifested in the flames. They think a ley-line was breached."

Mason's gaze hardened as he turned to me. "You're going down there, aren't you?"

"You going to try and stop me?"

"Would it work if I did?"

"Nope."

"Then I'm coming too."

2

hankfully, I had a change of clothes in my truck. My job was messy, and extra pants, shirts and shoes were often a necessity. I dressed quickly, hoping the gloom in the courthouse parking lot would cover me, and then braided my hair. No matter how pretty Mason thought it was—and I still felt a little glow from his words—it was never a good idea to go into a fight with hair flying around. At best, it could blind me. At worst, it was an easy handhold for an enemy. Jacoby politely waited outside the truck. My sword lay on the seat beside me, blissfully quiet.

"You can come in now," I called out as I slipped on my work boots. Jacoby hopped into the passenger seat without opening the door. Dervishes can teleport short distances, so I didn't bother trying to keep him away.

"If you're going to come, you follow my rules, okay?"

He stared at me with wide eyes as I started the truck and navigated out of the lot.

"You stay close and at the first sign of danger, you teleport away. Understood?" I glared down at his earnest face and he nodded.

We parked near the water between the excavation site of the new railroad and a cluster of abandoned warehouses. The parking lot was a mess of emergency vehicles and Hub officer transports. The evacuation zone was a good hike from where I parked. I grabbed my emergency pack and headed toward the fires I could see burning in the distance.

GenPort, the conglomerate spearheading the new rail system had bought all this land. The warehouses were slated to be torn down and replaced with a snazzy new train station where GenPort could charge enormous fees to passengers looking for a quick and safe way through the Inbetween to Manhattan. A similar station was being built in Manhattan Ward by a company called Mansys. The two crews would meet in the middle, sharing the expenses and profits of the new railroad.

Digging through the Inbetween was expensive in both labor and magic. Terra had reclaimed the land, the water and the air. She left humans a few small spaces to live, and if we wanted to thrive, we had to learn to do so within those limitations.

So trying to create an empire by connecting two wards…well, that was just an exercise in hubris. For the past months, as GenPort broke ground and started digging under the river and into the Inbetween, we all waited for the hammer to fall. Surely Terra would manifest her displeasure and stop this encroachment? And now it seemed she had.

Somewhere in the excavations, the digging crew had breached a ley-line. The resulting explosion of magic had collapsed the tunnel, killing or trapping a dozen workers. And something had come out of the breach. All this I learned from frantic reports on the news as I drove to the site. When I got there, the reality was much worse.

Ahead of us, smoke filled the night sky and people screamed. Something roared.

"What in the hells is that?" Mason yelled over the noise as he ran to join me.

"I don't know. Ogre, maybe? Where's Dutch?"

"Gone to get the other Guardians." Not all the gargoyles could fly. I just hoped they got here in time.

We reached the construction site as a giant creature picked up a bulldozer and chucked it into the parking lot, flattening two cars. It turned its attention to a crane and shook it like a toy. A massive metal hook hung at the end of the crane's arm, and it smashed into the side of a nearby warehouse. Debris exploded like shrapnel.

The creature—whatever it was—stood before the construction site's main office, or what was left of it. The temporary building had been crushed like a tin can. Beside it, the entrance to the tunnel that would become the new railroad was now just a pile of rubble.

All construction was stopped. The site was in shambles. Fires burned in three places. The raging beast flung bricks, shards of wood and equipment while workers in hard hats dodged these missiles and tried to pull their wounded coworkers out of the way. A group of Hub officers in tactical gear mustered next to the abandoned warehouses, but they had yet to act.

I got a good look at the creature. It was easily twenty feet tall—taller than any giant or ogre I'd ever encountered. Grayish hide and wiry black hair covered thick slabs of muscle across its shoulders. Red eyes were almost lost under its overhanging brow. Blood stained the puckered skin around its lipless mouth, which was too round and had too many teeth.

While I watched, it seized one of the scurrying construction workers in a massive fist, bit off his head and swallowed it whole, hard hat and all.

Then it grew about a foot, its shoulders bulging even bigger.

Oh no.

I ran for the group of Hub officers.

"Who's in charge?" I demanded.

"Detective Lowe." Someone pointed to a swarthy woman with dark hair cut short in a military style who was giving out rapid-fire orders. They were going to shoot the beast with a synchronized burst of multiple blasters.

"Stop!" I yelled. "You'll make it worse! That's a snooker!"

Snookers fed off magic of any kind—life magic, blaster magic, they didn't care.

"Who are you?" Lowe frowned at me.

"Kyra Greene." I flashed my Hub credentials. "I work in pest control."

Lowe folded her arms. "And what exactly is a snooker?"

"It's something that manifested from the ley-line breach. If it gets any bigger, it will replicate and we'll have the beginnings of a snooker infestation."

"Mason, do you know this woman?" Lowe's tone was clipped. I wasn't surprised that she knew Mason. As captain of the Guardians, Mason had deeper connections to Hub than I did.

"Yeah, Glenda. She's legit. I would listen to her if I were you."

Captain Lowe squinted at me. "What do you mean by replicate?"

I took a deep breath and explained.

In the early days after the Flood Wars ended, pools of magic filled the space we now call the Inbetween. These were lakes of pure magic, from ruptured ley-lines or the residue from bombs dropped during the wars. A lot of really nasty things came out of those pools. Things like the snookers that rampaged the countryside, killing to feed and sometimes just for fun.

"Snookers are born of magic and they feed on magic. When it gets big enough, this sire will split into dupes."

Lowe scowled and I rushed on. "Dupes are duplicates of itself. They'll be smaller and easier to kill, but fast and sneaky. And—"

The snooker picked up a truck and bashed it against another truck.

"Just tell me how to kill it," Lowe growled. A few other Hub officers had gathered to listen.

"Blades, not guns. In this form it will only eat the blast magic and get stronger. Cut off enough parts and it will go down."

"And if it splits into these dupes?"

"Same," I said, "but you need to kill the sire, the master copy, so to speak. Then the others will die."

"You heard her!" Lowe barked. "Blades only!"

The officers dispersed. Mason pulled me aside, and we watched the snooker grab another construction worker as he ran by in a panic. It raked the man from head to foot with dagger-like claws and let the blood spray over its face, howling in pleasure. Then it tossed the body aside. The man lay in a crumpled heap against the broken office building. I turned away from this gruesome sight.

"Are you sure about this?" Mason asked.

"As sure as I can be." My blade was already singing as I swung it slowly to loosen my shoulder.

Behind us, Hub officers were re-arming with swords, maces and spears. This wasn't their first rodeo.

Then, before everyone was in formation, a thin man with crazy hair burst out of the broken office building, screaming and pointing a blast rifle at the snooker.

"You killed him! You killed him!" The man was hysterical. Tears, dirt and blood streaked his pale face. The beast turned at the noise and the man shot it. The blaster flared and hit the snooker in the chest. It would have been a killing shot to any other being, but the snooker only grunted and got bigger.

The man shot him again.

"Someone make him stop!" Captain Lowe yelled. Four officers rushed the shooter, but it was too late. The snooker was now taller than the office building and wider across than a bus. It roared, spraying blood and spittle, and stomped a foot. The ground shook under the impact.

Then it burst, like a seedpod exploding.

Where there was one snooker, now lay dozens of smaller versions of itself, no bigger than large dogs. They scattered like the wind, some disappearing into the ruins of the construction site, others into the vast warren of abandoned warehouses that stretched along the shoreline.

"Go after them!" Lowe snapped. "Buddy formation. No one goes alone!" The officers moved out.

"We'll take a section of the warehouses," Mason said, and Lowe nodded. But before we walked away, she stopped us.

"Give me the worst-case scenario," she said.

"If we don't find the host dupe and kill it, the others will grow and eventually be able to thrive on their own. When they grow big enough, they will replicate too. We'll be facing an infestation in a few months, tops. That's how Chicago ended after the war."

Lowe looked grim. "Find it."

THE WAREHOUSE PARK was bigger than a village. When the waters receded after the wars, most of the buildings were still standing. They'd been looted for anything usable to the budding new ward, then left to ruin. In the fifty years since, they'd been bought and sold, used, burned, rebuilt and left abandoned. Now they were a cluster of dirty, half-rotten structures with a million places for a dupe to hide. Captain Lowe had efficiently sectioned off the buildings, assigning each to a pair of officers and the farthest one to us.

We skirted around the last warehouse on the east side, looking for an entrance. No matter how much I pleaded, Jacoby wouldn't wait outside. He had decided he was my protector and nothing would dissuade him.

Mason thought it was amusing. "You should get him one of your Valkyrie Pest Control shirts and make him your apprentice."

"Very funny." But really, that wasn't a bad idea. If the little dervish was going to keep putting himself in danger on my account, I should give him some training.

"Remember, stay close to me," I said to Jacoby. "But port away at the first sign of danger. Don't wait for me."

He nodded, his eyes even bigger in the gloom. We found a door that was chained shut but broken near the bottom. I melted the lock with a bit of magic pushed through my sword and we went in.

The construction site was well lit, and some of that light filtered through the bank of high windows even though they were filmed with dirt. Rows of crates lined the walls, leaving narrow aisles to walk through, except at the center of the large space, which held three antique carousels. The horses and mythical beasts on the old rides were reared up, hooves poised to run, and eyes mischievous in the shadows. We snuck past them, listening for any sound that could mean a dupe was inside with us. The wind banged a loose shingle on the roof and we all stopped. Jacoby slipped his tiny hand in mine. I squeezed his fingers once, but didn't let on that I knew he was scared. Or that I was too.

Mason motioned for me to go clockwise around the last carousel while he went the other way. I stopped halfway to peer underneath but could make out nothing in the darkness. The skin on the back of my neck tingled, as I imagined the dupe jumping out at us. He would be smaller than the sire, but he could still do a lot of damage with those claws. I reached with my keening, and felt only the tiny magics of crawling things as I moved on to join Mason at the far end of the warehouse.

We stood staring into lines of piled up crates holding abandoned goods. The warehouse was big enough that we couldn't see the far end. Many of the crates were rotted and their contents spilled out. Navigating around all this junk in the dark would be dangerous.

Something giggled. The sound was too deep and throaty to be human.

"He's taunting us," Mason said.

I nodded, then realized he couldn't see me and said, "They're crafty."

The sire had been content to bash things, but the dupes would be like mischievous kids finding their way in their new bodies and testing their limits.

A crash and the sound of breaking wood had us moving again, me with my sword ready to strike. We ran, quick and silent, along a row of crates. The cement floor gave way to old wooden planks that shifted uneasily under my feet.

Mason stopped at the end to peer around the corner. We waited in silence. Jacoby pressed against my leg. Finally, Mason gestured for us to follow.

Debris filled the aisle ahead. A pile of crates had been toppled. Broken pallets blocked the way, and something had spilled out of them—shiny globes that caught the bit of stray light from the high windows.

"What are those?" I had an unsettling feeling, like a snake was coiled around my chest and starting to squeeze.

"I don't know," Mason whispered. "But he's getting away. Careful on that board. It's unsteady." Gingerly I stepped forward. Those odd glass balls were all around us and they made me queasy.

"They're magic. I can feel it."

"Just keep going. We'll get past them," Mason said. The board under my foot tipped, and I steadied myself before putting my full weight on it.

Something hit my shoulder, knocking me back.

"There!" Mason pointed. The dupe stood on top of a crate, breaking off slats of wood and lobbing them at us. It giggled again, and the sound chilled me.

It reached into the shadows to pull at the top crate, and the whole pile came crashing down. The dupe landed on Mason. The floor gave way and they disappeared.

"Mason!" The boards under my feet broke apart and I tumbled into darkness. Above me, the world exploded with magic. My psychic wards were shredded and my keening went into overload. Even before I hit the ground, a seizure took me.

3

My neck was bent at an odd angle and my head pounded as it dangled over someone's arm. Mason. He was carrying me. The swaying motion brought the contents of my stomach up to my throat, and I begged him to put me down.

As soon as I hit the ground, I rolled over and vomited. Sharp stones dug into my palms and my arms shook under my weight. A scuffling sound startled me. I tried to pinpoint the noise, but the darkness and pain were disorienting. I might have blacked out again.

Something tugged at my shoulders. Hands prodded me, pulling the pack from my back.

"Mason?" My voice quavered like an old woman's.

"Dammit, Kyra! All this stuff, and you don't have a flashlight!" He was digging through the pack, his tone gruff with alarm. Then a bright shaft of light sliced across my eyes. I knocked Mason's hand aside and groaned. Even that tiny movement was too much. I rolled and dry-heaved in the shadows again. My stomach had nothing left to offer.

Mason dropped the flashlight and held me while I shook with spasms. My hair had come loose, and he tucked it behind my ear. Then he touched my cheek with one finger, wiping away the gravel stuck to the fine sheen of sweat on my skin. I turned and leaned heavily on his shoulder.

"How long was I out?"

"Just a few minutes. Long enough for the dust to settle and for me to get you away. Why aren't you wearing that null bracelet I made you?"

"Didn't expect…" I took a deep breath and steadied my shaking nerves. "Didn't expect to be assaulted today." Then another thought froze me. "Jacoby?"

"He's gone. Must have ported away."

My throat ached. My joints throbbed. Mason touched my shoulder as if he didn't know what else to do. He handed me a bottle of water. I sat up and washed out my mouth before drinking down a big gulp.

I'd had seizures before, mostly in the early days of my keening, when I hadn't yet learned to set effective wards. I knew what to look for. Dizziness. Check. Bruises. Check. And the acid burn of vomit in my throat. Perfect.

"Why do you always get to see me covered in dirt, blood or vomit?" I asked.

"Don't forget green slime."

I sagged against him. I had nothing left.

"Just once I'd like to show off to my best affect. Maybe in a dress…"

"Sounds like a date. I don't date."

"Me neither. But just once…"

My eyes closed. Mason eased me down and arranged my head on his lap.

"Just take it easy," he said. "We're safe for the moment."

We sat in the near darkness. His heart beat against my ear. As usual, it tolled slow and steady, but my senses picked up something else going on inside him. A restlessness that would be hidden to anyone else. He sat against a cement wall, eyes closed, limbs still. Magic fluttered around him in anticipation…of what?

"Is it near dawn," I asked.

"No."

So he wasn't about to go all granite on me.

"Do you think we're trapped?" I said.

"No."

"We should try to get out of here."

"Yes."

He was going to mono-syllable me to death in payment for barfing on his shoes.

I sat up and drank more water.

"Is something wrong? I mean other than the murderous snooker hiding somewhere in here with us and you having to save the useless damsel in distress?"

"You're not useless," he said. "But yes, there is more going on here. That explosion? They were magic flash-bombs."

"But those were outlawed after the war."

"Outlawed but not destroyed." In the dim light, he looked even grimmer than usual.

Flash-bombs had been favorite weapons between warring city-states in the aftermath of the Flood Wars. They disrupted electricity and created pockets of rogue magic that were as unpredictable as they were dangerous. Alchemists still debated if magic bombs had been the catalyst that breached the ley-line, waking Terra. Or had Terra woken on her own and created the magic that allowed humans to make the bombs? It was a chicken or the egg argument that no one would ever solve. But the snooker dupe had just set off a crate-load of those bombs over our heads.

"The magic down here is erratic. It's affecting me in ways I can't explain," Mason said.

"Where exactly are we?"

"Under the warehouse, I guess. There's a hallway over there. We should follow it."

A scraping noise echoed through the cavern. It stopped, then started, stopped, and started again. Someone carrying a heavy burden was heading our way.

Mason rose, knife already out to face whatever was coming.

Scrape, scrape. Silence. Scrape, scrape. Silence.

He muffled the flashlight with his shirt, and darkness fell on us again.

Scrape, scrape. Silence.

The sound raked my frail nerves.

Scrape, scrape. Silence.

Mason whipped around and shone the light right in Jacoby's face. The dervish dropped my sword, screamed and disappeared.

Poor Jacoby.

I rose on unsteady legs and recovered my sword. The magic blast had really unsettled me. I hadn't even noticed it was missing.

"Can you walk?" Mason asked. "I want to get out of this place. The magic makes my skin itch."

Two hallways led away from the cavernous basement. Jacoby had come down the one to the left, but as we turned toward it, I heard that unearthly giggle from the other direction. The dupe had already dug its way out of the debris. We still had a job to do.

"Did he get dosed by the flash-bombs," I asked. That much magic could have forced a growth spurt on the dupe. We could be dealing with a full grown snooker again.

Mason shook his head. "I don't think so. We got hit with just the tail end of the blast."

Gods, if that was enough to send me into a seizure, I never wanted to be caught at ground zero for one of those bombs.

The dupe giggled again, taunting us to come for it in the darkness.

"Should we stay and fight it?" I really didn't want to. My muscles ached from the seizure.

"No. We need backup. Who knows how big that thing is now. Let's find a way to the surface."

We followed the hallway where we'd last seen Jacoby. It started off wide enough for us to walk side by side, but soon it narrowed and the cement walls gave way to rough-hewn rock. We continued single file and Mason had to stoop so he didn't scrape his head. The flashlight dimmed as the batteries wore out. We stopped while I scrounged in my bag for the gleam Mason had given me after our trip to the Inbetween. The silence was absolute. No city sounds reached down this far. We were completely cut off, alone, wedged in a tunnel that would come out who-knows-where with only the anemic flicker of a dying flashlight for comfort.

Just as panic won out, my fingers closed over the orb. I shook it, filling the tunnel with light. The gleam needed recharging from a ley-line, but in that absolute darkness, its dim glow was like a beacon.

After a deep breath to calm my nerves, we moved on. The path continued to narrow until I sucked in my chest to push past it. Mason must have nearly suffocated to get through, but he did it with only a grunt. On the other side, we came out to another long hallway with offshoots every few hundred feet. We walked quickly, looking for stairs back to the surface.

"Do you think these tunnels run under all the warehouses?" I asked.

"Probably. A lot of smuggling went on here in the early days of Montreal Ward. We'll come out at Old Port eventually."

Each time we came to another branch in the hall, we looked for a staircase, but found only more hallways. We took turns at random, having no idea where we were or how to get out of this dark maze. The pale light from the gleam did nothing to improve the decor. Trash littered the ground—plastic bags that had been banned in Montreal for over thirty years, old needles, broken bottles. Rodents rustled under the garbage. Now and then, the light caught their shining eyes. The graffiti-covered walls were made of chipped cement that held in the reek of urine and rot. We walked in and out of stagnant pools of magic. Each one felt like smog in my chest and oil on my skin. Either this place was a natural hotbed of magic or the ruptured ley-line that produced the snooker had flooded these tunnels.

Mason lagged behind me with unfocused eyes. He trailed one hand along the wall for support.

We stopped to catch our breath and take a sip of water.

"Are you all right?" I braced him as he stumbled into me, though I wasn't much steadier on my feet. A sheen of sweat covered his forehead and the crease between his eyes deepened.

"I don't feel right. Something's forcing me to turn." He rubbed the nape of his neck. "If I go to stone down here, I might never turn back." His voice seemed detached, like it came from somewhere far away.

"You don't seem too upset by that idea."

"It is what it is. I only want to be sure you get out." He motioned that we should continue walking. I was lost in the dark with a fatalistic gargoyle. My night just kept getting better.

I'd already checked my widget, but the flash-bomb had fried it. I couldn't even tell the time, but I guessed we'd been down here about an hour. It had to be near midnight.

We walked on through the unending darkness, with only the gleam to lead us. Jacoby didn't return, and I hoped he got out safely.

The tunnels became broader and more modern. We passed an old elevator cage and considered climbing the shaft. But staring up into the dark duct, I didn't have a good feeling. Broken cables hung from rusted struts. No telling how solid the structure was or even if it opened at the top.

"Let's continue," Mason said. "We'll come back if we don't find another way out."

I nodded. I had no heart left for arguing.

Several times, my regenerating wards shuddered as I stepped into pools of latent magic. These tunnels were a spell-caster's dream. So much untapped power. But I had no idea what to do with it. I could only feel it, like walking through waves of water that broke around me as I passed.

At one juncture in the never-ending tunnel, the air shimmered like a mirage. I stepped through a heavy fog of magic and turned to find Mason standing just beyond it.

"I don't think I should walk through that." He pointed to the shimmering spot of air. "Something keeps trying to force my change. That might do it."

"We go back then," I said without hesitation. We headed back down the tunnel and turned at the first branch. One turn was as good as another now.

Something skittered up ahead. I stopped. Not that I was afraid of whatever critters might be hiding down there. Bugs and rodents were my job, after all. But with stray magic flying around, rats and cockroaches could turn into something much worse.

I unsheathed my sword. Another light rap sounded ahead, like feet across a hard floor.

"Something's up there," I whispered.

"It was following us," Mason's dark eyes pierced the shadows. "It got ahead when we turned around."

We moved slower, stopping to listen every few steps. The cement walls were damp and somewhere up ahead, water dripped in a slow tap-tap-tap. Mason covered my shoulder with his hand as he walked behind me. I wasn't sure if the touch was meant to steady him or me.

A shadow flitted across the green light, and a clattering sound was followed by an eerie giggle.

The dupe dropped from the ceiling right in front of us.

4

He lunged. Pain lanced my shoulder, and I screamed as a claw bit deep. Mason punched him in the face and the dupe fell back. He opened his mouth to show off rings of sharp teeth and laughed again. In the faint light, his leering grin was hideous. He was bigger than the last time we saw him, but still no bigger than a man. In this smaller form, the snooker was more human like, but that only made the aberrations more disturbing—the extra teeth, the freakishly long arms that let fingers trail on the ground, the deep set yellow eyes, filled with madness.

I pushed Mason behind me. Armed with only a knife, he didn't stand a chance against the snooker. My sword was already out and primed by the magic all around us.

The snooker howled and threw himself at me. I barely lifted my arm before he was impaled on the end of my sword. The blade pierced his shoulder, but the momentum threw us both against the wall. He snapped his jaws at me and grinned. Then he grabbed the hilt of my sword, yanked the blade from his wounded shoulder and tossed it into the darkness.

He opened his mouth wide, and a double row of massive teeth filled my field of vision. A sound, halfway between laugh and cry, warbled from his throat.

"Gods, you stink." I kicked him in the stomach.

The dupe doubled over and Mason tackled him. They slammed into the wall. Mason had the upper hand only for a moment. He stabbed the dupe in the gut, but the creature took the hit with a grin. Only thin lines of dark blood leaked from his wounds. His long arms reached around Mason and squeezed. Mason grunted and his face turned red.

I scrambled through my bag, looking for a weapon. Knives would be useless against the dupe until I could get it away from Mason. I needed time to find my sword so I could cut his gods-damned head off. My hand closed around the handle of a small gun. Excellent.

I yanked out the taser, pressed it to the side of the dupe's head and pulled the trigger. He spasmed and released Mason, who dropped to the floor with a thud. The dupe stood to his full height and stretched. He grew again and now stood at least eight feet tall.

"What did you do?" Mason coughed and rose on hands and knees.

"I had to make him let go. He was choking you!"

We both scrambled backward as the dupe shook out his arms and legs, adjusting to his new growth. He leaned forward and roared.

"By the One-eyed God, that's disgusting." I covered my nose with an elbow, looking around for my sword. Mason grabbed me, pulling backward, but we had no more room. Our backs pressed against a wall.

The dupe charged. Mason pushed me aside and shoved his arm into the beast's mouth. Teeth cracked on stone. The dupe gurgled out a scream of pain, but didn't let go.

I'd seen Mason turn just one arm to stone before. The effort was costing him though, and sweat streamed down his face. Mason punched him with his other hand. I regained my wits, found my small utility blade and drove it into the dupe's throat. Blood spattered, but the stinking beast held on, the three of us locked in a morbid dance.

Then there was a tiny pop in the surrounding magic, and the dupe disappeared, leaving only his stench and flecks of blood on our clothes.

"What the..." Mason stumbled back. His arm slowly changed back to flesh. "Where did he go? Did you kill him?"

"No. It was a dupe. Someone up top must have killed the sire. They're still linked at this stage. Kill that one, kill them all."

I hung onto Mason's shoulders, panting with the rush of the short, brutal fight.

"So that's it?" he asked. "We can get out of here now?"

"Kind of anticlimactic after all that, isn't it?" I leaned my head against his collarbone and breathed him in.

"Yeah, I feel cheated, like a hyena who's just had his kill taken by a lion."

"That's why I love you. You remember lions." I tensed as soon as the words came out of my mouth. What in the hells was I thinking?

After a moment, we broke apart. He watched me with dark, unfathomable eyes. His gaze drifted down my face and snagged on my lips, then he stepped away.

"I hope you have some antiseptic in that pack. Your shoulder is bleeding, and who knows what was on those claws."

And just like that, we were back to the efficient but cold version of Henry Mason.

We met Angus and a couple of other Guardians as we left the warehouse. Mason spoke to them quietly, and they headed back inside the building. We went on to find Captain Lowe.

I let Mason fill her in and found a quiet spot to rest. My head still spun from the flash bomb, and my many bruises started to make themselves known. I crumpled to the ground at the edge of the parking lot where the gravel met grass. Hub trucks lit the scene in stark white light that hurt my eyes. Officers had cordoned off the site, but a crowd had already gathered to watch paramedics load bodies into ambulances.

It was hot, even for June, with that muggy air that hinted at rain. Sweat mingled with the blood and dirt on my face and dripped under my collar. A hub tech came by and gave me a bottle of water. I drank most of it and then splashed my face with the rest.

In front of me, a large slug oozed across the gravel. The humidity had made him optimistic that he could cover the expanse of the parking lot before drying up. He wasn't going to make it.

I plucked him off the gravel and dropped him into a patch of weeds and grass on the edge of the lot. I looked up at the sound of feet coming across the gravel.

"Did you just save a slug?" Mason asked.

"Uh-huh."

"Of course you did."

"I sure hope that's not a smirk I see on your face."

"No, ma'am. Never. And not after that fight. You were amazing."

"Yep, I'm a killer with a taser."

"Not that."

"Oh, you mean when I threw up in the dark."

He pinched the skin between his brows.

"Why can't you just take a well-deserved compliment with grace?"

I shrugged, feeling childish but not knowing how to stop.

He sat on the grass beside me.

"I'm just trying to say I'm sorry."

I picked through the clovers in the grass looking for four-leafers.

"Sorry for what?"

"At the courthouse." He rubbed the back of his neck with a dusty hand. "I was too harsh."

"But not wrong?"

He took a deep breath. "No. Not wrong. When I say I want you to stay out of my business, it's not because I think you can't handle the fight. But there's a battle coming that won't be won with a sword."

"What do you mean?"

"Do you know who owns GenPort?" He waved a hand at the construction site, now burning with a dozen small fires.

"Gerard Golovin." He let that sink in for a moment.

"You think he wants the bloodstone for this? What for?"

Mason shook his head. He looked as tired as I felt. "I don't know. But it's all tangled together somehow. I wasn't put on trial because I violated the Black Hat Act. That's a joke. We all have relics we shouldn't have. No way Hub could police that. I was tried because Gerard wants the bloodstone. I don't know why, but I can't let him keep it. It's too dangerous, and I don't trust his motives."

"So we get it back." Mason had had my back during the whole dragon fiasco. He'd earned my loyalty, even if he didn't want it.

"That's what I've been trying to make clear." His dark eyes hid all emotion. "There is no 'we.' Not this time. Golovin is a prime minister. He won't give in without a fight. It's going to get messy, and I want you to stay out of it."

I stood up to leave, then turned on him. "And I want you to stop treating me like some delicate flower! I think I've proven myself!" Later, I would understand that raising my voice was not the best way to deal with Mason, but I was exhausted, and bruised in heart and spirit.

Mason stood, rising to the bait and yelled back. "The only thing you've proven is that you're reckless!"

We were standing close enough that I could feel the warmth coming off his skin. Behind him, to the east, the sky was beginning to lighten. He'd win this argument just by turning to stone, and in that moment, I was unreasonably bitter about that.

I backed away. "Look. I don't want to fight. There is a whole lot more going on here. Do you see those fires?" I pointed to the smoky haze over the construction site. "And all this mess? This is Terra fighting back. She won't let us dig into her heart without consequences. So while you and Gerard Golovin squabble over your toys, someone needs to watch your back."

He stepped in closer and ran his fingers along my cheek. His eyes were dark and sad. "You're right. But it can't be you."

DERVISH GOES NOVA

(April 14, 2078)

A fire dervish has been pestering people in Pointe-Claire lately. I chased him from the chimney of one of my clients again today. She thought she had raccoons. This is only the second dervish I've met in over ten years of critter wrangling. They're that rare.

For those of you who don't know, a fire dervish isn't really a dervish any more than a Tasmanian devil is a devil. The name refers to the whirling. They like to spin. Sometimes for fun, sometimes in agitation. The spinning seems to ramp up their magic potential, causing a maelstrom of power.

Dervishes have often been mistaken for brownies or gnomes. They are similar in stature and mostly humanoid, but covered in curly fur, usually gray or brown, but sometimes black or brindled. The first time I saw one, I thought, "Wow, a poodle mated with a gnome." Would that make it a gnoodle?

My first encounter was about six years ago. That dervish was old even by fae standards, and he walked with a cane. Some kids had cornered him in an alley and thought it would be fun to taunt him into spinning. Probably the same kind of kids that like to squash stinkbugs just to see if they smell bad.

I was walking by the alley on my way to a job when the wind suddenly picked up, tossing debris in the air like a mini tornado. I heard the kids whooping and hollering and went to investigate. They were poking the dervish with sticks. One kid shook a bottle of soda and sprayed it over him. The poor creature was disoriented and scared. As he spun, smoke streamed from his ears. Though I'd never encountered a dervish before, I could sense the build-up of power coming off him.

The kids were too dumb to realize they were in the line of fire. I used my best angry adult voice to scatter them, and then I tackled the dervish, like smothering a fire with my body.

Thinking back now, that was really foolish. I've read a lot more about dervishes since and know that my actions could have made things worse. Much worse. I think the only reason I escaped with nothing but a few scrapes was because of the dervish's advanced age.

So my questions for you good reader are these:

Have you ever seen a fire dervish go nova?

What's the best way to de-escalate a pre-nova dervish spin?

I ask only to be ready for my next encounter. This new dervish is young and healthy. I have a feeling I'll be seeing more of him.

COMMENTS (7)

Unfortunately, there will always be dumb kids around, looking for fun at the expense of another living creature :(
Cornucopia277 (April 14, 2078)

Give those kids medals! Making our streets safe from fae scum!
CurtWad (April 15, 2078)

It takes a lot to make a dervish go nova. But when they do, it's deadly. One took down half a block of apartments in my ward last year. I didn't see it, but there were eye-witnesses. Said it was like a fiery tornado!
BeverageBaker (April 20, 2078)

I'm sorry to hear that. Were there many casualties? Did the dervish survive?

Valkyrie367 (April 21, 2078)

> 3 dead that I know of. They never found the dervish. The building collapsed on top of him.
>
> *BeverageBaker (April 21, 2078)*

Best way to stop a dervish from going nova? A bullet between the eyes. Works on fairies too.

Holierthan666 (May 1, 2078)

Wow! A dervish? I've heard of those, but never seen one. They sound dangerous.

DaddysGirl (June 10, 2080)

5

Five months later…

I dumped my sword in the umbrella stand beside my door, happy to be home after a long workday. I found Gabe and Jacoby in the large area that was once a garage. We used it as a gym and to store extra cages, traps and tools. A nerve-jangling soundtrack that instantly made me feel old blasted from a portable speaker.

Gabe, stripped to the waist, was busy cleaning cages. He held a scrub brush like a microphone and sang along to the screeching notes. Jacoby danced beside him, holding the spray nozzle of a hose.

I took a moment to drink in the sight of wet Gabe, his bare shoulders flexing, butt prominently displayed in tight jeans as he leaned over the cage.

Wow. And I mean…wow.

Not that I would ever act on the hormones that spiked in me every time I saw him engaged in manual labor. Gabriel Devi was gorgeous but he was also a mystery. And my employee, so off limits.

After a long string of unsuccessful assistants, I was lucky to have him. Not once had he shrunk away at the sight of blood or bug guts. And he was a computer wiz. I was so well organized, I couldn't go to the bathroom without checking my schedule. He worked hard. The customers liked him and so did I. But I just couldn't figure him out.

He stood over six feet and his black curly hair begged to be touched. With his rich golden skin and dark eyes fringed in lashes longer than any man had a right to, he could model in any of the best net-zines. His magic resonated with divine power. I guessed he was some sort of godling. With a name like Devi, he was probably part of the growing Hindu pantheon in Montreal. And he had money. Or at least he came from money because he drove a sleek silver car, one with the new hands-free drive systems that cost more than I paid him in a year.

So why was he working as an office manager for a small pest control operation? I'd asked him that very question and he said, "Because I need to *do* something," putting weight on the word "do" as if the alternative was unthinkable.

Yes, he was an enigma.

I put that thought on hold when I realized that Jacoby was spinning to the increasingly aggressive music. A little whirlwind had blown up around him. Stray leaves and dirt swirled around his feet.

The music beat faster, building to a discordant crescendo, and Jacoby was caught in its spell. Gabe seemed oblivious to the danger of a fire dervish going nova right beside him.

"Gabe! Stop him!" I ran forward, but skidded on the wet floor. Gabe looked up, startled. "Turn off the music!" I shouted.

Smoke billowed from Jacoby's ears, and his eyes glazed over. The twister spiraling around him sparked like a firecracker. I dove at him, trapping his arms to his sides, even as sparks zapped my hair and face. Jacoby strained to keep spinning, his legs scrabbling against the cement floor.

The music cut to blissful silence.

"What the hell?" Gabe asked, crouching at my side.

"He's a dervish…you can't…" I struggled to speak while trying to restrain Jacoby without hurting him. Last time this happened, Nesi had drugged him.

"The hose! Drench him now!"

Gabe grabbed the nozzle and sprayed us both. Steam blistered from Jacoby, but the cold and wet calmed him and he fell limply into my arms.

"Get Gita!"

Gabe rushed away. Moments later Gita arrived and clucked like an angry hen when she took in the scene.

"'Tis nothing but ill fortune to have such a creature about. Death will be coming to this house, for sure."

I just nodded and laid Jacoby in a puddle on the floor. His poodle fur was bedraggled and his limbs still twitched.

"Do you have something to make him sleep?" I asked. Gita made all kinds of tinctures from our tiny herb garden. She nodded and left. Gabe returned with a pile of towels. He propped Jacoby up while I wrapped him in terry cloth. Smoke seeped from his ears.

"What happened?" Gabe asked.

I was irrationally angry and had to take a minute to breathe and sort my thoughts.

Gabe was a terrific assistant, I reminded myself. This near miss was my fault. Gabe was so competent at so many things, I had been lax in his training. He'd had no idea that a dervish could be dangerous. Jacoby's peculiar magic was the reason I had resisted letting him stay with us in the first place; the reason he had his own house in the yard rather than a nook inside like the others.

"Did I hurt him somehow?" Gabe asked. "Was it the music?"

"It's not your fault," I said finally. "You didn't know. It's my fault for assuming you did."

"Know what?"

"Jacoby isn't just a regular dervish. He's a fire dervish. That means that if he gets too excited, he goes nova."

"Like a star?"

"Like a tiny exploding star."

"Shit."

"Yep."

"Have you seen this happen?"

"No, but I came close once. Some kids caught one in an alley and were tormenting him. I stopped them just in time."

"Jacoby?"

"No. Another dervish, a long time ago. He was much older. I'm not sure if Jacoby's youth makes him more or less unstable. But he's been following me around for years without a problem."

"So you thought it was a good idea to let this living bomb stay here."

Gabe leaned back as if the dervish might go off at any minute.

"Clearly, I didn't take your evil music into consideration." I smiled to downplay the danger. Gabe wasn't impressed.

"Look, it takes a lot to make a dervish go nova. Mostly he'll just smoke, but..."

"But you can never be sure."

I shrugged. "He probably wouldn't have exploded. It takes a real surge of emotion to bring him to that level of heat."

Gabe looked around the garage. Bits of leaves were soaked and stuck to the floor. The air smelled of smoke.

He shook his head. "Any other potential Armageddons I should know about around here?"

I thought of the various kinds of venom and other health hazards living in the cages that lined the walls of my apartment.

"Maybe we should make a list."

Gita returned with a small vial. In her no-nonsense way, she plugged Jacoby's nose until he gasped, then dumped the contents down his throat.

"We'll keep him inside for now," I said. "Let him dry off and rest." Jacoby had a tiny house in my yard, but even though the weather was oddly warm for November, I wanted him inside where I could keep an eye on him.

An hour later, I sat at the kitchen table watching the news and eating the ploughman's lunch that Gita had prepared for me as a late dinner. In my youth, I'd been a vegetarian, but in the post-war era, protein was scarce. I took what I could get. Which meant I didn't look too closely at Gita's homemade sausage. She dumped another wedge of cheese on my plate. She wouldn't be happy until I had fat, jolly cheeks. Luckily, my job let me burn off the calories she insisted on force-feeding me.

I stopped her when she started slicing another huge chunk of crusty French bread to go along with the cheese.

"You need to eat more," she rasped. When I refused again, she pouted and stomped off to her closet.

No, I wasn't some cruel dictator that forced my banshee housekeeper to live in a shoe closet. Gita preferred small, dark places. She'd built her nest in there, and nothing I could say would change her mind. At least she didn't cry.

After her scream-to-end-all-screams that brought down a condo, Gita had slept for a week. Her voice didn't come back for a month and another five months later, it was still frail. But she didn't cry anymore, as if that one scream had fulfilled her wailing quota for a year.

After dinner, I checked on the critters. Willow, my gray cat, twined around my ankles, and I fed her some turkey hash. Clarence, my basilisk was curled up like a kitten on the couch and snoring softly. He looked a little ragged around the edges, like he was about to go into another molt. Hunter, the pygmy kraken, had snuck out of his tank to wrap around Clarence's serpent tail. He watched me with huge brown eyes as if daring me to try and pry off his suckers.

I poked my nose in on the rats, the eel, the various rodents and lizard-like things that I couldn't yet identify. Kur, my ice sprite, dozed on his bowl of ice cubes. With each snore, his blue lips trembled and the white feathery fur on his chest swayed. Bijou, the brilliantly-hued snail, munched through a head of lettuce. I let my thoughts stray for only a moment to the night that Mason had given him to me. It seemed so long ago.

A red balloon in the corner of the living room told me where Thomas the tortoise was. The balloon was another of Gabe's innovations. After losing the tortoise for nearly a week, we tied a balloon around him when we let him out to roam.

"Time to go back in your terrarium." I scooped him up and untied the string, letting the balloon float to the ceiling.

Next, I checked on Jacoby, who was still asleep in the office while Gabe rushed about, tidying up. He never left his desk unorganized at the end of the day. As I finished topping up the water bowls for the cages in the office, he pointed to his computer where the screen showed a calendar full of appointments.

"You're all booked tomorrow. Only two urgencies though. I told them you'd be there before noon. One is bats. The other might be brownies," he frowned. "Sorry about that." He knew I hated brownies. "The others can wait."

"Why are you in such a hurry? Hot date?"

Gabe said nothing, but turned to straighten the stapler on his desk for the third time.

"You do have a hot date! Who is it?"

He still didn't answer.

"Wait, is it someone I know? Are you meeting here?"

Gabe rubbed his palms down his immaculate pants. He'd changed out of his wet clothes and now looked runway-worthy in his designer jeans and black shirt. That was nothing new. The nerves were.

"You look like a kid ready to ask someone to the prom. What's up?"

"It's just that…I just really like this guy, so when he shows up, can you just try to be, you know, less you?"

"What does that mean?" I propped an arm on my hip and gave him a stern look. Somehow my air of authority was always lost on Gabe.

"I mean, don't shove an ice sprite into his hands the minute he arrives." He looked me up and down. "At least you don't have blood on your shirt or cobwebs in your hair."

"I don't…I mean…" I looked down at my clothes. I'd showered and my jeans were the second cleanest pair I owned. I'd even spent some time with a scrub brush to get at the dirt under my nails. Was I really that bad? It had been so long since I'd had anyone to impress, I had no inner filth filter anymore. I thought of all the times Mason had pulled wads of chewed hay from my hair or wiped a smear of dirt off my face. He'd even seen me puking my guts out. No wonder he was making himself scarce.

"Fine. I'll play nice."

The office door opened and Dutch walked in.

"Hey, is everything okay?" I asked. I hadn't seen or heard from Mason in five months. Seeing Dutch made my heart clutch for a second as I imagined the worst.

Then I saw the look pass between them.

"He's here for me." Gabe smiled tightly. "Dutch is my date."

"Unfortunately, we have to postpone," Dutch said. "There's been an incident."

Dutch would give me little else. Only that Mason was safe, but a Guardian was dead. Mason had asked that I come to the scene. I thought about refusing. Last June he'd made such a big deal about me staying out of his business. But my bitterness could not outweigh my worry and curiosity.

I followed Dutch and Gabe in my truck. We drove east along the old highway that once cut through the heart of Montreal. Now it wove around the ruins of expressway ramps and a tunnel that was destroyed during the wars.

The Old Port of Montreal had once been an important trading post for the European settlers of this land. Later, it turned into a tourist attraction with huge theaters juxtaposed against quaint cobbled streets and eighteenth-century buildings turned into restaurants. Now it was home to an eclectic, though poorer set. Humans and fae mixed freely here, but mostly class two fae like goblins, imps and trolls or those class one fae with weaker magic. The ward was set a kilometer offshore in the deep channel to accommodate the ships coming into port. It was far enough that it didn't register on my keening.

Old Port was a magnet for artists, musicians and their hangers-on. The narrow roads often switched back on themselves, and many had been given over to pedestrian traffic. You never knew, walking on those twisted paths, when you might turn a corner and find yourself in the middle of a pop-up music club tucked away in a little alcove or an impromptu art class right in the street.

As I parked, I thought about leaving my sword in the truck, but I couldn't bear its whining, so I strapped it to my back and followed Dutch through the winding cobblestone streets.

"You're dating Dutch?" I nudged Gabe with my elbow. His hands were shoved deep in the pockets of his jeans.

"He's sexy as hell."

I watched the slender man stalk up the sloping road ahead of us. He did have that whole silver fox thing going.

"Besides, you told me I couldn't date customers. He's not a customer."

"Well, he might be after tonight. Do you have any idea why Mason wants us here?"

"Only that the death was suspicious, and you might be able to help with the interrogations."

We turned into a gated courtyard. Angus stood guard at the open gate.

"Ah, Kyra! Aren't you a sight for crusty eyes!" He took my hand and swept over it for a kiss. Angus was a gargoyle, created through traditional alchemical magic during the Renaissance. Mason had carved him in the form of a green man, a figure of fertility and growing things. Holding Angus's hand was like clutching a rough-barked branch. The brambles that passed for hair on his head jabbed my arm as his lips brushed my knuckles.

"What's going on here?" I asked.

"Nothing good." His leafy brows lowered. "Go on in. Mason's waitin' on you."

Past the gate, the path opened to a cobbled courtyard surrounded on all sides by three-story stone buildings with slate-tile roofs. The building at the far end boasted a belfry with architecture that could only be called Gothic Ministry. The buildings on the long sides of the courtyard had once served as dormitories for a nunnery. In the last century, they'd been converted to apartments.

The night was warm and the air still. Only a few lights were on behind closed blinds in the apartments. Classical music wafted through the cracks of stone. I spotted three gargoyles perched on the roof, watching the scene below.

My hair was still damp from my shower, and it hung loose around my shoulders. I pulled it away from my neck and searched my belt kit for a hair tie as I headed toward the light from a gleam that floated over several crouched figures. My stomach twisted in knots and my lips wavered somewhere between a smile and a frown.

Five months. I hadn't seen him for five whole months.

The figures stood as I approached. Mason's eyes roved over me from head to foot. Feeling self-conscious, I quickly tied my hair back and turned to the man beside him.

"Kyra Greene," I offered my hand but he ignored it.

"This is Detective Kesik," Mason said.

Kesik was a short white guy with blond hair trimmed in straight bangs across his forehead. He nodded at me, but his mouth pinched in a frown. I knew what he was thinking. He didn't want a civilian mucking up his crime scene.

I'd worked with Hub before, usually with Detective Benoit Giroux. It took half a dozen cases before Ben trusted me not to step in blood or otherwise contaminate evidence. But Ben was dead. A lot of good officers had died during Prince Alvar's attempted coup last spring. That meant new people had stepped into their shoes, people I didn't know. People who didn't know me.

"And this is Susanna Coulter. She's an alchemist working with Hub."

"We've met." I smiled at Susanna and she smiled back faintly. We hadn't met under the best circumstances. Seeing me probably stirred up memories of death and being hurried out of a crumbling condo in shock while fending off vampires. I couldn't blame her for the unenthusiastic greeting.

Ignoring the weight of Mason's eyes on me, I turned and got my first good look at the body. Except it wasn't a body. It was a mess of stone and dust. The torso was mostly intact, but the limbs were broken and scattered. A long-fingered hand pointed into the sky, the arm cut off at the wrist and the inner flesh nothing more than jagged stone. The head lay off to the side, partially crushed in the fall.

"What happened?" I asked.

"If you believe the detective, suicide." Mason crossed his arms and glared at Kesik.

"He jumped?" I looked up at the roof.

"Or he was pushed."

"There's no proof of that," Kesik said. He tilted his head and squinted as if we stood in bright sunlight.

Gargoyles are hard to kill. Any wounds taken in their human form heal as soon as they turn to stone. Only decapitation works, and I've even heard rumors of gargoyles surviving that. But in their stone form, they are surprisingly fragile, if you could call anything that weighs half a ton "fragile." Break them into enough pieces and they won't come back. A fall from a three-story roof would do the trick.

"You think someone did this on purpose?" I asked. "How? That would be like trying to push over a horse." I couldn't see how that could happen in broad daylight.

"Makes more sense than suicide," Mason said. "Gargoyles can't generally leap in their stone form."

Susanna shone a powerful light at the roof, startling a stray cat that hissed at us.

"There is a rope or something dangling from that chimney. He could have rigged it so he fell after sunup."

Mason turned away and spoke into his widget. A gargoyle on the roof broke from the shadows and moved toward the chimney. A few seconds later, Mason's screen lit up with an incoming message.

"It is a rope, but too old and frayed to hold a gargoyle. And short. If it snapped, where's the rest of it?" He pointed at the ground. There was no evidence of rope.

I thought over all the possibilities: suicide, murder, accident. None of them seemed plausible.

"Who is he?" I leaned over the body, pushing the gleam to illuminate what was left of his face. He was a classic "grotesque" gargoyle with a wide mouth and vaguely simian features.

"His name is Cyril. He was a Guardian and an alchemist." Mason nodded to the others standing vigil on the roof. "They found him on their patrol."

The Guardians were a group of gargoyles that kept watch on the parts of the city that Hub ignored. Some people called them vigilantes. Some called them saviors. Mason was their captain, which caused friction with his alchemist cohorts.

"I was an alchemist before I was a gargoyle," he'd once told me. "And they can't take that away from me."

But they could make life difficult for him. Gargoylism had no classification with the fae. And though they were originally made by alchemists, that sect didn't want to claim them either. They were a species apart, as Mason's trial had proven. Compounding the problem, the Guardians had set themselves up as folk heroes who often tweaked the noses of authority. Could this incident be an attack against the Guardians or their captain? I kept my suspicions to myself. For now.

Susanna rose, packing away her thaumagauge.

"First tests show no magical residue, other than Mr…uh, Cyril's signature."

I could have told her that, but alchemists only trusted their gadgets. They would consider my keening as something less than hedge-witch hocus-pocus, but I had sensed the lack of stray magic from the entrance of the courtyard. I gave her points for at least remembering Cyril's name, and that he was a person, not just a pile of rock dust.

Detective Kesik scrolled through something on his widget. He stopped and read the screen for a moment, then turned to Mason.

"Isn't it true that gargoyles are in constant pain, a side-effect of their conception?" He weighted his stare with lead.

Mason's lip curled as if he almost blurted an obscenity, then he raked a hand through his hair.

"Pain is a strong word. A gargoyle may experience discomfort, but we get used to it with age. And Cyril was over two-hundred years old."

I understood what they were talking about. Except for Mason, the magic of every gargoyle I'd met resonated badly, like a square peg mashed into a round hole. I didn't understand the mechanics of it, and the art of creating gargoyles was lost, but the discord had something to do with the way the original stone was imbued with life. Angus had explained it to me.

Life could not be created. It could only be stolen. And the alchemists had stolen the spirits of dead fae to bring their stone creations to life. It left a spiritual dissonance in the new creations and was one of the reasons there were so few gargoyles left. Most either killed themselves or went mad and had to be put down.

Kesik said, "But you agree that this discomfort could lead to depression." It wasn't a question.

"Not Cyril. He was working with me on an experiment to fix the problem."

"So you admit, this is a problem for all gargoyles."

Mason's nod was sharp enough to cut glass.

"And is your experiment on the verge of any great breakthrough?"

Even I withered under Mason's glare and it wasn't directed at me, but Detective Kesik just shrugged it off.

"So, Mr. Mason, could it be possible that your experiment gave new hope to Mr. Cyril? Hope that his constant agonizing pain would end? Hope that turned out to be false? Sounds like a good reason to throw yourself off a roof."

A nerve twitched in Mason's jaw.

Susanna opened a case of glass vials. She removed one and held it up.

"I'd like to examine the body more closely. It might provide more clues, but it would also help with my research. May I have permission to take samples?" She looked to Kesik.

"No crime here as far as I can see. I've got no claim to the body. You'll have to take that up with the next of kin."

Susanna turned to Mason. She held up a small tool, ready to scrape some of the dust into the glass vial. "May I?"

"No." Mason's voice was flat.

Susanna's expression wilted, but she didn't protest.

"We're done here then," Kesik said. "Do you want me to call the coroner?" Just the fact that he had to ask implied that Cyril was less than human in his eyes.

Mason shook his head. "No. We'll take care of him."

Kesik turned and left. Susanna finished packing her kit. She smiled and shrugged as if to apologize for the detective's behavior, then followed him out of the courtyard.

More lights had come on in the apartments. Faces appeared silhouetted in the windows. Dutch and Gabe, who had been loitering near the gate, now came over.

"Berto should be here soon with the truck," Dutch said, even as I heard the beep-beep of a vehicle backing up into the courtyard. The van pulled right up to the remains and stopped.

Berto jumped out of the driver's seat and opened the back doors. He was a taller-than-average gargoyle with wide-set eyes and a pointed mouth that hinted at a duck bill. He pressed a button and a gurney-like contraption floated out of the van, then lowered to hover about two feet off the ground.

"I thought you'd want to examine him back in the lab," Berto said.

"Agreed. Let's get him home." Mason bent to gather the remains.

Feeling that this was a deeply personal moment, I left the Guardians to pack away their brother and wandered to the edge of the yard, looking for…I didn't know what exactly—that big glaring clue that pointed to foul play, clearly defined boot prints at the base of the wall, or a monogrammed handkerchief left by the assailant.

I found none of those, not even a whiff of stray magic. I glanced up at the rooftops. If there had been a crime, it had happened up there. A lone bench tucked away in the corner of the courtyard was a good spot to wait. The night was warm enough that I felt the need to remove my jacket. If this heat wave didn't end soon, we'd have unrest in the streets. The weather could easily be interpreted as Terra's displeasure.

Mason joined me on the bench, and we watched the others carefully pack Cyril into the van. Berto and Angus drove it away. Dutch and Gabe waved to us before heading out.

"Right about now, Gabe is thinking 'Worst first date ever,'" I said.

"Dutch will make it up to him." Mason leaned back on the bench. I wanted to comfort him, but any words I thought of seemed unequal to the task.

One by one, the lights in the apartments went out now that the excitement was over. We sat side by side, listening to the muted noises of a city. Our legs were close but not touching. Only his magic bumped against me, familiar and exciting at the same time.

"I'm surprised you asked me to come," I said before the silence between us became overwhelming.

"You mean because I told you to butt out of my business." His voice was flat, giving me no hint of his emotions.

"You were rather adamant about it. And this is definitely gargoyle business." The five months of silence spoke louder than his words.

He grunted quietly. "I understand the urge to commit suicide."

Whoa! That change of subject nearly gave me whiplash. I glanced sideways, trying to gauge his mood. Was that anger, frustration or sadness that made his shoulders tense and his magic clang like a church bell announcing an invasion?

Mason rubbed his temples with stiff fingers as if he could massage away the last few hours.

"I'm sorry. I'm doing this all wrong." He turned to me, and I saw real pain in his eyes. "I asked you here to help. You didn't have to come. And now I'm being an ass."

"Your words, not mine." I nudged his knee with mine and he smiled.

"It's just that Detective Kesik is not wrong. Being a gargoyle isn't easy. After a while, so much of daily life seems pointless. Washing dishes, cleaning house. It all just has to be redone. The small talk conversations, the same words repeated over and over for centuries. It wears on an immortal."

My heart seized. I'd once loved a man who made that same argument right before he forced me to stab him through the chest.

A mosquito buzzed in my ear. The warm weather had kept the bloodsuckers around late in the season.

"Did you know that only female mosquitoes bite?" I followed the buzz until it landed on Mason's arm, then squashed it with a slap. "Take that, little lady."

Mason quirked an eyebrow at me.

"How about this? I promise never to bore you with small talk. Only relevant information."

"Like the gender of biting insects?" He chuckled, a deep throaty sound, and I realized how much I missed making him laugh.

"Exactly. And in return, you promise not to kill yourself."

"Deal."

It felt so right to be sitting there with him, swapping morbid banter. I let the feeling go on for a bit before I asked, "Why did you really ask me here?"

"Because I don't believe Cyril committed suicide, and I want your help finding the person who did this."

"Me? I'm not a detective."

"And you saw how much help they were. No, you aren't Hub, but you have a different skill-set. You know the dark corners of this city, and the fae that lurk in them."

"You think a fae did this?"

Mason leaned forward and examined his hands. They were covered in rock dust. Cyril dust.

"I think it would take someone with inhuman strength to push a gargoyle off a roof."

"Or several someones with plain old human strength."

"Maybe. Or an alchemist with a clever gadget."

Well, that narrowed the suspect list down to everyone in the city.

"Even if your theory is true, wouldn't the Guardians have a better chance of finding the killer?"

Mason said nothing. A siren blared somewhere in the city. Seconds passed.

Finally I said, "You don't trust the Guardians."

"I trust them with my life. It's not that. The Guardians are the police in neighborhoods Hub doesn't bother to protect. We could ask questions, but we won't get the right answers. I need someone from the outside. Someone with connections to the fae world…"

"…particularly the class two fae," I finished for him. He nodded. Class two fae were often overlooked. They were small and could fit into tight spaces. And they knew things, like a vast spy network, if one knew how to tap into it.

"Could you just ask around?" Mason said. "Maybe someone saw something. I'll pay your daily rate, whatever that is."

I waved away that suggestion. "Let's call it a barter for you helping me to find the dragons." I wouldn't take his money. Not for finding out who killed Cyril. "Can someone get me into Cyril's apartment? I'd like to start there."

"I'll ask Angus. He has the keys."

I nodded and rose, but Mason held me back with one warm hand on my arm.

"I didn't mean that I want you entirely out of my business." He sighed. "Well, maybe I did at the time. But that doesn't work for me. I can't stop thinking about you."

I turned to meet his gaze. He was so gods-damned gorgeous. Dark hair slightly messed, silver-gray eyes softened by the crinkles at the edges.

He grabbed my hand and tugged me toward him. His face tilted up to gaze at me and the stray bit of moonlight lit his eyes. "I'm trying to wrap my head around this, but honestly, I'm a little rusty. I want you in my life. I just don't know how. But I'll figure it out if you give me time."

Time to a gargoyle could mean weeks, months or even years, but I nodded.

"Just stop shutting me out. The rest will come."

"I'm going to try. That's all I can promise."

That was good enough for me. He pulled me down to sit on his knee, and I wrapped my arms around him, my head resting on his shoulder. His magic rumbled through me, slow and steady like his heart. I could smell his skin, the scent of hot summer sun on sand. I thought of everything we'd been through already, and I knew I'd wait for him, no matter how long it took.

7

Protesters crowded the GenPort construction zone just east of Mercy bridge on the south end of the ward. I'd been called to the site to investigate a possible knocker infestation. A metal barrier separated the crowd from a temporary modular building. The GenPort logo—a stylized "G" with a lightning bolt serif—was freshly painted across one side of this new building. The old site headquarters hadn't survived the snooker attack.

In the five months since the ley-line rupture that produced the snooker, GenPort had reorganized, cleared the debris, and mourned the loss of its workers. Then they moved on with constructing the new railroad system. The warehouses around the site were being demolished to make way for the train station. Alchemic specialists had even siphoned off the magic overflow from the ruptured ley-line. That didn't surprise me. A company like GenPort, with its vast resources, wouldn't let such power go to waste. They'd harness it and use it to their advantage.

The cleared-away site meant that little was left to remember that dreadful night when good people died. But certain citizens of Montreal weren't ready to forget the fiasco. Protesters were permanently camped on the ground just outside the construction zone, and today their numbers had swelled as rumors circulated that Golovin was going to address a recent rash of accidents on site.

The construction headquarters was deceptively small for the scope of the project. Most of the work went on underground. GenPort's railroad was a revolutionary project. Not since the Flood Wars had two wards worked together on a joint endeavor. Soon, travel through the Inbetween would be fast and safe, at least between Montreal and Manhattan.

Of course, no bold idea ever went unpunished. Change was hard. Especially in the post-war world.

As I pushed through the crowd, I saw signs like "Terra will fight back!" and "Leave our ley-lines alone!" and "Build walls, not doors!" My favorite was "Magic is my right, not your profit!"

I couldn't blame them. History had proven that when people got too ambitious, Terra slapped them down with a firm hand. Expand the farming communities too far outside a ward and you could expect the forest to reclaim any newly cleared land within weeks. No one dug for fossil fuels anymore. The earth spirit simply caved in the mines or swallowed drilling rigs whole.

Everyone expected the GenPort-Mansys operation to fail spectacularly. So far, they had succeeded in digging under the river and a few kilometers into the Inbetween, but lives had been lost. The snooker incident was only the most disastrous. Despite GenPort trying to lock down the site, stories leaked out. Small accidents plagued the work site. Tools went missing, vehicles wouldn't start, vermin chewed through electrical wires, and crew members were constantly being treated for minor injuries.

Terra worked in mysterious and subtle ways. At least that's what the protesters wanted us to believe. I didn't disagree.

Reporters had set up cameras in front of an empty podium. An expectant hush fell over the crowd as they waited for Golovin's morning briefing. I didn't want to wait around to hear it. I could watch Golovin's platitudes on the news feed later. With a full roster of jobs today, I needed to get inside the GenPort site, wrangle whatever critter they were complaining about and move on.

I wasn't that lucky. Just as I pushed through the press of people, the door to the GenPort office opened and Golovin stepped out. The crowd started shouting, "Terra rules!" and "Stop killing us!" and a dozen other claims that all melded into one incomprehensible roar.

Golovin ignored the shouting crowd as he approached the podium. He smiled once for the cameras and then started to speak in a quiet reasoned voice, pitched for the dozens of microphones pointed at him. The protesters, realizing they would miss his speech, quieted. Golovin smiled again at their sudden attention but didn't break his flow of words.

"...we must continue to strive for excellence, for new connections. We are not solitary creatures and can only progress as a community, not as individuals. Soon our community will grow as we add a new connection to old allies in Manhattan. The benefits of such an alliance will be felt by all. New markets to sell our goods. New access to foods and technologies. Safe travel through the Inbetween..."

I tuned out his privileged hype when I saw three figures emerging from the tunnel leading to the new rail system. Two of them were construction workers, dressed in overalls and hardhats. A giant walked between them.

I squinted. Was that some kind of ogre? A troll? Robot? It stood on two legs and was man-shaped, but drawn in rough lines, as if a child had formed a man out of clay. It moved slowly with a lumbering gait. As it approached, I could make out its face, or at least, I could see where its face should have been. It was a blank roundness with the vague impressions of eyes and nose. Something was tattooed into its forehead, but I was too far away to make it out.

Gasps and shouts rang out in the crowd. A child started to cry.

"At GenPort we hear your concerns. Revolution is dangerous. And building a rail system into the Inbetween is nothing if not revolutionary. Lives have been lost. People have been hurt. And we feel each of those wounds dearly. That's why I'm proud to introduce you to GenPort's newest crew member. This fully automated labor machine will speed up the construction and save lives. Ladies and gentlemen, I give you the Gencrew 80x."

He waved his arm backward in a flourish to point at the monster now lurking behind the podium. The crowd was dead silent.

Oh, man. They really should have given that thing a face.

The reporters recovered from their collective surprise, and fired a dozen questions at Golovin. I pushed through to the metal barrier and spoke to a guard, showing him my work permit.

"I'm supposed to meet the supervisor, Debra Housing." The guard allowed me through the gate and pointed at the opening to the tunnel.

"Take the elevator down and ask for directions at the bottom."

I could do that.

I left the crowd to decide the fate of our ward and headed into the tunnel. "Elevator" was a generous word for the metal box that hurtled me hundreds of feet into the earth, coming to an abrupt stop that rattled my teeth.

At the bottom, I asked another crewman where I could find Debra Housing.

"You here about the knockers?" he said.

"Yes."

He grunted. "Good. Can't stand the racket anymore."

He looked me up and down.

"Those steel-toed?" he pointed at my boots.

"Yes."

"Hard hat's mandatory from here on." He grabbed one from a peg on the wall and jammed it on my head.

"Housing is at the command center." He pointed down the long dim tunnel. "You aren't claustrophobic, are you? I don't have time to come rescue you."

"I'll be fine."

"Good. Take the scooter. Straight on that way. You can't miss it." Then he jumped into the elevator cage and left me alone.

The scooter was little more than two fat wheels with a footpad and a long handle, but it was fast and I zipped along at a good clip. The dark road was about as wide as the old metro tunnels. Lights were fixed to the ceiling at intervals, so that I rolled into and out of shadows. The first section was finished with a cement floor and tile walls, but these soon gave way to bare stone and steel supports.

The scooter's quiet hum and the crackle of gravel under the tires were the only sounds until I hit a dark section where the light was out. A loud clang echoed through the tunnel. I stopped, listening in the dark and now total silence.

I scanned the shadows, but found no movement, not even the scuttle of rats. The dead air smelled faintly of fish and rotting vegetation. Overhead, the rough ceiling was bare, but I could imagine its weight pressing down on me. Tons of rock and above that, the St. Lawrence River.

I'm not afraid of enclosed spaces. I couldn't do my job if I was, but I had to take a deep breath to calm my nerves.

Then something banged again, this time a staccato beat, like someone taking a wrench to a steel beam and tapping out a tune. The echo made it impossible to sense the sound's origin.

Most people think that knockers are mischievous gnome-like creatures who run through mines with tiny hardhats and pickaxes, causing trouble and taunting miners by banging on rocks.

That's not true. The reality is much worse. The good thing was that a true knocker infestation would give my sword a good workout and maybe quiet its whining for a while.

I pushed the scooter into gear again and finished the trek through the increasingly rough tunnel until I came to a makeshift command center, a large room excavated from stone and finished in fresh white tiles. The tunnel continued into the dark at the other end of the room, and I could hear the distant rumble of machines at work. Another elevator shaft climbed into the ceiling which meant I'd passed under the river.

The last reports had said that the tunnel now drove right under Hedge, the shanty town that surrounded the south gate. The plan was to dig underground for a few kilometers then surface in the Inbetween and continue the railway above ground, warding it with a series of Apex towers in the same fashion as the city. Residents of Hedge didn't like this idea. Many had been displaced during the construction for fear of cave-ins. They'd protested, of course, but Hedge residents weren't citizens of any ward, and they had no rights.

Two workers stood near a table with a coffee urn and water cooler. The woman was small and wiry with a pale, hard face and lips pressed thin. Her coworker was a tall black man, easily twice her size, but she seemed to be the one calling the shots as they flipped through screens on a widget. They looked up as I parked my scooter and approached.

"I'm Kyra Greene from Valkyrie Pest Control. I'm here about—" The banging cut off my words. Both workers winced at the noise. The man looked up at the ceiling with genuine fear in his eyes.

"I'm here about that. Supposed to talk to Debra Housing."

"That's me," the woman said. "Can you find the creatures? We haven't seen them once, but as you can hear, they're very active."

"Knockers are bad luck," the man said. "Real bad."

Housing frowned. "Can't be sure they're knockers. We left out some milk and cakes. They didn't eat it."

"No, they wouldn't." I looked around. Other than the elevator and the refreshment table, a desk sat in one corner along with another table and a few chairs where workers probably rested and ate lunch. One of Gerard's gencrew automatons stood inactive against the tiled wall, its faceless expression even creepier because it was so still. Several smaller tunnels branched off from this larger room. I let my keening out, but felt nothing other than cold stone.

"So how do you catch them then? Traps?" Debra asked.

"No. Can I ask, where did the cave-in happen?"

Debra frowned. "The other side of the river. Why?"

Well, that made no sense. I'd only heard the knockers near this end, but I had to ask, "Were the bodies all recovered?"

"Every one." She seemed annoyed by my prodding.

"Have you found any other human remains during the excavation?"

She squinted at me and crossed her arms over her chest, a sure sign that the next words out of her mouth would be a lie.

"No."

"I'll just have a look around then. See if I can find the source."

Housing pinched her lips.

"You can't just go poking around on an active site. It's not safe."

I hiked my pack over my shoulder and turned toward my scooter.

"I'll be going then."

A clanging noise echoed around us. Housing and the man glanced up like the ceiling might fall in.

"Fine!" Housing threw up her hands. "But you can't wander around alone. Bones, escort her."

"Hey, boss, I've been here all night. I'm off."

"I don't have time for this! At least show her how to take a genny." Housing clamped her helmet on and stalked off down the largest tunnel.

The man nodded at me. "Name's Hank. Everyone just calls me Bones. Follow me."

He led me to the gencrew.

"It's voice activated, you see? Genny, on," Bones said sharply. The automaton came awake, but without my keening, I wouldn't have known because it didn't move and had no expression to change. Standing close to it now, I could see the symbol carved into its forehead—the GenPort logo. It glowed with a faint pulsing light.

"Bring this lady…what's your name again?"

"Kyra Greene,"

"Right. It's good to be precise with the gennys when you can," Bones said. "Escort Kyra Greene. Stay with her until she's finished her work, then escort her back here. Understood?"

The genny nodded slowly.

"Good." Bones turned to me. "You need anything else, just ask it. If you run into trouble, it has a direct link back to Debra. Call for help."

"Thanks. I'm sure we'll be fine."

Bones turned to leave, then paused as if wanting to say more. He looked down the access tunnel, then back at me and shrugged before heading to the elevator.

Alone with the genny, I took a moment to study it. During my time in Asgard, I'd seen plenty of giants. As a pest controller, I'd dealt with all kinds of trolls, ogres and other oddities that lumbered out of the Laval floodplains when the magic was hot. This creature didn't resemble any of those. It was something else entirely. Something unnatural. My best guess was that it was a golem, a homunculus, imbued with magic to animate it. But even that assessment seemed off.

The creature stood well over seven feet tall and was made out of some kind of pliable putty. Bulky arms tapered to strangely delicate hands with fingers that looked quite nimble. The facelessness intrigued me. How did it see and hear? I let my magic wrap around it, tasting the life-force that burned from that glowing logo on its forehead.

Its magic stank of death. It tasted of burned flesh and iron, like someone had left a steak cooking too long in a cast-iron pan. I thought of Angus with his dryad spirit locked in stone and my stomach soured.

I looked back. Bones had already gone up the elevator. I was alone with the golem.

"Lead the way." I stepped aside, letting the genny lumber into the access tunnel so I could keep my eye on it.

Critter wrangler rule number five: Just because something smells dead, doesn't mean it can't kill you.

The fresh tiles and good lighting only lasted for a few steps, and then we moved through a darker tunnel, its walls propped with metal bracers and only a few gleams to light the way at wide intervals.

The genny walked at a steady pace. A ghost popped out of the wall and floated down the tunnel ahead of us. The genny paused, as if sensing its disturbance. Curious.

"Keep going," I said and the genny plodded on. The banging sounds continued, getting more agitated as we delved deeper into the excavations. I poked my head into any offshoots, but I was snooping rather than searching. The ghost would show me the way.

We followed the unearthly glow until it disappeared into a larger cavern. It was natural, by the looks of it, though digging had enlarged it at one end. A machine sat silently in the middle of the open space. It was a digger, abandoned here when the work halted. A huge mound of rock and dirt butted up against the far wall, as if it had caved in.

The knockers were going crazy now, and I could barely think with all the noise. A stray wind buffeted me, something that shouldn't happen in this enclosed space. And then I saw them.

Knockers aren't little grumbly gnomes. They are spirits of the restless dead. Souls that want to be acknowledged for one reason or another.

"All right!" I shouted. "I'm here."

The knocking stopped but the unnatural wind picked up, blowing through my thin shirt as more ghosts whipped around me.

I stepped around the digger. It had disturbed a grave site. Bones were tossed in a heap to one side. Others were scattered across the open ground. I counted five skulls. The leg bones all looked adult-sized. Who were these people? I looked at the ceiling and the mass of stone above me as if I could find the secret to this odd burial ground.

Traveling through the tunnels had turned me around, but I thought we were under the outskirts of Hedge. Had a homesteader family strayed into this cave and become trapped? More likely, the bones were older than that, possibly from the Flood Wars. Back then, people tried to hide from the magic bombs underground.

These people hadn't found refuge here, only death. And their spirits lingered. They hovered nearby, invisible now, but I could still keen their presence.

If you'd asked me last spring to use my sword's power to release a group of excavated souls, I would have balked.

Valkyrie were the battlefield cleanup crew of old. We followed in the wake of wars between gods and giants and dispatched to Valhalla those who had died honorably.

I hadn't wanted that power. It seemed…presumptuous. How could I judge which death was honorable? If a man thought of his wife in the last moments of battle and fled so he could live and feed his family, was that dishonor? If a man wept in fear as his blood leaked onto the field, was he a coward?

I refused to be that judge and Dana, Freya of the Valkyrie, decided to teach me a lesson in blood and broken bones, so I would remember my duty. The lesson hadn't stuck and I left Asgard soon after.

For years, I skirted around the issue of my sword. So even when I'd cut Joran by accident and watched him turn into a walking corpse, I'd been loathe to finish him off. I didn't want to choose his afterlife. But in the end, I'd done it. I'd released his soul. And I didn't regret it.

Joran taught me an important lesson. I was not a god—benevolent, vengeful or otherwise. I didn't decide what happened to Joran when he left this earth anymore than I decided what he did with his time here. Now I looked at myself as more of a priestess, giving last rites and a little push in the right direction.

My Aunt Dana would be proud. Well, probably not. She didn't like me enough for that. But she'd grunt something like "I told you so" and make me run fifty laps around the training yard, just for questioning her.

I no longer refused to let my sword do its job. I wouldn't be hunting down victims to satisfy its blood lust any time soon, but I could help these lost souls, regardless of who they were. They could have been a family, a band of smugglers or human traffickers. But I didn't need to decide their immortal fate. I only needed to get them to stop harassing the locals.

I unsheathed my sword and scraped it against a skull. A ghost burst from the bone. It loomed over me, a great wash of blue light only faintly reminiscent of a human form. Then it seemed to shatter against the rocks, exploding into a million little shards of light, and it was gone.

My sword sang with glee. This was what it was forged for. A Valkyrie blade cleaning up the stray dead.

I poked another skull, releasing another soul. I repeated the process four more times until only one ghost remained. It zipped around me in agitation. I dug around in the dirt, letting my sword lead me. I was sweating in the cool, damp air when I finally uncovered its bones and sent it home.

I sheathed my vibrating blade and wearily turned to the genny, thinking I was done.

Two more ghosts sat on the fallen rocks. These wore modern construction clothes and hard hats.

I counted the skulls: six in all. I'd released all the spirits here. So where were the bodies for these two men?

"Where?" I asked, but the ghosts melted into the rubble and were gone.

I turned to the genny and stopped short. Its expressionless face somehow looked sad. My keening was picking up its emotion. Again, curious.

"Genny, contact Debra Housing."

A half hour later, Housing made an entrance. She was alone, though I'd asked her to bring a digging crew.

I pointed at the rockfall.

"There are at least two more bodies under there, but you know that already, don't you?" I didn't give her time to make excuses. "The cave-in five months ago. It wasn't the first one, was it?"

Housing glared at me, but I pushed on. "Let me guess, you found this old burial site and while excavating it, the roof caved in. So you just left them. How many men died here?"

I waited a long moment before she answered.

"Four."

"Strange that I didn't hear that on the news. Because you never reported it, right?"

She gave her head one curt shake.

"Because it's just more fuel for the Terra protesters. I get it. But you still have to do the right thing and retrieve the bodies."

"This cave is unstable," Housing said. "Why should we dig them up just so we can bury them again?"

It was a good question for someone who didn't see ghosts. So I explained to her the origin of the knockers.

"I released these spirits." I pointed to the ancient bones. "But you may find yourself with another knocker problem if you don't do the right thing and retrieve the bodies of your colleagues. When you do, call me."

I turned to the genny. "Get me out of here." It wasn't a precise instruction, but the genny understood me just fine.

8

For the rest of the day, after leaving the GenPort site, my sword's hum was a constant background irritation.

"You ought to be ashamed of yourself," I grumbled. It wasn't. It liked poking bones and sending spirits onto the afterlife. Now it purred while I watched the sun set in a wash of morbid purples.

I leaned against the brick wall beside the front door to Cyril's building, waiting for Angus, and thought that if—by some slim chance—I ever ended up with Mason, I'd be doing this a lot. Waiting for the sun to fall below the horizon. Waiting for Mason to come alive again.

And what did Mason do all day long, petrified in his own body? Did he play word games to pass the time? Did he sit in front of his video screen, never able to change the feed? Or maybe he sat by the window and counted the seconds until the sun set.

Gods, it was enough to make you throw yourself off a roof.

I glanced up at the roof in question, where Cyril had met his end. A Guardian perched on the eave, facing the window of Cyril's apartment. As I watched, he stretched, fanning wings behind him.

The sun had gone down. Angus would be here soon. We'd made a date to search Cyril's apartment, though I had no idea what we were looking for. Perhaps we'd know it when we saw it.

A screech and a hiss came from the shadows, and then an orange tabby flew by, followed by Jacoby. I grabbed him by the arm.

"Leave the stray cats alone!"

"But they makes funny noises when I chases them." He pouted.

"That's because they want to scratch your eyes out."

Maybe it wasn't a good idea to bring him along, but Jacoby had a lot of energy. He needed a job to keep him busy.

"Why don't you walk around the building and report back to me if there are any fae living nearby. Underground dens and the like."

Jacoby scratched his furry belly. "You wants that I brings them to you?"

I had visions of him hog-tying some poor garden gnome and hauling him back here.

"No. Just make a note about where they live for later. I might want to question them."

Jacoby grumbled something rude about questioning vermin and wandered off. Well, I'd always wanted an assistant, and he was cheap labor.

"Aren't you as pretty as a peach pit," Angus said, strolling up to the building entrance. "Standing there in the last light of the day. You're a gift to these old eyes."

I curtsied. "Thank you. I put on my best jeans just for you."

"Ah, don't flirt with an old man. My heart can't take it." He pressed a hand to his chest.

"Oh, you can take it better than most."

Angus lowered his twiggy eyebrows. "Mason been his usual ornery self, I take it?"

"Ornery isn't the word I'd use."

"Frustrating? Stubborn? Morose?"

"Now you're getting closer." I leaned against the stone building, still warm from the day's heat. "I just never know what to expect from him."

"Give him time. He's an old stone. Unmovable until you put the right force under him. I can tell you that when Mason loves, he does it with his entire being. He won't be able to stop that force." Angus winked. "He's already a rolling stone. He just doesn't know it yet."

He dangled keys to unlock the apartment as Jacoby rushed around the corner and nearly bowled me over.

"Did you find anything?" I asked as I steadied him.

"Brownies." He wrinkled his nose in disgust. "Just a den. Filthy brownies not home."

"Okay." I could come back tomorrow to question them. Brownies were worse than little old ladies for gossip. They might have heard something.

We climbed three stories. This old building had no elevator. Angus fluttered his stubby wings and lightly bounded up the stairs. I had to move fast to keep up. That was fine; I didn't want to spend any more time than necessary in the stairwell. It stank of rotten food and mold. The walls hadn't seen paint in the last century. Scuff marks and graffiti made it difficult to tell what color they had originally been. I didn't touch the banister that was covered in something sticky-looking.

"Why would Cyril live in a place like this?" I asked, stepping over a broken bag of garbage spilling used tissues and fruit peelings down the stairs.

"It's as good a place as any around here. Old Port was Cyril's turf. He patrolled this area every night."

"I saw a gargoyle on the roof before you arrived."

Angus hopped onto the top floor landing and headed for a door with a brass "3B" hanging at an odd angle.

"Aye, we've got someone watching the place. Can't imagine Cyril was killed for something in his apartment, but…" He shrugged and opened the door, "if so they might come back."

"You really believe that Cyril was murdered?"

He turned in the open doorway and smiled sadly. "I believe it's a possibility."

"And so is suicide, you mean."

He stretched his wings and scratched under the waistband of his pants. "Let's just search the place so we have all our ducks on the same page."

"Right."

Inside, the apartment was a complete contrast to the dingy hall. Cyril was either a neat freak, or he spent little time there. The door opened right into a living room and kitchen separated by an island counter. To the right, a short hall led to a bedroom and bathroom. Ahead, the far wall of the living room was all glass with a narrow balcony beyond. Curiously, a plain wooden chair sat beside the window, pointing toward the glass.

I studied the space. One throw pillow lay flat on the couch while the others were propped nicely. On the kitchen counter, a row of containers marked *flour, sugar* and *coffee* were misaligned, with the sugar too far forward. In my apartment, those details would be nothing, but this space was exceedingly tidy, and they stood out.

"Does it look like someone searched it already?" I asked.

"Maybe," Angus said. "If so, they were careful."

"You take the living room. We'll do the bedroom."

Angus nodded. "What are we looking for exactly?"

"Dunno. I'm no detective. Look for anything that seems wrong."

"Well, those drapes are just wrong with that sofa print, but I expect you're looking for something more substantial."

"Decor aside, letters would be nice. Or pictures. And look for his widget. Let's see who he spoke to last."

Jacoby was running up and down the short hall, so I nabbed him on my way to the bedroom.

"Start in the closet," I said. "Look through all his clothes. Check the pockets."

The dervish nodded and went to work. I looked over the room. It seemed undisturbed. A twin bed was pushed against the wall, looking like it was never used. Another plain chair sat beside the window. Now it made sense to me. Cyril wouldn't sleep in a bed. He was stone during the day. What need for comfort did he have? No, he would spend his stone hours sitting on one of those chairs, watching the sky outside his window.

I opened the drawers in a dresser and quickly searched them, feeling dirty at having to paw through Cyril's personal things. He had just a few changes of underclothes and shirts. Behind a pile of balled up socks, I found a wad of bank notes.

Did anyone even use this stuff anymore? I counted forty-five twenty-dollar bills in the old United States currency. Nearly a thousand dollars, but no one would accept it. I wondered why Cyril even kept it. Beside the money, I found a small pouch of gemstones. These had real value. At least we could be sure that no one had burgled the apartment. I left the stash out for Angus. He would know if Cyril had any family to give it to.

I moved on to inspecting the rest of the room. The walls were covered in photos of sunny landscapes—beaches, snowy mountainsides, rolling pastures, and city parks. I guessed that for someone who lived in darkness, those vistas were exotic.

One digital frame on his bedside table caught my eye. I picked it up. It flicked through a series of images—Cyril with a blond woman, Cyril with a group of fae and humans, party-goers laughing into the camera and so on. Most were of the same gang of friends, all smiling for the group selfies. Cyril, with his wide gargoyle mouth and heavy brow, didn't look out of place in this gang. One was a troll of some sort, another had the look of an elf. They were an eclectic bunch for sure, and they seemed to be having a grand old time at various night clubs around town.

I put the frame down and tapped it with my widget to upload the images. It was hard to imagine a Guardian with such a busy social life. Gargoyles tended to be solitary creatures. Or maybe I was projecting that idea onto Cyril because I was so used to Mason's introverted ways.

A crash came from inside the closet, then a muffled, "I'ms fine!" Jacoby staggered out with a scarf wrapped around his waist. A large shirt was draped over his head and one arm.

"You weren't supposed to try on the clothes," I said. "Just search them." I helped him untangle the twisted shirt. "Did you find anything?" He nodded, ducked back into the closet and came out with a bedraggled teddy bear of brown, threadbare plush with fake glass eyes and a plastic nose that was bent to one side. It was a much-loved bear. Jacoby turned it over and showed me the straps. It was a bear backpack. I unzipped its small pocket and searched inside. Nothing. I handed it back to Jacoby.

"I haves it?" He cuddled the thing against his chest.

"If Angus says it's okay." Jacoby dashed into the other room with his treasure. I rifled through the rest of the closet. There was nothing here. Cyril had led a spartan life. If he'd been killed, it wasn't for a teddy bear and a few gemstones.

I found Angus in the living room going through the contacts on Cyril's widget. I handed him the wad of antique money and the pouch of gemstones.

"If Cyril had any heirs, they might want those. I don't know if the cash is worth anything."

Angus whistled and took the money and pouch. "No family, other than the Guardians. He was a good man, though. He'd want this to help someone in need. I'll be sure it does just that."

Jacoby was curled up with his bear on the chair by the window.

"Did he ask about the bear?"

"Aye, he can keep it. Better than throwing it in the bin. Guardians will come pack up the rest of his stuff and give it to charity. Did you find anything?"

I shook my head. We sat on the barstools by the kitchen island.

"Anything in his widget?"

"Nah. Lots of calls, but I recognize all the names. Cyril liked to party and he had a lot of friends."

"I gathered that." There were more pictures of Cyril with various people in frames in the living room. "He must have taken comfort from them."

"He was a good friend." Angus's woody lips flattened to a grim line. "This is a bad business. I don't know which I'm hoping for more, that we find a reason for his murder or his suicide." He shook his head, rustling the leaves in his brambly hair.

"What's it like to be a gargoyle?"

He squinted at me, and I rushed on. "I mean, I can feel your magic, you know that, right?" He nodded. "So I know a little bit about it."

One night when we were traveling through the Inbetween, Angus had brought out his "wee" bottle of whisky. I got a little tipsy and embarrassed myself by commenting on Angus's odd magic. His energy never seemed smooth and regular. It jarred. He'd said the dissonance was because gargoyles were created by man and brought to life with the stolen spirit of a dead fae—in Angus's case, a dryad.

Other than embarrassing myself for being so forward, I'd upset Mason, who had created Angus in the eighteenth century, before he understood the consequences of his alchemy. Angus didn't mind the questions though.

"It's hard to explain." He pointed to the chair at the window. "Even though we spend a lot of time thinking about it. Too much time, I suppose."

"But this dissonance you feel, would it be enough to make Cyril kill himself?"

"I dunno. You've got the same dichotomy warring inside of you. Why don't you tell me?"

"Me?"

He nodded. "Do you remember the deal we made in the Inbetween?"

"Yes. You offered to teach me dryad magic."

He watched me steadily. "Are you sure you want to learn? To welcome a very different magic into your mind?"

I thought about when my Valkyrie magic first came in—the seizures, the meltdowns. It hadn't been easy to master. How much worse would it be to incorporate an entirely different kind of power?

"I don't think I have a choice."

"That's true. And it was true for Cyril too. And me. We make do with what we are given."

"So you'll still help me learn to master my dryad magic?"

"Aye. And you're going to help me investigate Gerard Golovin." He pointed a gnarled finger at me.

That was the second part of our deal.

The alchemists were amazing inventors. They created all the wonders that kept our modern society running, from the cars we drove, to the ward that protected our city. And they all ran on magic tapped from the ley-lines running underground.

During our trip through the Inbetween, Mason had brought out an odd compass that used Montreal's Apex stones as a guide. It had resonated magic that was just a bit off, like a violin out of tune. Or like a fae soul stuck in a gargoyle's body. Angus had felt it too, and not surprisingly, he wanted to put a stop to it.

We both suspected that the alchemist prime minister was at least funding the research behind this new technomancy. But before we went to Mason with our claims, we had to be sure.

"Right. On that note, I had an interesting encounter this morning." I told him about the Gencrew 80x. The creature had been bugging me all day. It could have been an automaton as Golovin asserted, but I didn't believe it. There had been life trapped behind those sightless eyes. I was sure of it.

"So, you think Gerard's little robots are golems. You sure about that?" Angus growled.

"Not so I can prove it. And not like any golem I've ever encountered. It was alive. I'm not sure a thaumagauge could pick it up, but my keening is much more sensitive. The genny's magic felt, well…" I squirmed in my chair, trying to wrestle my thoughts into something less offensive.

But his tone was somber when he said, "It felt like my magic."

"Yes."

"You realize that you're accusing one of the prime ministers of Montreal of breaking the Black Hat Act. He could be sent to Grandill."

The creation of unnatural life was one of the few truly heinous crimes. Because there was no way to create life. It could only be stolen, in the way that Mason had stolen a soul to create Angus.

"If Gerard Golovin is behind the opji attacks—and now these golems—then Grandill prison is too good for him."

"And if you're wrong…" He let the thought trail off.

"If I'm wrong, I could be tried for treason too."

"Aye, Hub doesn't take kindly to false accusations that disturb the peace."

"So we need proof."

"We do."

"Without letting Mason know what we're doing."

"That too."

Mason wouldn't sit back and wait for proof if he knew we suspected Golovin of harvesting fae spirits to create his golems. I didn't like to lie to him, but Angus and I had already agreed to keep our suspicions quiet until we had concrete proof against Golovin.

"Mason knows that you're going to help me with my dryad magic?"

"Aye." He nodded slowly. "You think we can use that as a cover?"

I smiled. "Let's make it a date."

The world had gone a little mad. Montrealers were used to extremes—below freezing winters and blistering hot summers—but muggy heat in November made everyone antsy, myself included. It reminded me of the extreme weather swings we experienced back before the Flood Wars, an omen of things to come, if we'd been wise enough to listen.

I sat on the roof across from Cyril's nunnery-turned-apartment building, listening to cars honk, along with angry shouts and sirens in the streets nearby. I shifted in my little nook, trying to keep to the shade beside a chimney. The rooftops of Montreal were their own highway. That's how the Guardians moved around. And that's where Cyril had met his end. If anyone had seen his assailant, they would be the sort who moved along these rooftops with ease.

For three days, I'd come by this courtyard in between my pest control jobs, watching for any regulars who passed this way, and trying to stay cool. I'd already investigated the spot from where Cyril fell. A slate tile had come loose there and others showed unusual scuff marks, but that proved nothing. I needed a witness. Today was Saturday, and I vowed to stake-out the spot all day.

Few people used the courtyard below. In the morning, an elderly lady sat on the bench in the yellowing garden, but she stayed only until the sun shifted and the bench lost its shade.

The rest of the courtyard was silent. A tall cedar hedge hid the short wall that joined the two apartment buildings. I keened tiny magics running along the cooler earth under it, but nothing else moved.

The cobblestones in the courtyard were hot enough to bake bread. Jacoby, who could walk through fire unblemished, sprawled on the stones below, snoozing in the sun and enjoying the heat from above and below.

Just as I thought the heat was going to poach my brain in my head, a brownie appeared at the far end of the roof. He skipped along as if out for a summer stroll, humming off-key and sucking on a lollipop that was much too big for him.

When he reached the chimney, I stepped from the shadow and into his path.

The brownie froze, then crouched and shut his eyes tightly, as if hiding.

"I can see you." He opened an eye, grimaced and stood up. About two-and-a-half feet tall, the brownie was all arms and legs, like a toddler-sized gangly teenager. His hairless face hid under a hat made of rags, with bits of garbage dangling from it, tied in twine. Large, yellow eyes glowed from beneath this costume.

"What do you want?" He squinted at me. He was ready to run, and I held out a hand to stop him.

"I just want information."

The brownie bit me on the soft spot below my thumb.

"Dammit!" I clutched my hand to my chest. Blood already welled through my fingers as I watched the brownie slide down the drainpipe.

"Jacoby! Don't let him get away!"

I heard the dervish snort, the brownie hiss, and then I was scrambling down the drainpipe too.

"Where is he?" I pressed my bleeding hand against my thigh.

"I gots him trapped!" Jacoby jumped from foot to foot by the cedar hedge. He had the brownie pinned against the wall. At one end, the hedge butted up against the building with no easy handholds to get to the roof. The other end opened near the gate and Jacoby waited there. The brownie poked his head out, saw the angry dervish and dove back into the safety of the hedge.

I took the time to wrap my hand in a rag from my pack. Brownies were such a pain, but this one obviously had a nest around here. Even if he hadn't seen Cyril's killer (assuming there was one) he'd know the local gossip.

I crouched to peer under the hedge.

"I catches him for you!" Jacoby made a wringing motion with his hands. "No more brownie!"

"No! If you're going to be my apprentice, you need to follow my rules. Understand?"

"'Prentice?" The whiskers around his eyes twitched.

"Uh-huh."

That's right, you little whirlwind of trouble. Take the bait.

"I be's your 'prentice?"

"Only if you can obey my commands. We don't want to hurt the brownie. We just want to talk to him."

Jacoby pouted, but nodded. The brownie's lollipop was on the ground and Jacoby mashed it into the dirt.

The brownie crouched on the other side of the hedge. I peered into the shadows, and he hissed at me. If I tried to claw through the brambles, the little beast would attack with the ferocity of a pissed-off cat. I wouldn't be able to take him by force without shedding more blood.

"Come out of the hedge and I'll give you..." I thought about what I had to trade, dug into my pack and found a small bag of mints. I held them out to the brownie. "Candy!"

He sniffed the offer and hissed again. Apparently brownies didn't like mint.

"Kyra-lady shouldn't talks to filthy brownies," Jacoby said. The fae were as sensitive to social hierarchy as Victorian ladies, and brownies were way down the pecking order. Jacoby stood at least six inches taller, but more importantly, his magic would outclass a brownie's any day.

"I have to talk to him. I need to find out who hurt Cyril," I said through gritted teeth.

"Kyra-lady could sets fire to the hedge," he suggested. "Brownies don't likes fire." He grinned. Tendrils of smoke leaked from his ears.

"Uh, no thanks."

I tested the solidity of the bush. The branches were thick and intertwined. My sword would cut through it but not without considerable damage to the hedge.

"Kyra-lady could stabs 'em with her big sword. Stabs 'em right through the eye!"

The brownie peered through the branches and stuck out his tongue. Jacoby lunged at the hedge with a pretend sword. The brownie disappeared.

"Kyra-lady could poisons 'em." Jacoby stood back and scratched one ear with a long finger. "Or explodes 'em. Explodes 'em with a big bomb! Then chops 'em into tiny bits!" He made a chopping motion with one skinny hand. I was starting to think that Jacoby didn't like brownies.

In truth, brownies aren't the helpful creatures from fairy tales. They are the original trick or treaters. Instead of doing good deeds in exchange for milk and bread, they are more likely to throw eggs at your windows. Bug fogger and animal traps aren't sufficient for these critters. They only understand guile.

"I can wait here all day," I said in a sing-song voice. "You'll be hungry and bored. But if you come out now, I have just a few questions and you can go."

"How do I know you won't trick me?" asked the brownie.

Good question. I wouldn't trust me—a dirty, angry woman with a sword strapped across her back.

"Because I'm just like you." I brought my magic to the fore, letting it seep from me in a cloud. The brownie would taste it. He would feel the dryad in me and know that I wouldn't harm him. Dryads are wood-nymphs. They revere all life and wouldn't even pull weeds from a garden. He didn't have to know that the other half of my heritage descended from bloodthirsty vikings.

The brownie scented my magic. Then a face peered through the hole in the hedge again.

"I just want to ask you some questions." My hand was aching and I really wanted to go home.

The brownie's eyes perked up. "You want information? A forfeit then."

Ah, yes. The forfeit was a tried and true fae tradition. A test disguised as an offering. If I passed, he would know I was good people. If I didn't pass, I would owe the brownie a favor. Owing anything to the fae was never a good idea. They tended to seek payment in the form of your firstborn.

"Fine," I said. "A forfeit. But I don't sing."

The brownie considered this.

"A riddle, then. Charm me with a riddle."

"Fine, but if you can't solve my riddle, you come out willingly and answer my questions."

"One question."

"Five questions and you answer with only truth." You had to be really specific with brownies.

"Three questions."

"Fine."

I pretended to think hard, but I had several rock-solid riddles ready. My great-grandfather was Odin, the original riddle master.

"Who can hold a forest in his grasp and swallow a man whole, but is afraid of the wind?"

The brownie's face crinkled in a frown as he thought hard.

"A giant?" came the answer. "No! Wait! One of those big green meanies."

"An ogre?" I asked.

"Yes! Yes! Ogres! They're stinkers, so they hate the wind. Pew!" The brownie held his nose and waved his hand as if to fan away a stench.

"Wrong," I said. "You lose. Now come out."

The brownie groaned, but complied. Forfeits were sacrosanct. He scrambled through the small hole in the hedge. Thorns tore at his ragged clothes and elaborate headdress, but he didn't seem to notice.

"If not ogres, who then?" The brownie squinted up at me.

I waggled my finger. "Nah-uh. You know the rules. You didn't guess right, you don't get the answer. But I do. Three answers to three questions."

The brownie's eyes darted sideways as if he might make a run for it. Jacoby lunged at him and chomped his teeth.

"None of that," I said sharply, and Jacoby slunk away to wait in the sun.

I turned to the brownie. He was terrified. He clung to his ragged hat with one shaky hand. I dug in my pack again and came up with an emergency bag of trail mix. He sniffed the bag, then delicately took hold of it with two hands.

I had only three questions. I had to make them count. I could assume that he traveled this way often and would know the Guardians and the neighborhood.

"Can you tell me who pushed the Guardian off the roof?"

He smiled slyly. "Yes."

Crap. I'd just wasted one question.

"*Who* pushed the Guardian off the roof?"

His eyes shifted to the shadows, left and right, and his bare foot scraped at the dirt.

"You have to answer me."

"Them white coats. The takers!"

I had to be careful here. Only one question left. He might know who the takers were, but if not, I'd waste the question.

"Who do they take?"

His eyes were white all around and his hands spread against his chest.

"Me!" He pointed to Jacoby. "Him!"

Then he ducked through my legs and ran away with his bag of trail mix.

So these *takers* were nabbing fae off the streets? Why kill Cyril then? Did he see something? And why had no one reported the missing fae?

"Kyra-lady looks!"

I realized that Jacoby had been tugging at my pant leg for several seconds.

"What?"

"Looks!" He pointed at the rooftop.

A man stood on the ledge outside a third story apartment. The sun was behind me now, so his pale face and dark hair shone in the late afternoon brilliance.

He edged along the ledge which couldn't have been more than three inches wide, his fingers gripping the stone wall.

What the hells? I swept out with my magic to taste his and recoiled. He wasn't human. In fact, his magic was horrifyingly familiar.

Before I could react, he spread his arms wide.

"Goodbye assholes!"

And he dove.

RIDDLE ME A BROWNIE

(November 10, 2080)

If you came here looking for the "best chewy brownie recipe," you're in the wrong spot. Actually, I was amazed at the number of brownie recipes on the ley-web, especially considering my ward hasn't had real chocolate in over a decade. But that's a topic for a different blog. This is a discussion on the fae subspecies known as a brownie.

But first a rant:

Brownies are considered a class two fae of the gnome subspecies, along with bodachs, bogarts, blue-caps and bocans, to name a few. I have issues with this accepted form of classification.

Fae was once a broad term for any of the otherworldly beings documented by European folklore. Today, we lump almost any being with a touch of magic into this designation. Hub sorts them into three orders. Class one encompasses the fae court, beings who, with little or no glamor, can pass among the mundanes. Class two fae are also humanoid, though generally smaller or much larger than humans and speak with clear language. These are the gnomes, trolls, ogres, and so on. Beastkin make up the third class, the creatures that populated the forests of legend.

Hub uses these designations when doling out punishments for crime. A swarm of termites can do as much damage to a house as an arsonist, but the termites won't go to jail for it. Vampire slugs drink blood just like the monsters they're named for, but the council would never prosecute a slug for feeding on humans. It is an imperfect system of justice that the fae have been lobbying for years to change.

I agree with this need to change how we think of the fae. How should we rank a selkie, for instance? It is both beastkin and rational humanoid. And how can we measure the level of sentience in a will o'wisp? And where does that leave the other beings that can claim no fae heritage such as the gargoyles, shifters, vampires and godlings? All these creatures are part of our world now and here to stay. I think we do them an injustice by trying to box them into arbitrary classifications for our own purposes.

End of rant. Back to the regularly scheduled program about brownies.

We all know the myths of brownies. They're little helpers that come out at night to clean the house and do other good deeds. Don't forget to leave milk or other offering or your brownies will take affront and leave your house forever!

Seems simplistic, even for a fairytale.

They are not benevolent housekeepers. In fact, if you find one in your home, I suggest you check your silver. Brownies are pack rats and attracted to shiny things.

In my ward, I come across them almost weekly, squatting in old buildings and making nests out of anything they can find. They can be very territorial too, especially if they think their hoard of treasures (for "treasures," read "garbage") is being threatened. Don't bother bargaining with a brownie for goods or services in the normal way. They have no sense of monetary value. To a brownie, everything belongs to him as soon as he touches it.

The only true way to get what you want from a brownie is a forfeit. This means a tribute of some sort (which is probably where the stories of leaving milk came from). A forfeit means you must give them something they perceive as valuable to you. As I mentioned, they like baubles, but they also adhere to the old-world forfeit rules. You can pay them with a song, a story or a riddle.

Since I don't sing (at least not in any tone you'd want to hear), and stories can take too long, I keep a stash of riddles on hand for bargaining with brownies when I encounter them on a job.

Help a critter wrangler out. Hit me with your brownie-stumping riddle. Bonus points if I can't guess it.

COMMENTS (11)

Without fists I strike, without fingers I point, without legs I run, what am I?
justme5869 (November 10, 2080)

> A clock?
> *cchedgewitch (November 10, 2080)*

If a man carried my burden, he would break his back. I am not rich, but leave silver in my track. What am I?
cchedgewitch (November 11, 2080)

> I got this. Snail.
> *Valkyrie367 (November 11, 2080)*

>> :)
>> *cchedgewitch (November 11, 2080)*

Turn me once, what is out will not get in. Turn me again, what is in will not get out. What am I?
sqirtzburger (November 14, 2080)

> A key?
> *Valkyrie367 (November 14, 2080)*

I have no life, but I can die. What am I?
DaddysGirl (November 12, 2080)

> A vampire or a zombie?
> *Valkyrie367 (November 12, 2080)*

I was going to say a battery, but those work too. Please tell me
that zombies aren't real?
DaddysGirl (November 12, 2080)

> Not that I know of ;)
> *Valkyrie367 (November 12, 2080)*

10

studied the body splayed on the cobblestones. He'd landed on his left side, and one arm and leg were bent at bad angles. His nose was broken and a gash across his crumpled forehead oozed blood.

"Get up," I snapped.

The vampire blinked, wiped his face with his unbroken hand and sat up. He jerked his leg back into place. Already, the wound on his head was healing.

"Could you?" he pointed to his broken arm. "I can't reach."

He wanted me to straighten his broken arm so it could heal. My throat closed and my heart pounded. Memories betrayed me—fangs piercing my throat in the Inbetween, hordes of wojaks, the vampire drones, swarming over the human and fae defenses outside the gate to Underhill.

But Aunt Dana's voice was stronger than any memory. "You are weak when you stand in the shadow of your fear. It will be your death."

So I would try not to fear him. But neither would I be stupid. I pulled my sword and pointed it at his throat, then I leaned in and yanked his arm straight.

"Thank you." He forced his nose back into place with a crack.

I had a million questions, but only blurted, "You're opji!"

He smiled sadly. "Yes, I am. Still, and forever." He pulled a handkerchief from his pocket and mopped the blood off his face. I waited with muscles tensed, ready to impale him before his fangs could impale me.

He saw my fear, could probably smell it.

"Don't worry, I don't drink human blood."

Huh. I'd never heard of such a thing. He did look somewhat emaciated.

The high bones of his cheeks stood out prominently and his eyes bulged a bit as if the surrounding skin had shrunk.

"What do you eat then?" The question just popped out. It was rude to interrogate other species about their personal habits. The socially conscious part of my mind accepted that. The blogger of amazing creatures did not.

The opji shrugged. "Pig blood, mostly. Rats when I can't get that." He looked at the puddle of blood seeping into the cobblestones from his head wound and bared his fangs. "All this wasted blood will make things difficult for the next little while, so maybe you should run along."

He had a faint Irish lilt, which was just…wrong. The vampires in our area were a sect with roots in Poland and Hungary. They spoke with thick Eastern European accents that made me think of the counting vampire from a childhood TV show—a show that no human alive today would even remember.

Opji were always handsome, in the way that panthers were handsome, and despite his wasted look, this one was no exception. His dark hair seemed to glisten and his pale skin only emphasized the huge eyes. Despite the heat, he wore a long-sleeved silk shirt in a deep cobalt blue and black dress pants. They were now torn and dirty, but this somehow only added to his air of dashing menace.

He looked weak, but his eyes kept darting to the pulse at my throat. Oh, yes. He was hungry. I couldn't let a hungry vampire roam the streets of Old Port no matter how polite he was.

"Jacoby, run to the butcher and get some blood for the vamp." I didn't take my eyes off him. "Take my widget to pay for it." I felt Jacoby's deft hands in my pack as he fished for the widget. Then he was gone.

I still held the sword to the opji's throat. Something was definitely off about this guy.

"Now you're going to tell me how an opji ended up living in Montreal."

"My name is Emil Lughwaite." He held out his hand for me to shake, but I only nodded.

"Kyra Greene."

He sighed. "You see. This is why I jump."

I relaxed my stance and the blade dipped. This wasn't a regular opji. I wouldn't be baring my neck to him any time soon, but I'd give him a moment to prove himself.

"Every day, every person I meet, I must make them believe me—that I do not drink their blood."

"How are you here? Within the ward, I mean." Montreal Ward had been built to protect against the opji, after years of brutal warfare. Every gate into the city had fae scanners to be sure that no vampires snuck inside. It shouldn't be possible that he was even here.

Emil finished wiping blood off his face and tucked the handkerchief in his pocket before leaning back on his elbows—both of which were perfectly functional now. I knew opji healed fast, but I'd never seen their healing power in action.

Then I realized what was nagging at me. I could sense his heart beating. Opji hearts beat so slowly, the pulses were nearly undetectable. But Emil's heart thrummed almost as fast as a human's.

"I was stolen by a fae as a baby," he said in a resigned tone, as if he'd told this story before. "I don't know why. He was a minor noble at the queen's court. Perhaps he wanted to keep me as a pet. But he died before I learned to speak. His sister, Lady Lughwaite, had always wanted a child but couldn't conceive. She raised me as her own, hiding me for many years, then finally seeking special dispensation from the queen. I am allowed to stay inside the ward so long as I drink only animal blood. The alchemists test me every few months." He gave a quarter smile.

"So you don't have anything to do with the opji who tried to break into the ward last spring."

"Nothing." His voice was flat, eyes troubled. "But since then…I have no rest. Everyone—the humans and the fae—they accuse me of colluding with the enemy or worse, stalking them to feed." He leaned toward me and whispered, "But in truth, they should be afraid. The cravings…they never go away."

His eyes had a haunted look. Strangely, this admission made me trust him more, and I sat on the grass beside him, my sword relaxed in my grip.

The sun had dropped below the apartments, and the courtyard filled with cooler shadow.

"I once knew a boy who ate rocks," I said. Emil smiled, seemingly happy just to have my company. "No one knew why. His teeth were all broken but he couldn't stop."

"What happened to him?"

"After years of intensive therapy, his parents thought he was cured."

"You think I can get therapy for my cravings?" The vampire looked skeptical.

"Then the kid ate a rock that pierced his intestines and he died floating in his own shit." I stared at the battered vampire. I suspected this wasn't his first attempted suicide, and it had little to do with the recent backlash against the opji.

He thought about my little parable and nodded. "This is how the cravings are. They never go away."

"So you need to make peace with it." I'd done the same with my demanding brand of magic. "Throwing yourself off a building is not a solution."

"Yes, of course, you're right." His focus had shifted. The agreeable words were just a formality as his senses honed in on my sword. His pupils dilated and he breathed in deeply, testing its scent.

Oh, hells.

I might have come to terms with my sword's heritage, but I would never let it be used for suicide. Not ever. Not again. But the look of pure rapture on Emil's face as he focused on my blade told me he was going to force the issue.

He pounced. For a half-dead thing, he was fast. Before I could react, he grabbed my sword and held it up in the dying afternoon light.

"So beautiful." His tired eyes came alive. "It sings to me."

I punched him, aiming for his nose which would hurt my hand less, but he turned at the last moment, and I felt the full brunt of my hit on his cheekbone.

"Ow! Why'd you do that?" He fell back, flinging his arms high, but not letting go of my sword.

I reached across him for the blade and immediately regretted it. As I stretched, my neck opened to his line of sight. I felt him suck in a deep breath—a breath of me.

"Don't even think it." I seized my sword and jumped up, pinning him down with the tip of the blade against his chest.

He smiled. "Yes." The word came out of him as a long, satisfied hiss. "Release me."

I stumbled backward, gripping my sword so tightly, my fingers ached. "No."

Jacoby saved me when he returned with the bottle of blood.

I shoved it at Emil. "Drink this and stay off the rooftops."

He wrapped long fingers around the bottle.

"Thank you, Kyra. Perhaps we will see each other again." His grin was inviting and just a bit cheeky.

"Not if I can help it."

As I left the courtyard, my sword hummed, and I could feel the opji's eyes on my back.

That night I dreamed about a funeral that never happened. It was an old dream, one that had haunted my nights for years. My mother lay in a casket looking withered from her long illness. In real life my mother had recovered, but it didn't take a psychoanalyst to understand that her illness and subsequent retreat to my grandfather's fort in Asgard had left me feeling orphaned.

In my dream, I stood alone by her casket atop a grassy knoll overlooking a barren terrain. Mom lay on a bed of white satin. Wind blew red clouds across the sky, but didn't move a hair on her head. I didn't cry or scream because I knew no one would hear me.

I woke to the smell of bacon cooking and cold dread in my gut. There was a cold lump at my hip too. Kur, my ice sprite, had broken out of his cage again and was curled up next to me. With his wings closed, he looked like a tiny sleeping yeti. I ran my fingers through his silky fur and stared out at the morning light.

I needed to be at Cyril's funeral, even though Mason hadn't asked me to attend. I didn't even know where it was taking place.

As I listened to Gita berating Willow in the kitchen, I tried to rationalize my need to be there. I wasn't so egocentric that I thought everything was about me. A funeral is a very private affair, a way to help family grieve. Mason needed to care for his people. But who cared for Mason? I was used to being the boss, used to having others rely on me and defer to my demands. I understood how this could be lonely at times, like sitting at a bar crowded with people and yet with no one you'd call a friend. How much worse was this for Mason as leader of the Guardians?

He was about to say goodbye to one of his brothers. No one should be alone at a time like that. And I refused to let him push me away again, simply because he'd forgotten how to be in a relationship. I had seen the pain in his eyes and wanted to be there to comfort him. I threw the blankets over my head.

Oh, gods. I was in love with a man who spent half his life as stone.

I hopped out of bed, dressed, and found Gabe in the office.

"Cyril's funeral is tonight. Are you going?"

Gabe shook his head curtly. "Dutch says it's for Guardians only. Some kind of ritual that's not for civilian eyes."

"Can't you wheedle the address out of him? I'd like to stop by, just to show my support."

Gabe frowned. "You want me to ask my potential new boyfriend to leak secrets so you can spy on his boss?"

"When you put it that way, it just sounds shifty."

"It is shifty." Gabe folded his arms across his chest and tried to look intimidating. It didn't work. I already knew he was as soft as Jacoby's new teddy bear.

"Just ask him. If he tells you, it's not such a secret is it?"

I left him mumbling something about female logic.

After lunch, Gabe returned to the office as I was cleaning out Clarence's pen. He wasn't happy about spilling the beans.

"The funeral will be at Union Church tonight. Or rather tomorrow morning, an hour before sunrise."

"What? Why so early?" That was actually late by gargoyle standards. I scooped a fresh load of straw into Clarence's pen while he slithered around my ankles, head-butting me with his rubbery comb.

"Look I got your information," Gabe said. "Don't ask me for more." He turned away to tidy his desk, as if I wouldn't notice that he was only trying to look busy.

"Did something happen between you and Dutch?"

Gabe gave me the full weight of his intense eyes. "As a matter of fact, my little fishing expedition led to our break-up. Dutch thinks I'm too clingy."

"Oh, Gabe! I'm sorry. I didn't mean to cause you any problems."

"Yeah, well. You couldn't know how touchy those Guardians are about their secret rituals. I should have left it alone when Dutch first refused to tell me the location. But it irked me, you know? He blows hot and cold. Sometimes he can't seem to get enough of me, and other times I'm barely an afterthought. So I pushed him."

"And he pushed back."

Gabe nodded. I knew exactly how he felt. Blowing hot and cold seemed to be the Guardian special.

"Maybe he'll change his mind." I laid my hand on his arm.

"The only reason he told me was because I said it was for you. He doesn't want me there."

Now I wasn't sure I should go either. But the vision of standing alone over my mother's body wouldn't leave me.

I set out for my first pest control job, intent on finishing early so I could get some sleep before crashing the gargoyle funeral.

Union Church was one of the oldest in my neighborhood. The town of Sayntanne squeezed up against the Gallop Bridge on the west end of the island, and the church wasn't far from the water's edge. Its main building fronted a warren of smaller structures that had grown up behind it over the years. The Guardians had taken over the complex as their precinct. Here they gathered to discuss crime in the lower echelons of the city and dole out schedules for their nightly prowls. Some gargoyles waited out the sunlight hours on rooftops within the city proper, but most returned to the church grounds, perhaps feeling there was safety in numbers.

A cloister paved in broken cement with weeds pushing through the cracks bordered the main yard. Behind that lay the ruins of an old school and a playground that was slowly sinking into the earth. No lights shone in the abandoned buildings.

Where were they? This was the Guardians' home and they wouldn't bury their dead too far away. The church graveyard was the obvious choice, but it was out in the open, easily viewed from the street, and I had checked it on my way in. No Guardians gathered there. Now I skirted through the shadows of the cloister, pausing to listen for voices. I wasn't exactly sneaking around, but I didn't want to run into any guards who might escort me off the property before I reached the funeral.

An old rectory filled the space at the far end of the cloisters. I peered in the windows. They were filmed with dirt, but I didn't sense movement inside.

Where to now? A small alley—too small for a car—ran between the rectory and the school. Shadows filled it, but I wasn't afraid of the dark. My footsteps sounded hollow on the fractured pavement. I trailed my fingers along the walls. The stones had worn down enough to feel like natural formations instead of masonry. I could see only a crack of sky overhead.

The skulking made me feel guilty, like I was committing a crime. I pushed that thought aside. I had every right to be here.

I continued down the alley until it opened to another, smaller courtyard where several Guardians stood immobile beside a coffin and a gaping hole in the ground. If I hadn't recognized Angus, I would have thought they were statues. I glanced at the sky. It was already starting to lighten toward dawn.

What were they waiting for? I hunkered down in the shadows and watched.

A few minutes later, more Guardians arrived, including Mason.

My legs cramped and my jeans were wet from the damp ground. I stood and shook out my muscles, careful to keep hidden, but my movement must have alerted Mason. His head turned and his eyes bore into the shadows. I felt like they pinned me to the wall, and I almost turned and fled.

He left the circle and crossed the yard, pulling me by the arm, back into the alley.

"You can't be here," he growled.

I yanked my arm away. "Why not?"

"Because this is Guardian business." He planted his feet and crossed his arms.

"Since when did Guardians get a franchise on death? I just want to pay my respects."

"So send flowers." His face was grim. In the shadows I couldn't see his eyes, but I knew they weren't friendly.

"What is your problem? Are you afraid I'll learn the super secret Guardian handshake or something?"

"My problem is that you keep sticking your nose where it doesn't belong."

"You're doing it again."

"What?"

"Pushing me away. I'm here because one of your brothers died. That's what friends do."

He blew out a long breath. "You're right. Just stay here. The others don't like to be seen when they change."

I glanced at the sky. It was noticeably lighter.

I reached for his hand as he turned away. He wouldn't look at me, but he squeezed my fingers before returning to stand vigil with the other Guardians.

Now I felt like a heel. I should have left well-enough alone. I backed into the alley, intending to leave, but the Guardians began to chant and the sound rooted me to the spot.

Twelve Guardians now stood vigil over the casket. Other than Mason, they were all traditional gargoyles, some grotesques, the green man, one duck-faced creature, one fox-face and a few others that were vaguely simian. Their chant was low and solemn. The music grew until it hummed in my bones. I didn't recognize the language, but the song was vibrant and earthy, full of power.

I held my breath and watched as the chant built to a crescendo and then broke off, leaving an echo in the air.

Mason presided over the ceremony at the far end of the courtyard. None of the Guardians stood taller, and none had his dark presence. He held a closed book in his hand, the bible, I assumed. Four Guardians lifted the coffin and lowered it into the waiting grave. I watched as each Guardian tossed in a handful of dirt, then lowered their heads in prayer. Someone signaled the end of the prayer with an "Amen," and they all raised their eyes.

Then a voice rose in song. Mason sang a deep, low hymn in French. I recognized a few words of the lament. It spoke of darkness over the earth, like a mourning cloak, and trees weeping yellow leaves like the torn locks of a mourner.

He raised his face to the east, where the sky had lightened over the edge of the building and sang out loud and clear. His voice woke a strange longing in me. It was the sound of sorrow and brought memories of forgotten heartaches to the surface. The Guardians stood straight and tall, like soldiers at attention around the grave of their fallen brother. No one moved. The sky turned pink and Mason's song sped up as if racing the night.

I couldn't stand it anymore. I stepped away from my hiding spot. Mason turned his head and frowned at me. That's when the sun won the race. The song ended on a cut-off note. The Guardians were stone.

A ring of statues now circled the grave. One minute they had been alive, now they were still. Not dead. I keened the thrum of life coming off them.

And Mason still frowned. He would wear that expression until sunset.

I turned and wove through the alleys and church outbuildings, rehearsing apologies in my head. It seemed very important to me that Mason forgive my intrusion. I decided the best vindication would be to hand him the head of Cyril's killer.

12

My feet squelched inside wet socks with every step. My toes were probably wrinkled prunes by now. I'd just come from the south bridge, where I'd tracked down a tribe of nixies that were damming up the river.

Inside my office, I greeted Gabe's brilliant smile with a scowl. He seemed to have recovered from his split with Dutch.

"There's a gargoyle in your living room." He winked at me. My stomach did a little flutter. "The brambly one, not the broody one."

"Oh. Good." I hadn't faced Mason since the funeral. I wanted to go to him with something concrete about Cyril. Until I had that, I'd stay away.

I dropped my kit beside my desk, unbuckled my tool belt and let it drop too.

Gods, I was tired. Barely any sleep the night before because I was too busy poking my nose in gargoyle business and then a full day hunting shape-shifting water sprites. I wasn't up for company.

"Well, at least one of us has a hot date," Gabe said. His smile had a sharp edge. Maybe he wasn't getting over the breakup as well as I'd thought.

"Tomorrow, you can take me on a hot date to get ice-cream," I said.

He nodded like he knew I was just trying to make him feel better.

"Hub asked for you in the morning, so I pushed everything else back."

"Great. What do they want?" I often did jobs for Hub that their normal exterminators or animal control couldn't handle.

"With the day you had, I'm afraid to tell you."

"Just spill."

"They've got a grubber."

I winced. "Do they need me there tonight?"

"No. I spoke to that new detective. That hard-nosed j—" he checked himself. "That blond guy we met at Old Port. Detective Kesik."

Kesik *was* a hard-nosed jerk. I couldn't fault him there.

"Anyway, he said they contained the grubber for now. And the site isn't stable yet anyway. Some kind of explosion. So best to come first thing in the morning."

"Got it." I resisted the urge to sag into my chair. I might not be able to stand again. "You heading out?"

"Unless you want me to stay?" He cocked an eyebrow at the door to my apartment and the gargoyle waiting beyond. I had the irrational image of Gabe and Angus in a fight and couldn't fathom which one would end up on top. I stifled a giggle into a sigh.

"No, you go. I'll be fine."

I found Angus peering into a terrarium on one of the many shelves full of critter habitats that lined the walls of my apartment.

"Is that the wee snail that Mason brought back from the Inbetween?" Angus asked.

"Yep."

"He's grown."

That was an understatement. Bijou had been about the size of a walnut when Mason found him stowed away in his pack. In the six months since, he'd doubled in size.

"Is he singing?" Angus's craggy face beamed with delight.

"Yes. He does that. I'm not sure if it's a voluntary sound or not." In the quiet of the night, I'd noticed that the little snail made a sound halfway between a whistle and a squeak. "I think he likes you."

Bijou seemed as curious as the spectator, and his multi-hued eye stalks stretched up to get a better look. Angus stuck one twig-like finger in the case and waggled it. Bijou's eyes waggled back. Angus laughed and pulled his hand away.

"Damnation and roses, but you've got yer hands full with this lot." He turned slowly around the room. Dozens of eyes inspected the new visitor.

Kur reached his tiny, strangely human hand through the bars of his cage. My rats chased each other on their wheel. A pair of troll bats fluttered their wings and hung upside-down on their perch. Willow yawned, then tucked her nose under her tail and went back to sleep.

Angus turned to the terrarium beside Bijou's, and his expression scrunched in disgust when he saw the purple gelatinous blobs sitting on a rock inside.

"What on God's black earth are those?"

"Vampire slugs."

"And for what purpose do you keep them?"

The slugs were more like giant leeches that moved on land instead of in the water. They latched onto larger beasts and drank blood. One vampire slug could drain a cow.

"You'd be surprised at how helpful they can be in my line of work. Besides, I think they're fascinating in a morbid way."

Angus shook his head. "To each his own." Then he looked at me for a full minute without speaking. A full minute. That's a long time to stand still under anyone's scrutiny, and near impossible with Angus's twiggy brows furrowed over his intense eyes. I broke first.

"On a scale of one to livid, how mad is he?"

"Madder than a box of three-legged cats."

"That mad, huh?"

"Girlie, you should be proud. I haven't seen him this broody since…well, never."

"Just because I intruded on Cyril's funeral? That seems a bit excessive, even for Mason."

"Oh, it is that. Which makes me believe there is more going on in his stubborn granite head. You've really got under his crust."

I crossed my arms and changed the subject. "I assume you're here for a reason."

"Aye. Magic lessons, remember?"

I sighed. Shower and bed would have to wait. "Coffee?"

"By the gods, yes. It's too early for decent folk." In fact, it was just past six in the evening, but that was the crack of dawn to a gargoyle.

I pulled the pot off the coffee maker and got a familiar whiff of fishiness. Hunter eyed me from the bottom of the pot. I sighed, dumped him into his tank, threw in fresh crayfish to keep him busy, then scrubbed the pot well.

"Well isn't he just as cute as a button on a hog's arse." Angus tapped the glass. Hunter popped his head out of the water and threw a mangled crayfish in Angus's face.

"What in the hells?" Angus picked a bit of shell off his cheek.

I threw him a towel to dry off. "Bad crayfish."

Hunter slunk back to the bottom of the tank.

"I like him." Angus wiped his face. "He's sassy."

Once settled at my rickety kitchen table—that was now propped on a wooden block since Joran had bent one of the legs as he trashed my apartment—with two cups of fresh coffee, I studied Angus in the glow of the pendant light hanging over the table.

He really was beautiful, but also frightening and a little bit ridiculous. His face looked like it was carved from a solid block of oak. Twigs twined around his head, woven in a complex pattern to resemble an untidy wig. A few green leaves poked through this mess. When he opened his mouth to speak, the hollow inside was pure black, except for his slate-gray tongue.

I pulled out a bottle of whisky and offered him a shot in his coffee. He nodded and sipped the hot brew with an expression of pure contentment on his face.

I sipped my coffee and waited for him to speak. He seemed troubled.

"So are you ready to dig up dirt on Gerard Golovin," he said finally.

"That's why you're here, right? You teach me, and I snoop for you."

He nodded. "But I got the easy end of the bargain. You realize that spying on Golovin will be dangerous?" His bushy eyebrows lowered, almost masking his eyes. "I shouldn'av forced you into it. And I wouldn'a hold you to the bargain."

Angus was really troubled by all this.

"I'm not backing out. I'm just not sure how we can go about spying on him. He's a prime minister after all."

Angus scratched the bark-like skin where his shirt opened on his chest.

"Aye, it's a stumper. He's got a lab on Perrot Island and another at Abbott's Agora, but they're both locked down tighter than a virgin's corset."

"He must have an office at Hub too. I'll be there tomorrow. Maybe I can get a peek inside."

"Don't do anything rash. I'll ask around with the alchemists and see if I can find an excuse to get inside his lab on the island. If there's any alchemy shenanigans going on, it'll be there." He stood and rubbed his hands together. "So, let's get this magic party started."

"Wait. I have an off-topic question for you. Do you know of any opji living within the ward?"

Angus sat down again. "Oh, you've met Emil, have you?"

"You know him?"

"'Course. He's an old friend of the Guardians. Helps us out with surveillance sometimes. How did you meet?"

"He threw himself off a roof in front of me."

"Ah! He does like to impress the girls." Angus grinned.

"A bit melodramatic for my taste. But there was something odd about him. He was alive. At least I could sense his heart beating."

Angus watched me with a grim expression. "And you're worried about this?"

I nodded. "He seemed very taken with my sword. Like he could sense its potential. But the blade is unpredictable when it comes to immortals. I'd like to understand Emil's deal before he forces the issue."

"Forces the issue? You mean before he forces you to kill him."

I nodded. Angus poured more whisky into his empty coffee mug.

"This has been a problem for you in the past?"

I nodded again.

"By hell's sweet teats, that's a raw deal." He shook his head. "Well, I don't know much about the opji, they're a secretive bunch, but I know that they are not truly undead."

"But I've felt their hearts start beating. In the Inbetween when I fought that wojak, my blade broke its immortality and for a moment, before I lopped its head off, its heart was beating."

"The wojaks, yes. They are just walking carcasses. The opji breed them to be killed and brought back to life with dark magic. But the opji are a bit different. They're still alive, though their hearts beat barely at all."

"How is that possible?"

"More dark magic. They are masters at it. Opji are born with that superhuman healing power you saw with Emil. But at puberty the blood lust kicks in. That's when they perform the *zycha*—a rite that both kills them and lets them live forever."

"Sounds like a curse."

Angus shrugged. "One man's curse is another man's baptism."

"So Emil, raised in Montreal, never had this zycha rite performed on him?"

"Probably not. Poor kid. The zycha helps to control the blood lust, without it…" Angus shook his head. "Anyway, let's get this showboat on the road. Time to learn some magic."

I put away my vampire worries for now.

We went over to Gita's plant rack, where she grew herbs for all her concoctions.

"I worried we'd have to go out and find us some plants to experiment on, but you've got a whole jungle in here." Angus eyed the pots.

"Wait. You won't hurt them, will you?" Gita would never forgive me. Some of those herbs were rare, and she fussed over them like they were her babies.

"I'm not gonna do anything to them. You are." He held up a gnarled finger when I started to protest. "Calm your horses. We're not doing battle magic here. Just a little communing with nature is all."

I stared at him dubiously. My only experience with flora magic involved a giant man-eating plant that we had somehow subdued together.

"Here, now. Pick one of these pots and bring it to the kitchen," he instructed.

"Just a minute." I went over to Gita's closet and peeked inside. She was curled up on her bed using her widget as a flashlight to read from an old paperback of "Barometer Rising." I'd told her she could read the book on the widget instead, but Gita did things her way.

"Angus is here to teach me some flora magic. Is it okay if we use one of your plants. He promises that we won't hurt it." I waited for the waterworks but she just waved me away.

"Use the parsley. It grows like a weed anyway." Then she flipped a page in her book and I shut the door.

"We're good to go," I said to Angus. I settled the pot of parsley on the kitchen table and sat in front of it. "How do I do this?"

"You talk to it." Angus eased himself into the seat opposite from me.

"Right."

Angus saw my hesitation. "You can't ask the wee greenie to fight for you, if you don't know how to talk to it. Now, settle your mind and focus on the leaves. What do you see? And don't just tell me it's green. Really look at it."

I focused on one leaf—vaguely trefoil, with a deckled edge, and variegated with a lighter green along the veining. The veins themselves were mesmerizing, and I soon lost myself in the branching patterns.

"Good, good," Angus said quietly. "You can feel it, can't you."

"Feel what?"

"The lifeblood. The magic. Reach for it."

I let out my keening hesitantly. Nothing.

"You're holding it as tight as a bull's butt in fly season. Let loose, girl."

"It's not that easy."

"It would be if you weren't so uptight about your magic. I only got to listen to that damnation sword screaming to know you're afraid of the power the gods gave you."

So Angus could keen too. Made sense if that part of my magic came from my dryad side.

"Just drop those walls you've built around you. You're better protected than the gold in old Fort Knockers."

"That was Fort Knox."

"Whatever. Just drop it."

I sighed and tried to comply. It wasn't easy, no matter what Angus thought. I'd spent the last sixty-five years fortifying those walls. They'd need a magic jackhammer to break them down.

I leaned in closer so the parsley filled my vision. The green leaves were beautiful in their symmetry and variegation. I tried to block out all other thoughts—the rustling of little feet in the cages, the rasp of Angus's shoe on the floor, the tiny splashes as Hunter ate dinner in his tank, and the faint hum of my slumbering sword.

I could do this. I could drop my wards completely. I was safe here. This was my space. I let magic slip through my fingers, draining it away like water from a tub. The psychic noise around me grew, humming and buzzing, filling every space between my atoms. And under all that noise was the deep thrum of Terra's heart—the magic of the land itself.

Now the trick was to find one tiny parsley voice within that din. No, not one voice. Dozens of voices, as if each leaf sang a harmony of a greater song. Of course, I'd been aware of plant magic before, but I'd never paid attention to it. Always, it had just been a drone of magic in the background of all the other magics. Now I sensed the uniqueness of this one pot of parsley. Its song was a bit cheeky, like it was having fun.

"I hear it!" I almost pulled back in my excitement, but Angus urged me on.

"Go on. Don't stop now. Reach for it."

Instinctively, my hand reached forward, even though I knew he meant for me to reach with my magic. I let my hand drop and tried to release a bit of my magic, like I did with my sword when I needed to prime it. The parsley leaves shot straight up in rigid spikes then wilted flat.

Suddenly the magic around me was overwhelming, like the racket of a million cicadas coming out of their seventeen-year hibernation. My fingers went rigid. I wanted to be holding my sword. Too…much…magic.

I panicked and slammed my wards back down hard. Hard enough that Angus winced. My sword wailed its anxiety from the umbrella stand by the door.

I laid my head on my arms that rested on the table.

Angus patted my back. "It's okay. We'll figure it out."

I wasn't so sure. I glanced at the parsley that hung like wet noodles over the edge of the pot.

"You said I wouldn't hurt it!"

"Well, now I didna expect you to blast it so. Where did you learn to do that?"

"I…I don't know. It's just something I can do with my sword."

Angus whistled. "Remind me never to spar wit' you."

I could tell my magical outburst ruffled him because his accent got thicker. He patted the parsley and hummed a little tune. The leaves perked up.

"Give her some water and she'll be fine."

I slumped in my chair. "Clearly my dryad nature can never beat out the Valkyrie warrior in me."

"Nonsense. It just takes practice. If you can hear the wee greenie, you can talk to it." He rose to leave. "For now, just practice listening. We'll try again in a few days. But now, I'm off to do my rounds. No rest for us Guardians."

I gripped his hand, and he looked a bit startled. I didn't think that many people were ever brave enough to touch a green-man gargoyle.

"Thanks." I tried to fill that one word with true gratefulness.

Angus smiled. "Oh, aye."

13

Wednesday morning greeted me like a kick in the face. After Angus left, I practiced dropping my wards until my head pounded, but got no closer to success. Now I felt hungover, though I hadn't had the fun of drinking.

I shuffled through my morning chores like a zombie. Gita force-fed me oatmeal with raisins, and it sat in my stomach like cement. Gabe watched me with worried eyes as he handed off the morning job manifests. I scanned my widget and groaned. I'd forgotten about Hub's grubber problem.

"You want me to cancel?" Gabe asked.

"No." Hub was a priority. They gave me too much business to just blow them off.

I grabbed the large cooler Gabe had packed for me, my travel mug filled with Gita's jet-fuel brew, and my sword before heading out to the truck. Just gripping my sword's sheath eased my headache. Usually, the magic was a one-way street—from the ley-lines, through me and into the sword. But ours was an odd symbiotic relationship, even if I rarely took advantage of its power. Today, I welcomed the boost. Along with the caffeine, it might just get me through the morning.

Jacoby popped his head out of his little house beside the garage.

"You needs 'prentice today?"

"Sure, hop in." I held open the door and he jumped into the passenger seat. Jacoby was about to get a real dose of what pest control meant in the brave new world.

A Hub cleanup crew met me at the site of an explosion in Carterville, a neighborhood in the north end of the ward. An illegal magic amplifier had been found at the scene, and detectives were trying to figure out who had initiated the blast. I had little to do with the investigation, but Hub had called me in to tackle the grubber that emerged from the flood plains, attracted to the burst of magic.

Grubbers are translucent, gelatinous creatures about the size of a compact car. They have dozens of stubby legs that leave trails of slime as they move. They're harmless to humans because they feed only on corpses. But there were a lot of corpses in the wake of the explosion. My job was to neutralize the slimy beast and recover anything it ate.

Woo-hoo.

The crew chief met me wearing a thaumasuit that would insulate him from magic contamination. He had yet to don the hood and mask, but his long red hair was pulled back in a ponytail and his beard was braided like a Viking's. The sight of him shoved a tiny splinter into my heart because he looked a whole lot like Aaric, my first love.

"Matt Kender." He didn't hold out a hand to shake mine. People who worked with hazmat rarely did. "You can suit up in there." He pointed to a large tent.

"Is it really necessary? I can take a lot of magic."

He leaned in close and bared his perfect white teeth.

"I don't care if you're the equivalent of a magic sponge. On my site, everyone suits up."

"Fine."

Inside the crew hut, I found a suit more or less in my size. Another crew member was just starting her shift and she helped me tape up my wrists and ankles. By the time she sealed me in, I was already sweating. This was going to be a long day.

There were no suits in Jacoby's size, but he would have just teleported out of it anyway. Dervishes could take a lot of heat, magic or otherwise, so I wasn't worried about him.

Outside, I approached the perimeter of the site which was blocked off with yellow rope and also protected by a powerful ward that extended a full city block. Whatever had exploded inside wasn't good.

The crew chief watched the coroner haul out two covered bodies on stretchers.

"Anyone know what happened?" I asked.

Matt frowned, then his expression turned to stone.

"Some moron had an unauthorized lab in a residential area. Experiment went bad and *boom!* Suddenly we've got a ruptured ley-line and creatures breaking out of the flood plains to feed on it. Not to mention a dozen fatalities and twice as many wounded."

Technically, the Laval flood plains were inside Montreal ward. After the war, a vast section of the city fell into the water. In the fifty years since, Laval had been partially drained, but it was still unusable swampland. The ruling ministers had big plans to reclaim it, but draining the water was only part of the problem. So much magic had been expelled on the site, it was a perfect breeding ground for manifestations of all kinds. The royal fae court was situated nearest to Laval, and they patrolled the border, keeping the nastier swamp creatures in their place.

"What else broke through the border?" I asked.

Matt puffed up his chest. "So far we've taken down a griffin, a bear-like creature and something my tech called a wendigo. I don't believe it, but the thing bit off the tech's arm before we could blast it."

"You killed them all? Why did no one call me in sooner?" If it truly was a wendigo—which I doubted—I couldn't have done much. But a griffin? I could have saved that.

Matt's eyes slid sideways at me. "With all due respect, ma'am. We had it under control."

Did he just "ma'am" me?

"Fine. Whatever. Show me where the grubber is."

"Southeast quadrant. Near the church." He corrected himself. "Near where the church used to be. The explosion happened during the knitting circle's monthly meeting and three senior ladies died in the blast. Then, before we could recover the bodies, the grubber rolled over them like a steamroller—a Mrs. Dulyle, Mrs. Wardynski and a Miss Poole." He checked his widget. "Another knitter is being treated for a heart attack after seeing her friends sucked inside the beast. It's a gruesome thing." Matt frowned.

"Oh, I don't know. Sounds like an efficient way to clean up the dead," I said.

"You're kidding, right?"

"Sure. Let's go with that."

I headed for the ward gate, carrying my cooler and my sword. Jacoby skipped along behind me.

"Who's that? He can't go inside." Matt pointed at the dervish.

"You just try and keep him out," I said over my shoulder.

I ducked under the rope and walked down the street to a kind of town square, bracketed on all sides with duplexes. Fires had scorched one section of buildings, but the rest looked untouched. Except for the glass that crunched like gravel under my feet. Every window in every building was shattered.

We walked past the epicenter of the blast zone. The home that had stood there was flattened. Those on either side sustained heavy damage too. Rescue workers were still picking through the debris, looking for bodies. Even with the thaumasuit, I could keen the rush of magic coming through the ruptured ley-line. It howled like hurricane-force winds, and I couldn't believe that the rescue workers were deaf to it.

"Whose house was this?" I asked a tech who was making scans of the wreckage with a thaumagauge.

"Some alchemist moron," he muttered.

"Does the moron have a name?"

The tech checked his widget. "Peter Sewel."

"Was it an accident?"

"Seems to be." The tech shrugged. "Shouldn't have had a lab here. There's a park just across the street.

A second tech approached. His face was red inside his mask. "What are you doing giving out classified information to a civie?"

"She's not a civie. She works here." He pointed to my thaumasuit as if it were an official badge.

I left them arguing and slipped away before they could question my credentials.

Peter Sewel. I would ask Angus about him on the off chance he was one of the alchemists working with Gerard Golovin.

The church on the southeast corner was one of these modern designs that looked more like a community center, at least what was left of it. The back end of the building was nothing more than a pile of crumpled siding.

I found the grubber sitting like a bloated bag of clear pudding on the front lawn. It had eaten so much in the last few hours that its pudgy feet no longer reached the ground, and they twitched in the air while the grubber went about digesting the knitting club.

Because the beast was translucent, I could see the bodies floating in its digestive juices. One face pressed against the inside of the stomach. She wore an expression of surprise, even in death.

I set down my cooler, opened it and pulled out a vampire slug.

"Take this." I handed it to Jacoby, who pulled a face. "Just take it. Press it to the side of the grubber." I pulled out two more slugs. "We're going to juice this thing."

An hour later, I was exhausted, covered in slime and nicely broiled inside my suit.

Vampire slugs are amazing. They can drink ten times their weight in liquid. And they happen to find grubber juice delicious. When latching onto an animal in the wild, the slugs will drink until they became too heavy, then drop off to digest their booty. But grubber slime short-circuits their instincts, and they would keep drinking until they burst. After an hour, we pulled them off the grubber and let the slugs rest and digest in the shade.

Jacoby looked a little green as he watched the slugs that were now each as fat as prized hogs.

"We'll need a wheelbarrow to get them home," I said. "Go see if you can find one." Jacoby nodded and dashed off.

I walked around the grubber, which was much deflated. I didn't want to kill it. The poor thing was just doing what grubbers do. But humans are twitchy about their dead. If I didn't retrieve the knitting club ladies, someone else would and that would go much worse for the grubber.

I primed my sword and made a two-foot slit on its belly. The grubber didn't even flinch. I shoved my arm inside, searching through the goo until my hand closed around something solid and I pulled. The body popped out with a gush of viscous liquid that soaked me to the ankles. She was still clutching her knitting.

I love my job. I love my job. I kept repeating that mantra, hoping I'd believe it as I dug in for the next body.

After stitching its wound, I dropped the deflated grubber at the edge of the Laval flood plains. It would recover and slink back into the magic-rich waters of the swamp. I didn't worry about it breaking out again. The fae were swarming the border, guarding it in the aftermath of the explosion in Carterville.

At Hub Station, I left Jacoby to watch the vampire slugs in the truck and headed inside. I kept a locker there, so at least I could shower and change before I had to fill out my report. Working for Hub paid the bills, but I didn't love the documentation, especially when there were deaths involved. Hub would investigate this event from every angle, and my report needed to be exacting.

After cleaning up, I grabbed a tablet from the dispatch office to detail the gory account of my morning and headed for the cafeteria.

Susanna Coulter was getting her tray when I stepped in line.

"Hey, anything good on the menu today?" I asked.

She turned her bright smile on me. We weren't exactly friends, but I'd helped her through the opji attack last spring, and we'd bonded over Cyril's corpse, so I felt that we were close enough acquaintances to have lunch together.

She pointed to my wet hair. "You just come off a job?"

"Yeah. A grubber."

"Eww. I don't know how you do it."

I shrugged. "The work keeps me in cat food." When she looked at me oddly, I added, "I have a lot of rescues."

Still thinking about the grubber, I avoided anything pudding-like and added a spring salad with grated beets and turnip to my plate. You couldn't eat a bad meal in Montreal. It was part of our civic pride. But the cafeteria at Hub was a hidden gem. The chefs were a married couple—human and fae—who brought as much passion to their food as they did to their kitchen. Even now I could hear them arguing hotly behind the kitchen's swinging doors. A sound rang out, like a metal bowl hitting the wall.

"Looks like Penny and Cedric are at it again," Susanna said with a smile.

"They can argue all they want as long as they keep making this amazing bread." I added an extra deep brown pumpernickel bun to my tray. I'd earned it with that grubber.

As we sat at an empty table with our loaded trays, I said, "So did you know the alchemist who blew himself up in Carterville last night?" I wasn't good at small talk. Susanna didn't seem to mind.

"Peter? I didn't know him well, but it's a shame. He was a good alchemist."

"In what way?"

Susanna stirred her soup, thinking before she spoke. "I heard he was working on the swamp problem. Had a new device that would speed up reclaiming the flood plains by decades. His theories are supposed to revolutionize the way we use magic. I guess it didn't work out."

Not so much.

"He was working for Gerard Golovin though, right?"

Susanna's eyes jerked up to meet mine.

"Who told you that?"

You just did, I thought, but I only shrugged.

"I saw the excavations at his new railway. Isn't he also looking for some new engine to make the digging go faster? Seems natural that the two alchemists would work together."

Susanna peered around the cafeteria as if looking for eavesdroppers. Then she leaned in and spoke softly.

"Don't get me wrong. Golovin's brilliant. And kind of sexy too, if you like old guys." She grinned, and I played along, pretending that Golovin was a girl's dream.

"But he's very strict about research protocols. Don't go around asking questions or you'll find yourself being questioned in return." She leaned in and whispered, "In a Hub interrogation room."

I nodded and chewed my salad for a few minutes, looking for something to say that would change the topic.

The silence stretched. This was why I didn't have a lot of close friends. I sucked at the whole social interaction thing. Animals were so much easier.

"So you said you take in rescues? What's that like?" Susanna finally asked. I eyed her to see if she was really interested, or just making noise to fill the space. She smiled, so I gave it a shot.

"I get a lot of class three fae creatures that need caring for. Most of them can't survive in the city. And then a few I can't even classify. Lately, I've had a dervish attach himself to me. I couldn't shake him, so I made him my apprentice."

Susanna's eyes were wide, and her fork stopped halfway to her mouth. "A dervish? Aren't those things dangerous?"

I shrugged. "Only if you get them excited." I didn't enjoy talking about my critters face-to-face like this. I could blog about them all day long, but hearing the words aloud—*I made a dervish my apprentice*—just made me realize how crazy I sounded to other, normal people.

"So what are you working on?" I asked. Work was usually a safe topic with alchemists.

Susanna's eyes lit up. "It's pretty cool. I've recreated the Renaissance era blazing alembic, but with a modern twist, of course."

"I thought your work had something to do with gargoyles. Isn't that why you wanted to examine Cyril's body?"

"Oh, it does. Hey," she paused, spoon half way to her mouth, "you know that Guardian captain guy, Mason? Can you ask him to let me see the body? I just want to do a few scans. I sent a request to the Guardians, but they just returned it with a no. Didn't even give me a reason."

"They like their privacy." I thought about Mason and the look of betrayal on his face when he saw me at the funeral. "In any case, the funeral was last night. Cyril's been buried."

"That's too bad."

"Why do you think examining his body would help with your research?" Anything that would help me understand the gargoyles better—and Mason, by extension—was welcome information.

Susanna scooped up the last mouthfuls of her soup before answering. "It's kind of complicated."

"I would love to know more about your work. Maybe we could…um… meet for lunch sometime and you could show me your lab." I twirled my fork, just to keep my fingers busy and forced myself to meet Susanna's eyes.

She quirked a smile that brought out the dimple on her cheek and said, "Sorry, but I'm into guys."

I wanted to bang my head on the table to knock some social grace into myself. I hadn't had a female friend since Asgard. And that was Gunora, Aaric's little sister, so it was more like a friendship of convenience. I just didn't know how to do this girlfriend thing.

"No, I mean not like that," I said too forcefully and Susanna frowned.

"Not that you aren't attractive or anything…" I took a deep breath and started again. "Look, I'm just interested in your work. It sounds fascinating and I thought we could be friends. Maybe. If that works for you."

Kyra, stop talking.

Susanna studied me for a minute, then laughed. "Okay. But I work at Hub in the mornings, then at my lab behind Abbott's Agora in the afternoons. Dinner would be better. How about we meet at that little cafe as you enter the market then we can go to my lab after?"

"Sure. That'll work."

We ate in awkward silence, and I was much too grateful when a uniformed officer poked his head into the cafeteria to interrupt us.

"Lowe is calling for all hands on deck. Some big announcement. That means all of you in the ready room in five."

I wasn't technically a Hub employee, more like a contractor, but I wanted to hear what Detective Lowe had to say too. Maybe it had something to do with these takers the brownies had mentioned.

Captain Glenda Lowe wasn't happy. In fact, it looked like unhappy had taken up residence in her nasolabial folds. She scowled at the gathering of officers, alchemist techs and other Hub workers who were now shuffling into a room too small to hold them. Susanna and I slipped in and stood with our backs against the far wall.

Under Lowe's glare, the crowd settled down.

"By now you've all heard about the explosion in Carterville last night. The clean up of the site is ongoing. But a ley-line was ruptured and until alchemist crews contain it, we need to be on the lookout for odd manifestations. You all know what that means."

Ley-line ruptures were bad. The ward around the city not only kept out aggressive neighbors like the opji, it moderated the magic by siphoning off the ley-lines. Odd things still happened. One block on the east end of the city was permanently stuck in winter. Sometimes, for no reason at all, small forests would pop up overnight and engulf entire neighborhoods. And once, a crystal formation had grown around a west-end deli. It grew so fast that it blocked the doors and trapped diners inside. But these oddities were mostly controlled.

A ruptured ley-line meant that pure magic was spilling into the city. Until the alchemists could cap it, anything could happen.

From her podium, Captain Lowe continued. "So be on the lookout for anything unusual and report it immediately. We've set up a special task force to respond as needed."

Someone from the front of the room spoke up. "What about the flood plains? I heard a bunch of nasties came out of there last night." General murmurs of discontent answered that.

Lowe raised a hand for quiet. "The fae have increased their patrols on the border of the swamp. I've been assured that they will catch anything attracted to the magic." More grumbling. A few people here weren't convinced of the fae's ability to stop things bursting out of the flood plains.

"When will the ley-line be capped?" said another voice.

"As soon as the alchemists can," Lowe said. "By tomorrow latest. But we can expect the manifestations to go on for some weeks."

"Will we be getting overtime?" someone else asked.

Lowe's lips pinched tight. "Overtime is not on the table yet."

The discussion continued with more questions about logistics. I was about to slip out the door and head home when one woman stood up and spoke over the noise.

"Does this mean that the investigation into the missing fae is on hold?"

The room went quiet. I craned my neck to see who had spoken, but could only see the top of the woman's head.

Lowe didn't look pleased about the question.

"Constable Hughes, there is no investigation. Fae go missing all the time. The queen's court isn't concerned, and so we're not concerned. In fact, you seem to be the only one bothered here. I would even say you're obsessed. Let me make it simple for you. Until further orders, all your energy will be spent walking your beat, looking for odd magic, not missing fae. If you can't do that, let me know now, and I'll find someone who can. Is that clear?"

"Yes, ma'am," came the quiet answer.

Detective Lowe dismissed the meeting. I said my goodbyes to Susanna, and she headed back up to her lab. But I hung around the station lobby until I saw the dark-haired officer leaving.

I caught up to her as she strode out the front doors.

"Hey! Can I talk to you for a minute?"

She turned to me, frowning. Dark curls framed a pretty pale face with beads of sweat already glistening on her forehead from the heat. She was shorter than me by a good four inches, but she was curvier, and the curves looked good in her Hub uniform. A few eyes turned our way as we walked past, and I was pretty sure they weren't looking at me in my grubby jeans and work boots.

"I saw you in there." I thumbed back at Hub Station. "Heard you ask about the missing fae."

She stopped in her tracks and turned to me. "Who are you?"

"Kyra Greene. I work on contract for Hub sometimes. I was at the blast site this morning. And you are?"

"Constable Hughes. Valerie." She looked me up and down, then started walking again. "I shouldn't be talking about that. You heard the captain."

"Does the name 'takers' mean anything to you?"

That stopped her again. "Yes! Where did you hear that?"

"From a brownie. It could be meaningless."

"It's not. The fae are all whispering about them."

I wondered how a human officer would know about fae whisperings, but then I saw something I should have noticed right away. Her magic had that lilting, joyful beat that was common to the fae. She was human with some fae blood or a full blood fae wearing a good glamor. I voted for the latter.

"So who are the takers?" I asked.

"Dunno. But they've got the fae community around Talon Street locking their doors even during the day. That's my usual beat—Talon Street from Dennis Boulevard all the way to Fleet. So far, I calculate that a dozen people have gone missing, but they're mostly homeless or addicts, so no one at the station wants to hear it. This is me." We stopped at a bicycle parked in one of the bike racks that were all over town. She touched her widget to the rack to unlock it and mounted.

"If I find out anything more about the takers, do you want to know?" I asked.

She shrugged. "You can ask around, but no one will talk, especially not to a human." She nodded and pedaled off.

It seemed I would have to visit Talon Street soon.

14

Coaxing Clarence to lick hairball remedy off my fingers required some acrobatics. He hated the stuff. I needed more than two arms to hold him down and force the gooey paste into his mouth.

Every few months, Clarence grew noticeably. The snake half of him shed his skin. The chicken half went through a full molt. During this time, he often groomed himself to excess and his digestive tract became blocked with feathers and skin. I'd discovered that cat hairball remedy helped. And since he was looking a bit scruffy, I assumed he was about to go into a molt. I was trying to be proactive, but he didn't appreciate it. I reminded myself that this was one of the joys of caring for animals. No point getting mad at him for resisting my care. He didn't know any better.

"Come on, buddy. It's greasy goodness. Willow likes it." The cat opened her eye when she heard her name but declined to comment.

"Gobble! Gobble!" Clarence slipped out of my hands—which were now sticky with paste—and tore around the cage.

"Here," I shoved the tube at Gita. "I'll force open his beak, and you squirt some in." I wrestled with him, getting a mouth full of feathers, but managed to secure him under one arm and pry his beak open with my other hand. Gita smeared the paste onto the roof of his mouth and I let go. He snorted and shook his head, spattering the cage—and me—with goo.

I sighed. Hopefully he got enough down to make a difference.

"You need a bath." Gita sniffed. "Can't meet the queen smelling like chicken-lizard."

"No, I can't." I headed for my bathroom, trying to ignore the flutter in my stomach brought on by Gita's reminder.

Today I had an important meeting with Queen Leighna. The stories warn you never to accept a favor from a fae. They don't mention that the fae don't like owing a debt any better. They're a tricksy lot, and that makes them suspicious of others. It's best to accept payment for any favors done. So when I helped to uncover Prince Alvar's plot to overthrow the Winter Court, Leighna offered me a boon.

I'd contacted her office in the weeks after the opji attack, but Merrow, the queen's advisor, told me she'd call when Leighna was well enough to receive visitors. The queen had been seriously hurt when the old condo collapsed on her after the battle, but she'd closed the last door between our world and Underhill, blocking further raids by the opji. I'd waited six long months to hear back from Merrow, and today I would get my boon.

After showering and drying my hair, I found Gita in my bedroom pulling clothes out of my closet.

"I already have an outfit picked out." I pointed to the beige pants and short-sleeved sweater on my bed.

Gita squinted one eye at me. "You can't wear that to see the queen."

"Why not? Last time we met, I was mostly wearing blood and dirt. She didn't seem to mind."

"Which is why you need to show up dressed like a normal person today." Gita pulled out a cream-colored summer dress with a red poppy print. "This one."

How had that even survived in my closet? It should have died of fright long ago, all alone in the dark, surrounded by my blood-encrusted jeans and faded work shirts.

"I wore that ten years ago. It can't possibly fit." I touched the soft fabric, remembering the only time I'd worn it to a friend's wedding. What was her name? Bethany? It was the first year I returned to Montreal and knew next to no one, had no plan for my life going forward and no job. At least I still wore pretty clothes.

"Try it." Gita actually smiled. I thought her face might break. This new, happy Gita was still freaking me out a bit. She saw my expression and shoved the dress at me.

"Fine, but it won't fit." I slipped the dress over my head. It fell around my body like it was meant to be there. The fabric was a soft cotton blend that fell just below my knees, with enough skirt to flare if I twirled.

I twirled, and felt just like a girl.

"I remember this being too snug." I tugged at the bodice. If anything the fit was a touch too loose.

"You don't eat enough. You work too hard. This is what happens." She poked me in the hip. "You lose all the good parts."

I found the red sandals that went with the dress squashed under my old running shoes and slipped them on. My sword, in its ratty old sheath, didn't go with the ensemble, but I had no choice. I had to bring it. I decided to carry it, rather than strap it on and glamored it to look like an umbrella. A dash of lipstick and Gita pronounced me ready to go.

"You look beautiful."

I reached out and hugged her, not caring if she smelled of brine and musty rags.

"Thanks."

She gave a dry-eyed sniff. "Oh, be gone with you now." And she headed back to her closet.

Gabe's eyes lit up as I walked through the office, and he let out a low whistle.

"Damn. You should dress like that every day."

I laughed. "It's hardly practical, though I suppose the poppies would hide the blood splatter."

Jacoby slipped his hand in mine. His fingers were warm and bony.

"I comes with you, Kyra-lady?"

"Not today."

"But I ams your 'prentice!"

"You are, but I'm not working today. I have a meeting and it's personal. Something I have to do by myself. Understand?"

Jacoby frowned but nodded. I crouched to meet his eye.

"Can you help Clarence while I'm out? He needs a friend right now. Maybe you could coax him to drink a bit of water."

"Yes! I be's a good friend."

"I shouldn't be too late." I squeezed his hand and headed out for my date with the winter queen.

THE COURT GARDENS were a glorious array of wildflowers, even this late in the season. I suspected fae magic at work. The fae didn't believe in confining the earth's bounty in beds. Better to let nature dictate the color scheme and design. A narrow cobbled path leading from the parking lot to the main entrance was the only concession to order.

Right by the front door, I stopped to move a snail off the path so he wouldn't be squashed, then took a deep breath. I was stalling. It was time to face the queen.

Contrary to popular belief, the Winter Court was not housed in an ice palace, but a large municipal building on the east end of the island. Built in the early twentieth century, the limestone and granite building was one of the tallest in the city, ten stories high. Its top floor scraped the underbelly of the ward. Outside, the style was all business, but inside, the fae had redecorated the old offices to suit their tastes. It was all soft lines, pale wood and natural textures. No chrome or glass.

A smartly dressed goblin greeted me at the entry. When he glanced suspiciously at the umbrella in my hand, I expected him to demand that I relinquish my sword. I let the glamor drop. He nodded at the weapon but said nothing. The fae are less fragile than humans. It would take more than a single sword strike to take down anyone in this building.

"Leighna is expecting you," he said with a toothy smile. Not for the first time, I marveled at the familiarity. Leighna ruled the fae absolutely, and yet they all referred to her like a friend.

I, however, was not fae and I wouldn't make that mistake. When the goblin led me up to the penthouse apartment and presented me to the queen, I made sure to pull out the best curtsy in my repertoire.

"Your Grace." I wobbled in the pose and Leighna smiled.

"Please, none of that pomp today. Let us simply take tea and chat like sisters." She invited me to sit on a couch in front of a low table.

I studied Leighna as another goblin poured the tea. She'd been reading reports on a tablet when I entered, and she still clutched it on her lap. Her hands trembled. The skin on her knuckles looked too big for her bones. She wore an ice-white tunic dress that did nothing to hide her thinness. Her hair had grown out since Mason's trial and it hung in a neat bob, but her complexion had a sallow tint except around her eyes where it deepened to bruise-purple.

Closing the gate to Underhill had taken a lot from her. I reached out with my keening and felt the weariness in her magic.

She smiled. "Do I taste sweet or sour?"

I reeled it in as if she'd slapped me. Few people ever sensed my magical scans. Her keening abilities were off the charts.

"I'm sorry. I didn't mean to offend."

"It's quite all right. You can't live with a bunch of fae and not expect to get magically probed once in a while. So, did I stand up to measure or are you going to tell me I don't eat enough like Merrow?"

I laughed. "My banshee roommate says the same about me."

"You live with a banshee? Ah, yes, the one who brought the condo down on my head."

I felt the need to apologize again.

"Nonsense. We all did what we had to that day. And your friend's actions saved a lot of lives. Among the courtiers, they're calling it the Great Scream."

"It was that." I sipped my tea. It was fruity, flowery and earthy all at once, a signature fae blend that no one else could replicate.

The lights flickered. I glanced up, but Leighna ignored it as a goblin came in with a tablet and a brief needing her signature.

While she dealt with the interruption, I peered around the room. Like the offices below, her private chambers were decorated in light woods and neutral colors that appealed to my Scandinavian roots. We sat in a large parlor. Windows flanked by thin drapes in a bronze material dominated one wall. Three closed doors on the shorter walls probably led to bedrooms, baths or offices. In the corner by the window, a small shrine was set up—a stone basin with a fountain splashing quietly. A statue of a young boy stood under the spray with his back to the room. Fresh flowers had been laid along the basin some hours ago, and they were wilting.

Something about the angle of the stone boy's head sparked a memory. It was Alvar's cocky stance.

Leighna caught me looking. "He was such a happy child. I don't know what happened."

I didn't know what to say. Alvar had betrayed her, and we'd all watched his new allies murder him, but she'd built a shrine to him in her rooms.

"He was a twilight baby, you know. Our parents were already eight-hundred years old when they had him. They'd forgotten how to be parents, really. I practically raised him." She clutched her teacup as if needing its warmth. "But you're not here to talk about my family, are you? You're here to learn about your father."

"You were gracious to offer me a boon. I did nothing but bring you news that broke your heart."

"News that gave us a fighting chance." She sat up straighter, and I sensed a bit of her old confidence. The lights flickered again. This time, Leighna glanced up and frowned before continuing. "And you were gracious enough to ask for a worthy gift in return. In truth, you should have been told about your father years ago."

"I don't understand why his name provokes such strong reactions in the fae. Some seem to revere him and others despise him."

Leighna sipped her tea and took her time to answer.

"How much do you know about Timberfoot's death?"

"Very little. I never met him. So I know next to nothing about his life or death. Only what I hear the fae whispering sometimes." And the few grudging bits I had pulled from my mother and grandmother. Neither liked to talk about him and didn't see any reason I should be curious.

"You have his eyes, you know. The same speckling like blue quartz."

I shifted in my chair. Leighna's gaze was on a horizon that no longer existed, and I was suddenly curious about how well the queen knew my father.

"He was a handsome man. Strong, but tender. Tall and broad shouldered with huge hands that were delicate enough to hold a butterfly."

Yep, my dad and the queen totally got it on.

"You're right that most fae revere him. He was our savior. Only a few misinformed miscreants believe he had anything to do with the demon. It was pure coincidence that they arrived around the same time."

"Demon? Here in Montreal?"

Leighna shook her head. "In Underhill. This was during the Flood Wars. The demon Horak. You remember him."

I didn't.

"I spent the Flood Wars in Asgard. Didn't return to Montreal until just a few years ago. I should know this history, but I don't."

"You were lucky. Terra was hell back then. Magic burgeoned and at first, we fae welcomed it. With the ley-lines swelling we could easily move between the two worlds. But then humans learned to tap the magic, and they did what humans always do. They weaponized it. They learned quickly to summon vicious creatures from other realms to wage their wars. And the fae retreated to Underhill to wait out the madness."

She looked thoughtful. "I thought we'd return to Terra one day and find a desolation overrun by demons. Many times, the humans begged my father, the king, to join the fight, but he declined. And so we hid.

"During this time, your father found his way to Underhill. It had become a haven not just for the fae, but for others like the dryads and some godlings. Timberfoot was not a fighting man. Like most dryads, he preferred the gentler arts. But he was as strong as he was poetic, like an oak." She smiled, remembering some personal joy.

"The demon showed up about this same time. My father sent soldiers to fight him but they never returned. It seems Horak had a taste for fae."

I swallowed my tea in a lump. "He ate them?"

"He ate their magic, which amounts to the same thing. And every fae he consumed only made him stronger. By the time he reached the Winter Court, he was unstoppable. And so we fled. Alvar, Timberfoot and I. My parents stayed to fight him, to give us a chance to escape." She closed her eyes. "I never saw them again."

"That must have been terrible." I'd fled my home too, leaving my mother and my grandfather. No matter the reason for leaving, family always tugs on you.

"Terrible was still ahead of us," Leighna said. "We rode through Underhill, urging all the fae to return to Terra, but Horak's minions had already been through most of the countryside. So much death." She shook her head and her eyes gleamed with tears even though she spoke of events that happened half a century ago.

"As we rode, we closed every door from Underhill to Terra. We knew that if Horak followed us into the new world, there would be no stopping him. His minions harried us the entire way—small, vicious creatures like angry spiders. And at the last gate, we made our stand. The last gate to Terra. If I closed it, I would sever the connection between the worlds. We could never return."

She paused, and the only sound was the burble of the fountain on Alvar's shrine.

"I waited as long as I could, hoping against hope that my parents would come. But Horak came instead, and I knew they were lost. I was ready to close the door. It would have killed me. The severing of two worlds requires enormous energy. But Timberfoot had other ideas. We came through the gate. He kissed me and I knew by the look in his eye I'd lost him too."

She reached for a pendant hanging on the chain around her neck. It was a tree of life carved from green stone. I'd thought it a pretty ornament, now I suspected it held deeper meaning.

"Alvar knew what Timberfoot was up to, and he pulled me away, but in truth, it happened so fast, I couldn't have stopped him."

She looked me right in the eye. "Your father sacrificed himself to close the last gate to Underhill, but because of him the link between our worlds wasn't permanently severed. In true dryad fashion, he transformed into a tree and his roots pierced the veil, connecting the two worlds. As long as his oak stands, we can go home."

There were a whole lot of feels to unpack in that story. I didn't know where to start. Should I be proud of my father for saving so many fae? Should I resent him for leaving my mother and I and finding a new family to love?

Leighna watched me with an intense stare. She expected some reaction from me. I chose my words, focusing on the logic and not my stunted emotions.

"But Alvar went back to Underhill. I was there. What about this Horak? Maybe he's already gone."

"Perhaps. I think it more likely that he slumbers after glutting himself on fae magic. Alvar was lucky. Stupid and lucky. If they'd stayed longer, the demon would have eventually felt the fae presence and come for them."

I shivered, thinking of my near miss.

"That means you planned to sacrifice yourself that night at the condo," I said. "To close the door to Underhill."

"I knew it was a risk. But as long as Timberfoot's oak stands—and it does—it's not a true severing."

In the silence that followed that story, I felt acutely my sword's agitation.

"I would like to see Timberfoot's tree one day."

"And so you should." She unhooked the necklace and held it in a fist. "He would want you to have this."

I stared at her closed fist with the bit of silver chain dangling down and gently pushed it aside.

"No. I think he would like you to have it." Timberfoot had sacrificed his life for this woman. That was a stronger love than I could claim from him.

She smiled and held onto the necklace. I could see relief in her eyes. It was probably the last piece of him she could hold onto.

My sword had had enough of being abandoned, and its psychic wail grated across my nerves. I winced.

"That's quite the vocal sword you have," Leighna said. "Bring it here and let's see if we can quiet it."

Embarrassed, I fetched the blade and laid it, still in the sheath, on the table between us.

"It's getting worse," I said. "I can't leave it behind anymore, and my glamor isn't strong enough to hide it from everyone. It's become a real problem."

Leighna reached forward but didn't touch it. Something unspoken passed between her and the blade.

"It needs to feed. You are Valkyrie?"

I nodded.

"This blade was made to ferry souls to the afterworld. You've been denying it its birthright."

I sighed. She sounded just like Aunt Dana.

"It's a little hard to find wounded warriors to poke with it," I said.

She raised her eyebrows in frank denial of my claim.

"Okay, so in the last few months, it may have seen a little too much death, but that seems to make it pine for more. I would just like it to be quiet long enough for me to leave it at home once in a while."

Leighna studied me.

"I can quiet it temporarily, but first tell me, what are your true motivations for wanting to silence the blade? Do you resist out of fear or some misguided sense of inferiority?"

I squirmed in my seat. Leighna was hitting a little too close.

"Maybe once I did. Not anymore." I wouldn't waste her time with my existential tale of woe. "Now it's more a matter of practicality. Apart from never being able to leave it behind, there are people in my life who might see the blade as an easy way out of their immortal ennui. I won't let that happen."

Leighna raised an eyebrow. "Are you talking about a certain handsome Guardian?"

"Maybe. But he's not the one I'm really worried about." I told her about my encounter with Emil and his look of longing toward my sword.

"This makes me unhappy." Leighna frowned. "Emil is the son of a good friend of mine. That's why I let him stay within the ward. Lady Lughwaite would be heartbroken if anything happened to her son."

She gripped my sword with both hands around the sheathed blade and closed her eyes. I felt the burst of magic from her and instantly, the sword quieted.

Leighna sighed. "I calmed it for now, but it's a temporary fix. Your best solution would be to embrace your Valkyrie heritage and do the sword's bidding. But I can see by your expression that won't happen. There is a ritual that will put the blade into a sort of stasis. I can teach it to you, but you must know that while in stasis the blade will be just like any other blade. Its magic will sleep."

"And what would I give you in return for this ritual?" I wouldn't take anything for free from the queen of the fae.

"Smart woman." The lights went out for several seconds and came back on. "As you can see, I seem to have a leech problem in the basement." Leighna nodded toward the light fixture on the ceiling. "I'll help you with your sword, and you can clear the building of those electricity leeches."

Vermin. I could deal with that. I agreed.

"Good. Barter is always favored in the eyes of the gods," she said. "Come back tomorrow for the leeches, and the instructions for the stasis spell will be waiting for you when you leave."

The goblin appeared again, though she hadn't summoned him. I picked up my sword and followed him out, stopping at the door for one last question.

"If I put the sword into stasis, but then need to…need its magic again. How do I bring it out?"

Leighna was standing by Alvar's shrine, still clutching the tree of life necklace in her fist. She smiled. "Like in any good fairytale. With a kiss."

15

kept my promise to Leighna and returned to the Winter Court the following day to rout the leeches that were wreaking havoc with her electrical system. My new apprentice tagged along. Jacoby had insisted on having his own tool belt, just like mine, but his hips were too scrawny and the belt kept slipping down around his knees. We stopped twice in the parking lot so he could hike it back up.

"That won't work," I said finally. Jacoby clutched his precious belt as if I might take it from him.

"Let's try it another way." I unclipped the belt and re-fastened it over one shoulder and around his skinny chest. "There. Now you look like a bad-ass commando."

"I haves bad ass?"

"Definitely."

He strutted the rest of the way, until we met the troll guard at the door, and then he scooted behind my legs.

I flashed my widget to the troll to prove my identification. She scanned her screen, looking for my name on the approved list of visitors. Her thick fingers worked the device with surprising ease. Trolls weren't the brightest bulbs on the string, so I was surprised to find one in such a position of authority. Deep-set black eyes stared at me from a flat, round face. She wore makeup—sparkly turquoise eyeshadow and vivid red lipstick. Deep wrinkles lined her green-gray cheeks and sprouted moss-like hair. The top of her head was covered in the same green fuzz, only longer. Some kind of small rock troll? I was too polite to ask, but I'd search my database when I got home. Collecting and identifying new species was a hobby that got me into trouble more than once.

"I have only you on the list," the troll said in a grinding voice. "Who's this?" She pointed at Jacoby.

"My assistant."

"Not on the list." Clearly the list was everything.

"Well, if you expect me to find leeches without an assistant, you'll have to come and do the dirty work." I smiled. "Fancy crawling into an air vent or two?"

She pinched her brightly painted lips and made a call. After getting approval for Jacoby, she pointed to a door. "Basement."

"Thanks." I wouldn't get any more help. That was fine. I preferred to work unsupervised.

Electricity leeches could be messy. They laid eggs on power lines, and when the babies hatched, they fed off the current. They were immune to most poisons, so foggers didn't work. The only way to eradicate them was to pull them off, one by one, like grubs. Usually, all the wiring needed to be replaced, and one missed leech meant the infestation could blossom again.

Most pest controllers wouldn't take on leeches because they couldn't guarantee success. They weren't my favorite job, but I had an advantage. I could keen the little buggers down to the last egg. So I was pretty confident that I could fix the problem.

Now I just had to find them.

The stairs to the basement were brightly lit, but as I descended, the lights whined and flickered. We halted on the staircase and waited it out. When the lights steadied, we moved on.

The basement opened into one large room with a narrow hall at the far end leading to a bunch of closed-off storage areas. The ceiling was low and oppressive, the walls lined with shelves that held office supplies, small appliances and linens. Everything was clean and orderly. I swiped a hand across one shelf. No dust.

As I moved to the far wall, the shelves became messier with boxes of miscellaneous junk.

Then the lights went out. The darkness was absolute. I fumbled in my pack for a gleam, shook it and let it hang in the air above us. Unlike some of the fancier alchemic gadgets, gleams didn't make me antsy. They were simple magic—power stored from a ley-line. Since our trip to the Inbetween, I'd been using the gleam on the job, but it didn't hold a charge for long, and now it barely lit a ten-foot radius.

I reached out with my keening, trying to feel the leeches. Nothing.

I walked on, searching until I found the breaker box at the end of the hall. It should have been a mecca for leeches, but the wiring was clear. To be sure, I unscrewed the plates on a couple of light switches to check their wiring. Still clean.

"Kyra-lady?" Jacoby hadn't been more than a step behind me the whole time.

"Yes?"

"I feels bad."

The lights flickered on, blinding me for a second before they went out again. I dropped my screwdriver and Jacoby yelped.

I keened out again, this time not focusing on the wiring in the walls, but just…reaching. The darkness pressed on me. My keening searched through the miasma of magic, as if pushing through a thick soup, and then…

We weren't alone in the basement.

"Something hummmongous," Jacoby whispered.

The lights flickered like a strobe. The extremes of brightness and darkness burned across my corneas. I could almost hear it, as if the light slapped me. Jacoby clutched my hand. I pulled him back to the breaker box and shut the breaker to the basement, plunging us into steady darkness again.

My heart raced. Jacoby's hand trembled in mine. Or maybe it was me trembling. My eyes adjusted slowly. The gleam was losing its charge fast. It floated at knee height twenty paces away and was no brighter than a dying match. I grabbed it out of the air before it crashed.

Jacoby danced from foot to foot. He could teleport away, but he took his apprenticeship seriously, and I would only insult him if I suggested that he leave. Instead, I moved back into the main storage area, rummaged through the boxes and found an old pillar candle with the wick burned down deep in the wax. I scrounged a match from my pack and lit it.

The good news for Leighna was that she wouldn't have to replace her wiring. Electricity leeches weren't to blame for her lighting problem. The bad news was…well, I was about to find out.

"Come on," I said. "Let's see who the bogeyman is."

If Jacoby's eyes opened any wider, they'd swallow his head. But he nodded. "Good man."

The candle was clunky to carry and the light only a dim erratic glow, but I wasn't searching with my eyes. Jacoby had a keening sense too. For some fae, sensing magic was as natural as smelling the wind. We both focused on the last door along the narrow hall. It opened to a stone staircase. Damp, earthy air wafted up from it.

Montreal was an old city, one of the oldest on the continent. Buildings were constructed over the ruins of older structures, and these ancient cellars weren't uncommon.

I'd have to go down there into the blackness. I looked at Jacoby and he shook his head.

"No, no, no, no…"

"You know, I think we're going to need a critter cage. Why don't you port back to the truck and get one? Then just wait for me at the top of the stairs."

He eyed me suspiciously.

"But I ams your 'prentice."

"Exactly. And that's what apprentices do. They fetch things. Now go. I'll be fine."

He grumbled a bit, but then ported away.

Good. I wasn't foolhardy. I wouldn't blindly stumble into an unknown cellar that housed a malicious creature calling out, "Is anyone there?" I'd seen the movies. I knew that's how the dumb blonds got slaughtered. But my keening was more sensitive to nuance than Jacoby's and I could tell that the humongous magic he sensed was all bluster. Something was in the cellar, but it wasn't mean. It was scared. I'd sent Jacoby away so he didn't set it off.

Because the magic wafting up the dark stairs was unbelievably strong.

"I'm coming down now," I said quietly. "Don't be scared. I won't hurt you."

The magic hummed like a swarm of bees, but it was no longer trying to scare the pants off me.

The stairs were slick and I nearly lost my footing. The candle flame rocked, filling the small space with leering shadows. At the bottom, I stood still, and focused with all my senses. My heart was the loudest thing in the room.

The magic centered on an old pot-bellied stove sitting in the corner, cold and dark. I had one glimpse of the tiny figure sitting on the stove, legs dangling over the side, before my candle went out.

"That's not nice," I said. "I can't see in the dark. I like the light."

A grumbling came out of the darkness, and then my candle flame was relit.

"Thank you."

I moved forward and sat on a rickety chair placed beside the stove, as if to catch its warmth. I studied the creature perched on the cast iron burner. He sat no more than three inches high. Skinny legs stuck out of short pants. His feet were abnormally large for his size and covered in boots so worn that one big toe stuck out. A red cap covered his bald head and a white scraggly beard fell to his waist. He held a walking stick—not more than a twig—in one hand.

I racked my brain to identify his species. Gnome-like but with powerful magic. I sifted through all the fae I could think of—boggart, bogle, miffie, hob, scrag, puckle…

"You're a bodach!"

"Gfheougthhbt," said the bodach. The words were unintelligible, but he'd placed their meaning in my head, clear as a bell. *Yes. My name is Errol.*

"I'm Kyra." I reached out a finger and he shook it.

"Why are you down here all alone?"

"Brgthiwgh."

Images flashed through my mind. City streets filled with noise, rushing buses and people—so many people. Then cold. Snowbanks as high as mountains, drifts too tall to walk through. Constant wet and cold.

"I understand." The city would be a frightening place when you were only three inches tall and a slush puddle could drown you.

"I don't like the cold either, but it's warm outside now. Warmer outside than this basement. Why don't you come with me and we'll find you a nice quiet place to live?"

More grumbling and images.

"No, I promise you won't be cold. And you won't be alone anymore. I have quite a few unusual friends living with me. You might like them. At least until we can find some place better for you."

Gita was going to kill me, bringing home another stray.

The bodach grumbled again, but I felt his acquiescence.

Jacoby waited for us at the top of the stairs with a pet carrier. His eyes widened when he saw the bodach riding on my shoulder.

"We won't be needing that," I said. "Errol is quite friendly."

The bodach grumbled a greeting and Jacoby grinned. I was glad that he could understand Errol's odd language too.

In the lobby, I checked in with the troll again to let her know that the electricity problem was solved.

"If you have any more trouble, just call me." With Errol no longer interfering with the current, I expected no more interruptions with the lights.

The troll nodded and handed me a sheet of paper. "This is from Leighna."

Wow. No one used real paper anymore. It was far too expensive. Even the rare paperbacks I found for Gita were relics from another time. I hadn't held a single sheet of pulped wood in years. It was heavier than I remembered. I gripped it carefully, not wanting to crease it, and studied the words written out in a scrolling hand.

It was the stasis spell. Leighna had given me a doubly priceless gift.

Bodachs: Looking at the Being Behind the Curtain

(November 17, 2080)

As usual, the information I can find about bodachs is antiquated and fairly useless when dealing with these beings in the modern, post-war world.

The origin of the term "bodach" may be derived from the old Irish word for peasant or from an old Norse term for cottage. In Gaelic, bodach is used as a familiar term of affection and simply means "old man."

None of this tells us what a bodach actually is, however. And unlike other class two fae such as the brownie, the bodach features in very few tales. When he does, he is often likened with a bugbear—a kind of boogie man that hides under children's beds. Or he is portrayed as a trickster, a devil or some other malevolent but more-or-less benign creature.

For our purposes, these tales are quite useless. What kind of magic can a bodach call upon? What is their lifespan? What do they eat? Anyone who is going to face a bodach will need to know these things.

Recently, I was fortunate enough to help a bodach out of a tough spot, and he blessed me with his company for a little while. I learned a few interesting tidbits about this unusual race. But I should qualify this post by saying that I have only met the one bodach, so this is not an exhaustive report on the topic.

Here's what I learned about bodachs (so far).

Bodachs are small class two fae. They stand only 2-3 inches high and look like tiny garden gnomes.

Their magic is mostly bluster. Their main ability seems to be instilling fear in others. That may be where the bugbear myth originates. Like a puffer fish, bodachs can puff up their magic so they seem much more powerful than they really are. It is pure defense.

They mind-speak in a peculiar way. My bodach friend speaks in an incomprehensible jumble of sounds, but somehow, I always know what he means. This has nothing to do with my skills at reading body language. The bodach seems to project his meaning right into my mind, without words. I just *know* what he's saying. It was a very unsettling experience at first. Because he doesn't use language in the normal way, he can communicate with any sentient species.

Bodachs and electricity don't mix. If you've read my blog before, you'll know that I often end up taking in stray creatures and lost fae. When I found a bodach who was down on his luck, I invited him to recuperate at my place. He settled into a little ceramic house beside my bonsai tree. However, when agitated, the bodach tends to blow all the fuses in my house. Sadly, as soon as spring comes, I will have to ask my bodach friend to move on.

If you've had a bodach encounter, I'd love to hear your input in the comments.

COMMENTS (11)

Bless you for looking past the myth to the true being beyond it. You are a source of inspiration.
cchedgewitch (November 19, 2080)

—— • ——

I think there was one living in my garden when I was a kid. But it could have been a gnome. They sound like interesting creatures.
DaddysGirl (November 19, 2080)

—— • ——

There was a bodach living in the barn on my family's farm. Scared the spit out of me until I finally saw him. Hard to be scared of such a little critter. After that, his magic didn't work on me anymore.

Homesteader898 (November 20, 2080)

> Agreed. My bodach hasn't tried his fear trick on me again. Maybe he knows it only works once.
>
> *Valkyrie367 (November 21, 2080)*

Skewer that critter! A little bbq sauce will fix him up good!

Oldtexdoneright (November 21, 2080)

I was blessed with a bodach friend for many years. I can attest that your experience with them is true. Also, did you know that they are great cultivators of mushrooms? Seems they can call them up from the earth.

poorpatty3 (November 23, 2080)

> Good to know. Thanks!
>
> *Valkyrie367 (November 23, 2080)*

I don't get it. Whos behind the curtin?

Sassfactor (November 23, 2080)

> It's a reference to *The Wizard of Oz*, a movie from the 1930s.
>
> *Valkyrie367 (November 23, 2080)*

> > Wow. Your really old.
> >
> > *Sassfactor (November 23, 2080)*

> > > *You're* right ;)
> > >
> > > *Valkyrie367 (November 23, 2080)*

16

fter a full week of fourteen-hour days, I quit early on Saturday. I wanted to go home to put my feet up, but that thought lasted for only a minute or two. I was still in the dark about Cyril's death. Though I'd been by his apartment a few more times, I learned nothing new. The disappointment frozen on Mason's face at the funeral still haunted me. We hadn't spoken since, and I felt like I needed a token of goodwill to break through his stony silence. The best way to do that would be to bring him irrefutable proof that Cyril was murdered. Or better yet, bring him Cyril's murderer.

And Constable Hughes had been adamant that a dozen or more fae had gone missing in the neighborhood around Talon Street, just like the brownies near Cyril's apartment. It was time to investigate these takers.

Talon Street cut through the most populous part of town and was home to twenty blocks of markets, shops and eateries. I avoided parking fees by stashing my truck at a charging station one block south. I handed my keys to Roy, a grizzled-looking scrag. Scrags are one of the few fae who can work iron and they make skilled mechanics.

"Thanks, Roy. I won't be long."

"I might have a look at those wheels while you're gone. They're looking unbalanced." He wiped grease off his hands with an even dirtier rag.

"Only if you have time." I knew he'd find the time. Roy had kept my truck running for longer than it should have, mostly because he was too stubborn to let it die.

After a call home to make sure Errol was playing nice with the rest of my pack, I headed north to Talon street and turned right into the busy pedestrian traffic. This section of Talon was closed to motor vehicles, but bikes zigzagged through the crowd, and several mule-drawn carts filled with the remnants of the day's farm market blocked the flow.

The afternoon heat packed around the buildings like insulation, but it took more than odd weather to keep Montrealers away from their entertainment, whether that be food, drink or music. I followed the flow of traffic with no real destination in mind and not knowing exactly what I was looking for.

Talon was on the border of the fae and human quarters. Here those class one fae who weren't court nobles mixed with lower class fae and mundanes. It was the one place in the city where everyone got along because they all agreed on one thing: keep to yourself.

That made questioning people difficult. The first pedestrians I encountered ignored my inquiries. I finally found someone willing to talk. Two old men sat outside a small mom-and-pop market that sold stale bread and eggs to locals at outrageous prices.

"I'm investigating a missing persons case," I lied. "Heard rumors that several people have gone missing from this neighborhood. Is that true?"

"You Hub?" one of the men asked. He chewed a cigar butt. Black glassy eyes peered at me from a round, inflated face.

"No."

"Private eye?"

"Just a concerned citizen." Clearly, I needed a better cover story.

"Well, aren't you sweet? Such a pretty thing. Coming here and bein' all concerned and stuff for us." He spat out the cigar and his friend cackled.

I stared at the two old codgers, letting them know that I wasn't afraid of their weak-assed attempt at harassment.

"Well, if you hear anything, here's my information." I didn't bother trying to transmit my data by widget. These two were old school. Every citizen of Montreal was required to carry a widget. It did everything from paying for goods and services, to holding our official documents of citizenship. But these two probably used their widgets as coasters. So I handed him a synthetic paper business card, which he promptly used to pick his teeth.

I had better luck when I started telling people that I was looking for my missing brother. I moved down Talon Street, giving out my contact info to anyone who would speak to me. A few listened, but no one had anything to say about the mysterious takers.

An hour later, I got stalled at the farmers' market. Hub officials had an entire section of the street cordoned off, and the air was heavy with the stench of death and decay. It was thick enough to taste and even covering my nose with my thin bandanna did nothing to quench it. After questioning a couple of bystanders, I found out that all the produce in the market had suddenly gone rotten. No one had an explanation for it, but with so much magic bursting through ley-lines around town recently, I thought we were getting off easy with a few rotten farm carts.

I wouldn't get past the blockade, so I ducked inside a tavern for a drink and to find some patrons willing to talk. The place was called Le Lion D'Or, and it had a medieval vibe going with decor that could kindly be labeled rustic—wooden tables and chairs, a great fieldstone hearth (still cold and bare despite the late season), and a long wooden bar held up by old beer kegs. The serving wenches dressed the part with long skirts and peasant blouses that showed off their ample bosoms.

All conversation ceased when I walked in. I stood in the doorway, letting my eyes adjust to the dim light. A half dozen fae and maybe twice as many humans sat at the tables, waiting out the afternoon heat with cold mugs of beer.

Everyone watched me.

I waved. "Hiya!"

A couple of bluecaps snarled at me. A table of pixie chicks laughed in that high-pitched pixie giggle.

I sat at the bar. The low buzz of conversation started up again, but I could still feel eyes on me.

"Can I have whatever is cold," I asked the bartender. He was a tall, fatherly man with an apron over his round belly.

"That's ten-fifty," he said as he placed the mug in front of me. I tapped my widget to his and he turned away.

"Hey," I said, catching his attention again. "I'm looking for my brother. He's missing."

"That's tough luck."

"Is it luck? I heard that a lot of people have gone missing from around here."

The bartender squinted at me, no longer jovial. He wiped the bar with a rag, then leaned in and spoke in a low tone.

"People come in here to forget. I don't ask what they're forgetting. That would be counter productive, wouldn't it? But I make sure they aren't disturbed while they're doing it. You understand? Questions are bad for business. Anything that's bad for business gets thrown out on its ass."

I smiled and sipped my beer, proving I could be good for business. The bartender moved off.

I was going about this all wrong. I was no investigator. Bugs and rodents rarely needed to be questioned. Talon was an insular neighborhood, and I stuck out as an outsider. Mason had wanted me to question the fae, but he overestimated my ability to connect with them.

The beer went down fast, and I left feeling over-full. The setting sun was too bright after the dark tavern, and I stood on the sidewalk blinking.

"Hey, missus?" a timid voice said. I turned to find one of the fae serving girls. As she hurried over to me, her blond ringlets bobbed, revealing the slight point to her ears. Probably only half fae. She grabbed my arm and pulled me into an alley beside the tavern. Her eyes darted across the shadows and up the brick wall at my back before she seemed satisfied that we were alone.

"My name's Betsy Lacroy." She tapped my widget with hers to trade contacts. "People *have* gone missing. My neighbor's daughter and the son of the grocer down that way." She pointed east along Talon Street. "Is it true that only those with exceptional magic are being taken?"

I studied her. Betsy was old enough to fill out her wench uniform, but her eyes betrayed the scared kid inside.

"I don't know. Is that what they're saying?" That's right, Detective Greene, ask leading questions only.

Betsy frowned. "You are here about the takers?"

"I heard of them. Don't know if they're involved in my…uh, brother's disappearance though. How do you know about them?"

"Everybody's talking about the takers. They snatch people right off the streets. No one wants to go out at night anymore. But my neighbor's kid was taken in broad daylight!"

She looked around again to be sure that we weren't overheard, then said, "Some say they're taking only kids with super magic, for experiments, you know? So it's gotta be those *alchemists*." She whispered that last word.

I'd had the same thought many times in the last few days.

A rogue fae was also a possibility. It wasn't unheard of for one of the stronger fae to break free of Leighna's strict rule and start rampaging the city. Some of the ancient ones had looser ideas of civilization. Some also had a deep yen for human flesh. But if a fae was stealing kids, he'd pick off the weak ones, not those with strong magic. No point fighting with your food if you didn't have to.

Who would want kids with off-the-charts magic ability? The alchemists were the obvious choice. They were the least populous arm of the triumvirate that ruled Montreal, but they held the keys to the technology that kept the ward humming. For that reason, they were well funded and given free rein to conduct all manner of experiments.

But there was another, more frightening option. What had Leighna said about the demon in Underhill? He ate magic. By the One-eyed Father, I didn't know which was worse, a demon loose in the ward or unsanctioned alchemy experiments.

"Are you worried that you'll be taken?" I asked.

"Not me. I'm a dud. I've got only one magic trick and it's pretty pathetic." She templed her fingers and concentrated on the space between her hands. Beads of sweat burst from her forehead, and her jaw set in a tight clench. A tiny storm cloud bloomed in the cavity between her hands. It swirled and flashed with mini lightning bolts. After a moment, Betsy let it drop and she sagged against the wall.

"That's your pathetic trick?" I knew Hub mages who couldn't call on that much magic. But the effort obviously took a lot out of her.

"My sister Maeve is much better. She's amazing." Her tired face lit up. "She can call the wind and make it rain just on our yard. We do that sometimes when it gets really hot." She looked shy, as if I might scold her for messing with the weather. "But Maeve's not like everyone else, you know?"

I let her explain before drawing conclusions.

"She's a little slow at some things. Doesn't like people. My ma used to say she had to be a changeling, left by hobgoblins when they took her real daughter. But Maeve's my sister. I feel it in my bones, you know?"

I nodded like I did know, but really, I'd never had that familial connection with anyone.

"Anyway, I try to keep her safe, but I can't watch her all day. I gotta work." She nodded toward the tavern. "And Maeve likes to roam. No matter how dangerous I tell her the streets are. She won't listen. These takers will get her. I just know it."

"Can you give me the names of the others who went missing?"

A door banged opened in the alley, and the scowling bartender came out.

"Break's over, missy. Get back inside. Someone puked in the bathroom. Go clean it up."

Betsy jumped and ran inside. The bartender looked me up and down and slammed the door behind him. I sighed. At least Betsy had given me her contact info. A minute later, a couple of names came through by message. The missing kids. Then another note that said, "Don't let them take Maeve!"

I decided that was enough detective work for one day and headed down the alley, hoping it would come out on the street where I'd parked. Four pookas huddled in the alcove of a door, whispering and generally looking suspicious. The throbbing beat of a rock-band came through the door, drowning out the pookas' words.

"Hey," I called out. Four round faces turned my way. Their baseball-sized eyes were full of shock and fear. And then they ran.

"Wait! I just have some questions!"

Running through an alley is never a good idea. Too easy to trip over garbage or slip in a puddle of unidentified fluids. Chasing fae through an increasingly dark alley was an exceptionally bad idea. The pookas knew this neighborhood better than me. They sprinted over debris I had to run around. I nearly lost them when the alley forked. Three pookas went one way, and I chased down the last one. He was an agile little guy and gave me a good run, but I finally cornered him behind a dumpster. He crouched like a primate, but his face was more feline, and a whip-like tail curled up behind him. His long ears flattened against his head, and his fur had already changed color to blend into the brick wall.

"Take it! Take it! I give up!" He thrust a candy bar at me. The paper was ripped, and a bite had been taken from it. Already, the pooka's hands shook, and the pupils in his enormous eyes dilated to fill the iris.

"Relax. I'm not Hub." I handed him back his chocolate. No shop keeper in their right mind would sell chocolate to a pooka. It was like crack to them. They hoarded it like street drugs, and I'd probably interrupted a trade.

The pooka clutched his dope to his chest. "What do you want?"

"Answers. Nothing about you and your friends. I want to know about the takers."

The pooka peered down the alley and nibbled the candy. His eyes were going glassy.

"When they come, they take. When they come, you hide." He shifted on his feet and his fur changed color again to blend into the rusted metal of the dumpster.

"They come, you hide. They come, you hide." He rocked back and forth, repeating this in a sing-song voice. He was already too far gone on the chocolate high. I couldn't leave him there, but when I reached down to help him up, the little beast went wild. He snarled and lunged, pointed teeth snapping at me. I scrambled out of the way, and he ran off.

Fine. I didn't want to be stuck with a stoned pooka anyway.

I backtracked down the alley. This section of town was a rabbit's warren of winding lanes that reeked of garbage and urine. The alleys mostly backed up onto businesses, but a clothesline of shirts and underwear strung from one window across to another told me that this one was inhabited. I turned a corner thinking I recognized a particular trash bin, walked another fifty meters and realized I was lost.

A car honked. Someone shouted and slammed a door. A TV was playing too loud, but these were distant sounds. In the alley—now almost completely dark—I turned to retrace my steps and keened that someone was lurking at the last intersection.

I was too far away to get a sense of their magic, but I didn't trust lurkers. I turned back, continuing down the strange alley, hoping it would merge with Talon Street. Behind me, the presence moved with stealth. And fast. I picked up my pace. Garbage was strewn in my path, and I kicked a bottle as I tramped through it. The sound of glass shattering against the stone wall was shockingly loud. I could hear my breathing, harsh and ragged with fear. My assailant—if I wasn't just jumping at shadows—was dead silent.

Panic made me choose badly at the next intersection. To the right was pure darkness, but a light shone distantly to the left. I ran toward it, only to find a dim bulb over a locked door and a dead end.

I banged on the door. Something scraped the asphalt behind me. I whirled, pulling my sword in one motion.

To find Emil grinning at me with arms held wide. The tip of my sword snagged his shirt just below his heart.

He smiled. "Do it."

"Charming." I started to lower my blade, but he stepped forward, wedging it against his breastbone.

"You really don't want to cut yourself with this sword."

"Don't I, Valkyrie?" He said that last word like a caress and ran a finger along my jaw. I jerked backward, coming up against a pile of crates left in the alley.

Emil let his hand drop. "I've done my research. I know what that blade does. It releases. It frees." His intense eyes pinned me, and he spoke like he was trying to seduce me. He leaned in and whispered, "Do it, Kyra. You know you want to."

A vision of Joran, skin rotting off him, flashed in my mind. Emil wasn't human, but my sword would do the job. I'd killed enough opji in that battle last spring. It might take two or three blows, but the blade would bring him a true death.

My sword hummed in anticipation. Emil smiled. He really was a handsome bugger. Hair curled in a messy mop, hazel eyes that never quite matched the humor in his sly grin.

I didn't want to kill him. He might want to die, but that didn't mean I wanted his death to be my burden for the rest of my life. I carried enough of those memories.

I backed away and lowered my sword. "I can't do it."

Emil tried to grab my hand in the sword's grip.

I'd been here before. He would plunge the blade into his own heart, forcing my hand to be the bearer of his death.

Not again!

I punched him and held the sword out of his reach. He lunged, his eyes manic and fingers grasping. I backed up, trod in something soft and fell, banging my knee on the cement. I put two hands on the ground to push up, and a yelp escaped me.

I was looking straight into the eyes of a dead woman.

Broken glass littered the ground around me. The pile of crates had toppled when I tripped over the body and now lay in a broken heap. Some kind of rodent rummaged under the debris.

Mason found me sitting against a dirty wall, with my chin resting on my knees—knees crusted in something foul from my fall. The body faced away from me so I could no longer see her eyes. Small mercies.

"Hey," Mason said as he crouched beside me.

"Hey." I refused to look at him.

"What's he doing lurking in the shadows?" He nodded toward Emil, who leaned against the far wall, feet crossed at the ankle and arms crossed against his chest. He nodded back at Mason.

"Emil? Just ignore him. We were having a chat when I found the body."

I'd called Mason first because the dead woman wore the distinctive white coat favored by the alchemists, and I recognized her from the pictures in Cyril's apartment. Cyril was also working with the alchemists. I didn't know if the two deaths were related or if they had anything to do with the takers, but I figured that Mason would want to see the scene before Hub took over. At least that's what I'd told myself. It was a gut reaction. When I was in trouble, he was the first person I thought of, and now I felt a sudden rush of relief to have him crouching beside me.

"Any idea who she is?" I asked.

Mason leaned over the body. "Lorraine Reed."

"You know her well?"

"Not really. I've seen her around Perrot Island. Her lab is in a different building than mine."

"Does she work with Gerard?"

"I don't know."

"Cyril knew her."

Mason quirked one eyebrow. "How do you know?"

I handed him my widget, open to the picture I'd downloaded in Cyril's apartment.

"That's her on the right, isn't it?"

Mason studied the picture and nodded. Then he took a pen from his pocket and used it to lift the victim's hair where it lay over her chest.

"She still has her ID badge." He pulled a gleam from his pack and shook it before tossing it up to hover overhead. The tiny globe lit the scene too well, highlighting gore that the shadows had hidden.

Lorraine Reed had been stabbed several times. Blood soaked the back of her coat and matted her hair. A gash split the skin under her unseeing right eye. It was crusted with dirt and gravel. Her lips were parted and lipstick smeared across her chin as if someone had tried to gag her. One hand partially covered a cracked widget.

"Doesn't look like a robbery gone bad." Mason's eyes took in every detail but he didn't touch her. "Those ID badges fetch a good price on the black market."

So not a mugging, unless the assailant was too dumb to know the value of tech. Not a sexual assault. There were many other reasons for murder, more personal reasons. Revenge, jealousy, love turned bad. Or someone could have wanted to silence Ms. Reed.

I could feel the weight of Mason's gaze as he watched me work through the possibilities.

"This is becoming a habit," he said. "You and me huddled over a cooling body."

I let out a harsh laugh. "At least we don't have to worry about boring small talk."

His smile didn't reach his eyes. That was all right. My laugh hadn't touched my heart either. There was nothing to be happy about here.

He took my hand, his fingers warm and solid, and he tugged me up.

He pulled too hard, and I fell against him before finding my feet. My chest bumped against his. We were so close. Close enough to kiss. His eyes flicked down to my mouth and back up again.

"Kyra, I'm sorry. I had no right to berate you at the funeral. I want you in my business. Truly. I just don't know how to let you in."

"You're doing a good job right now."

He grinned. My heart put on a tutu and did a little dance.

Gently, like I was made of spun sugar, he pushed me away and said, "Let's take some pictures, then we'd better call Hub."

I nodded and dusted gravel from my pants.

Emil jumped onto a dumpster. He didn't climb. He just bent his knees and launched six feet into the air to land on the metal lid with a bang.

Mason arched his brow and looked at me in surprise. I shook my head to say I had no idea what the vamp was up to.

"Your little dance is sweet," Emil said. "But I've got places to be." He started to climb. The wall of the four-story building was streaked with sludge from a broken eave. Emil didn't care. His fingers stuck to the brick like they had suckers. His booted toes found crannies for purchase, and he scampered up the wall like a spider to stand on the edge of the roof with his arms spread wide to the night.

"Not again," I groaned.

"You can take my body, but you can't take my soul!" The vamp tipped forward, arms still spread, and fell head-first onto the pavement.

I jumped at the impact.

"*Ciboire.*" Mason rolled his eyes and then nudged the gleam into the alley to hover over Emil's crumpled form.

His head was an indistinguishable pile of mash. One arm stuck straight up, broken at the shoulder. As we watched, it flopped over his wreck of a face.

"He's been doing that all week." I ran a hand over my tired eyes. "Every time I turn around. Today, he chased me here. He wants me to end him with my sword."

"Could you do that?"

I shrugged. "I killed a lot of opji last spring."

"So just do it, if that's what he wants."

"Really? Just because some jerk wants to die, I should play the grim reaper for him? I should carry that burden for the rest of my life?"

Mason held up his hands in defense. "I didn't mean to pull your trigger."

"Sorry." I turned away from the pile of vamp mush. "I just had a hard day…a hard week, really." Mason stared at me. He knew there was more to that outburst.

"I have a problem with suicide. I mean, everybody should have a problem with it, but I have…experience."

He watched me steadily, not prodding, just waiting.

"My cousin Aaric, a kissing-cousin, you could say…he was tired of the whole immortality thing too." Should I be telling this story to another immortal, one who already professed to being weary of this world? But the weight of his gaze bore down on me. He wouldn't let this go.

"Aaric forced me…forced my hand to be the one that killed him. My sword. Right into his heart."

"He needed a Valkyrie sword to die," Mason said, and I nodded. "And he needed a Valkyrie to wield the magic." I nodded again. He tipped my chin up, forcing me to meet his eyes. "And you loved him."

"Yes."

The memory of that fresh, innocent love was forever tainted by Aaric's last gasping breath.

"And this Emil guy?"

"Do I love Emil?" Was he serious? "He's just some whacko who's been following me around."

Mason nodded, but I could tell he was relieved.

"You still want to call Hub?" he asked.

"Yes, but we'd better go scrape vampire off the sidewalk first before someone slips in it."

Vikings loved a good sacrifice, the gorier the better. They spilled animal blood at every solstice and equinox to honor the gods. Enemies were sacrificed to Odin by gutting the victim from tailbone to neck and separating the backbone with an ax so his organs could be displayed in a delightful pose called the blood-eagle. So I wasn't surprised that the Viking ritual to put my blade into stasis required blood.

The recipe written in Leighna's neat handwriting on precious old-world paper lay on my counter. The ingredients included hemp seeds, licorice root, fresh mead and—because no Viking ritual was complete without it—the blood of a bull in rut.

I had a cutting from my pot plant, licorice root—thanks to Gita who liked to chew on it—a bottle of beer and a porterhouse steak. It would have to do.

I crushed the roots and leaves with a mortar and pestle by candlelight. The sun was just setting and my windowless kitchen was dim, but there was no point in turning on a light.

Since the wars, Terra had not allowed people to cut into her for fuel. Wind and solar power were acceptable, but limiting, for the new world order of small city states. Ley-lines were the go-to source of power. The magic that flowed through these veins seemed limitless, and so far, Terra didn't mind us tapping into them. The alchemists had created the new science of technomancy that blended ley-line power with state-of-the-art technology to power cars, heat homes and light the night. I had come to the conclusion that Errol didn't affect this electricity so much as the magic that fueled it.

He had settled into the ceramic house beside my bonsai tree, but the excitement of living with so many others made him jumpy, and the electrical breakers kept blowing out. I hoped this was something he would eventually get under control. For now—candles.

I set a timer for the root and leaf concoction to steep in the beer. Then I cleaned my blade with a soft cloth, looking for nicks. It had been with me for so long. Silencing the blade felt like a betrayal, but the days of the Valkyrie were long gone. I couldn't let the sword lust after blood any more than I could Emil. It wasn't safe for anyone.

I thought about Leighna's admonishment that I needed to embrace my heritage. And I thought about Angus trying to teach me about my dryad magic. Why was nothing ever easy?

The timer went off and I sighed. Time to get this done.

I washed the blade in the brew, covering its entire length. The next step called for coating the blade in blood. I glanced at the steak bleeding pink juice onto a plate. Would it be enough blood?

My mother was a terrific cook, one of those who could taste a stew and know instinctively what was missing. We hadn't been rich growing up. Mom's poor health made more than one job disappear, and we learned to make do in the kitchen. To improvise. I kept that skill into adulthood. It was an ability that made me good at my job.

So the sword wanted blood? I would give it blood.

I took a smaller blade from my first aid kit and washed it in the candle flame, then cut across my left forearm. The blood welled, and I held my arm over the steak, letting it drip into the meat. Then I folded the steak around the blade and rubbed it from hilt to tip while focusing my magic. Leighna hadn't included any ritual words to be spoken, only a note advising that I had to be calm and infuse the blade with my will, then tell it to sleep.

The blood, beer and herbs had woken the blade's curiosity. It tasted them and was partially sated. I dug deep into my life-force, enfolding the sword in an embrace of power. The sword's magic flared once, and it went still. Really still. I hadn't realized how irritating its constant buzzing was until it fell silent.

"That's disgusting." Gabe's big frame filled the kitchen doorway. Willow followed him in and jumped onto the table to lick the meat coated in my blood.

Gabe wrinkled his nose. "If you died and no one found you for days, she'd totally eat you."

"Totally," I agreed.

I shooed the cat away and dumped the meat and beer into a slop bucket for Clarence. He wouldn't touch it until the meat putrefied.

"I'm heading out for some errands. There's a girl waiting in the office for you," Gabe said. "She looks upset."

"A customer?"

"I don't think so. Said her name is Betsy."

The tavern wench. "I'll be right there."

"Sure. I'll tell her you'll see her after you clean the blood off your hands."

"You're lucky I already threw out that steak, buster, or you'd have gotten it right in the face."

Gabe backed away with his hands held out in surrender.

"Just go!" I laughed.

Before washing, I wiped down my blade with an oiled cloth. Just because I was tired of its neediness, didn't mean I wanted it to rust out. It was still a good weapon, even without magic.

I scrubbed my hands, rinsed them, scrubbed again, and then hurried to my office. Betsy was leaning over Clarence's cage when I arrived.

"Is that a snake or a chicken?" she asked.

"Both. He's a basilisk. And he's not feeling well." Clarence opened his eyes, let out a little wuffle and went back to sleep. Molting was hard work.

I steered Betsy to a chair. "What can I help you with?"

"It's Maeve. My sister. She's missing. Maybe." Betsy sat on the edge of the seat, clutching a small canvas sack. She still wore her tavern wench uniform, and the apron was stained with a day's worth of rushed food orders and spilled beer. "I get off early on Sundays, and I went home, hoping we could spend some time together, but she was gone."

"You said she likes to wander. When did you last see her?"

"About six hours ago. I know that doesn't sound like a lot, and yes, she often goes out alone, sometimes all day, but…" She wrestled with the bag to open the drawstrings and pulled out a ragged stuffed unicorn. "Maeve doesn't go anywhere without Mr. Pointy." The unicorn's head drooped as if it had lost most of its stuffing. "After my shift, I came home to find her gone. He was sitting on our front stoop. You probably think I'm silly for worrying. Maeve isn't a child, I know, but she's…special. She's too trusting."

Tears of frustration welled in her eyes. She looked down and one dripped onto the unicorn. "I had no one else to ask for help."

By the One-eyed God, this was exactly why I had a house full of strays. I needed to work on my saying-no skills.

"Why don't I drive you home and we'll see if Maeve has returned?"

Betsy nodded, clutching Mr. Pointy so hard that his head arched back. I swear he was grinning at me.

I LEFT MY sword in the umbrella stand with Jacoby babysitting it. It was a test. If the sword was truly dormant, great. If not, Jacoby would teleport it to me. He could find the truck anywhere in the city by now.

We drove east along the old highway toward Talon Street. I braced myself for the psychic scream of my sword, but it didn't come. I was still aware of it, like there was a trail of magic breadcrumbs leading back to it, but I felt no agitation from our separation.

Thank you, Leighna. That was one problem solved.

"Has Maeve ever been gone for more than a day?" I asked.

Sitting in the front seat of my truck, clutching the stuffed toy, Betsy looked like a scared kid.

"Once. That was before Mom died. We found her sleeping in the park. She said that Mr. Pointy wanted to watch the stars."

But she had left Mr. Pointy this time.

"Maybe she's finally outgrown toys."

Betsy shook her head. "You don't get it. Routine is important to Maeve. Really important. If we don't eat supper every night at exactly seven o'clock, she throws a tantrum. Once, when the shops were out of her regular soap, she refused to bathe for a week." She wrinkled her nose. "It was gross."

"That must be very stressful for you." I didn't imagine that Betsy had much of a social life.

She shrugged. "We manage."

We drove in silence until we neared her neighborhood.

"Turn here," Betsy said. "And the next left. My house is the third one on the right."

I pulled up in front of a single-story house with a neat lawn. Kids played street hockey in front of the next house. Rows of red brick bungalows and small cottages hid among old maples. Some had peeling paint, but most were well kept. It was an affluent neighborhood by the looks of it. Not the sort of place I'd expect a tavern server to be able to afford.

As Betsy reached for the passenger door, I stopped her, holding out my widget with the picture of Cyril and Lorraine.

"Do you know either of these people?"

Betsy studied the image and frowned. "No. Why? Are they missing too?"

"Not exactly." I didn't want to tell her they were dead. "Just another case I'm investigating." There was probably no connection to Betsy's missing sister. Probably.

Inside, Betsy called out for Maeve, but I could already tell the house was empty. It was silent on a level that went past normal hearing. The rooms smelled of years of home-cooked meals and the decor was decidedly old-fashioned for two young women living alone, with dark wood furniture and floral prints on the sofa and curtains.

"You inherited this place from your parents?" I asked.

"Yeah. Dad passed away eleven years ago and Mom four." Betsy bit her lip and looked around as if seeing the place for the first time. "I could sell it and move somewhere smaller, but Maeve likes it here…" She picked up a throw pillow that had fallen on the floor and placed it back on the couch, then fussed with some knickknacks on the side table. Her shoulders heaved as she tried to hold back tears.

"Why don't we start in Maeve's room?" I said gently. Betsy nodded and led me down a narrow hallway to the bedroom at the end. It was small and made smaller by all the clutter. A single bed was tucked in the corner by the window, with three rows of stuffed animals neatly lined up against the pillows. One entire bookcase housed dozens of snow globes, some simple, others with ornately carved pedestals. At first, it seemed like total chaos—a riot of toys, books, and junk piled on every surface—until I noticed the pattern. Items were sorted into clusters of five. Five snow globes to a shelf. Five books separated by a stuffed animal, then another five books. Five mobiles hung from the ceiling. Their arms dangled stars, planets, animals, fish and butterflies, and they twirled gently in the breeze from the open window.

A neat path in the clutter led from the door to the bed. Betsy indicated that I should go first. I walked in, careful to keep to the path so I didn't disturb anything. From Betsy's descriptions, it didn't sound like Maeve would be happy to have a stranger going through her things.

I bent over to examine the snow globes and found a terrarium on the lowest shelf. A basket was upturned on a base of sand, and as I peered into the enclosure, several small blue lights emerged to whip around the basket in a frenzy.

"What are those?" I asked.

Betsy shrugged "Maeve calls them fifollets. She found them at the park."

Fifollets. Interesting. That was the phonetic corruption of *feu folle* or false fire. They were will o'wisps, usually found in bogs or marshes. Some people believed they were a product of swamp gas, but on closer inspection, I could see that each light was actually a tiny, fat creature encased in blue light.

I stood up and turned to take in all the toys and childish art pinned to the walls.

"How old is Maeve?"

"Twenty-three." Betsy leaned against the door frame as if unwilling to step into the room. "But after Dad died, she sort of just stopped. I don't know. It's like she got stuck there as a twelve-year-old girl."

Now I realized what was bothering me. The room wasn't still. Apart from the mobiles swinging in the wind, other things were in perpetual motion too. Red and yellow lights swirled in the snow globes. A lava lamp standing in one corner continually morphed between purple, red and orange. A dipping bird, bowed to a pretend birdbath, stood straight up and bowed again. Over and over. Maeve liked motion. Several other kinetic sculptures were lined up on her desk, and, each sculpture seemed to be engulfed in flames. I leaned over and ran a finger through the fire but felt no heat. They were illusions. I looked into the snow globes. Each little winter scene was also on fire.

I pointed to a black scorch mark on the carpet. "What's that?"

Betsy shifted uncomfortably. "Maeve did that by accident a long time ago. I wanted to change the carpet, but she wouldn't let me."

I nodded. Maeve liked fire.

I let my keening out and tasted her brand of magic. It was spicy, like cayenne pepper, and agitated. The room was filled with magic. I glanced at the neatly made bed and imagined Maeve sleeping there every night, unconsciously emanating energy in her dreams until it seeped into the walls, the bedding, and the stuffed toys, like someone had taken a giant bucket and sloshed magic across every surface.

Unfortunately, this extra sense gave me no indication of where Maeve went, but if I ever met her, I'd know her magic signature as well as any bloodhound on the scent of a fox.

"Anything?" Betsy asked. The hope shining from her eyes made me feel like a heel. I'd led her to believe I was an investigator, when really I had no idea where to start looking for her sister.

"No. I'd like to interview the neighbors and then maybe you can show me the park that Maeve likes to go to."

Betsy nodded, but the light of hope in her eyes had dimmed. She didn't believe we'd find Maeve, and the wriggling doubt in my gut agreed.

19

As I got ready for my Thursday dinner date with Susanna, Angus showed up carrying a small potted plant. Gita greeted him while I dithered about which of my t-shirts to wear: the one with the angry hedgehog or the one with the cute dragon. I didn't know why it was so important. I was unreasonably nervous, like the unpopular girl in middle school who just got invited to her first boy-girl party. In the end, I dumped both t-shirts in favor of the one with the kitten in a wizard hat.

In the living room, Angus and Gita huddled together by the plant stand. Gita squeaked and jumped back in surprise, making Angus laugh.

"Don't that just beat a dead horse," he said.

"What are you guys so excited about?" I stuck my chin over their shoulders to see the plant Angus had brought. It looked like a fern, with clusters of small dark green fronds.

"Watch this." Gita touched one a frond and it closed up like an umbrella. She giggled.

My banshee giggled.

Angus leaned back and fluttered his wings, pleased with himself. Errol, who was sitting with his legs hanging over the rim of the bonsai's pot, thumped his walking twig in approval.

I couldn't resist. I reached out to touch one of the fronds and watched it shrink away.

"It's a mimosa plant." Gita wiped tears from her eyes and smiled.

"What's it for? Some new potion?" I asked.

"Only if you've got raging diarrhea," Angus said. "But no, I brought it for you to practice on."

"Me?"

"The wee plant will react to magic just as easily as the touch of a hand. Watch." He focused on the plant. I keened his magic lashing out, and another frond jerked closed.

"Amazing. And you think I'll be able to do that?"

"With practice. Every day." His bushy brows lowered over his eyes. "I want you to practice reaching for it. Don't talk to it. Just touch it with your magic. You'll know as soon as you do."

The green man was a genius.

"Thank you. I'll try it. But not right now. I'm meeting Susanna at her lab. It's in the same building as Gerard's, so I'm hoping to snoop a bit."

Angus frowned. "I should come with you."

"Not this time. Susanna isn't exactly a friend. At least not yet. She might find it odd if I have a gargoyle tagging along. And besides, this is just recon. If I find anything interesting, I'll let you know."

We walked toward the front door.

"That reminds me," he said. "You were right about Cyril and Lorraine. They were friends. And Lorraine was definitely working for Gerard, but on what project?" He shrugged, rustling the leaves on his head. "Who knows?"

"So what if Lorraine found out something…something that scared her? She didn't know what to do about it, so she went to her Guardian friend for advice. Gerard found out and killed them both."

"Oh, aye. You paint a pretty picture, but it's pure conjecture at this point."

"So, we'd better find some proof."

Angus stopped at the front door to skewer me with his best Guardian stare.

"You just be careful. People are dying like hotcakes."

The alchemists had taken over the old school buildings behind Abbott's Agora. These were offices and archives with a few labs. Most of their labs were on Perrot Island, ostensibly to protect the citizens of Montreal from any experiments that went horribly wrong. But keeping the labs outside the ward also meant that the alchemists had no oversight from Hub. They did as they pleased on their little island. And spying on them would be near impossible. So I had to settle for snooping at the more public offices.

Susanna had to work late and had called to ask if I would pick up dinner and bring it to her. Angus's arrival set me back, and it was almost eight o'clock by the time I paid for vegetarian curry and made my way through the winding path to the Penfield Building behind the market.

It was a boxy construction of red brick that only seemed quaint because it was old. Built in the early twentieth century, Penfield had originally been a college. To the right, as I walked up to the door, more red-brick buildings sat dark and abandoned. These were the old dormitories. The alchemists had bought the entire campus intending to expand into the other buildings eventually. For now, they sat empty but for the class two and three fae who dared to squat so close to the alchemist stronghold.

I buzzed the intercom on the door and a bored voice asked who I was there to see.

I leaned into the speaker. "Susanna Coulter."

"Please send your identification."

I tapped my widget to the pad beside the speaker and it beeped. Then I waited while the security guard checked that I actually existed. It always amazed me that one bit of encrypted code could validate my entire existence.

Eventually, the door clicked and opened slowly outward. I stepped inside and smiled at the guard sitting at a kiosk just past the doors. He scowled and pointed to my bag.

"Food must stay in designated areas. Labs marked with this sign," he held up an image of a person in full hazmat gear, "are off limits without proper escort. Basement is there." He pointed to a door marked "Stairs."

I thanked him and headed down. The stairwell was well lit, but I couldn't help feeling that I was being watched. Probably because I was. Cameras were fitted to every corner of the hall. I noted them all.

Susanna waited for me on the basement level.

"Hakim told me you were coming down," she said.

"And I brought supper." I held up my canvas tote with our curries inside.

"Great. I'm starving. We can eat in my lab."

"Really? The security guard made it sound like one sneeze might get me arrested."

"Hakim's just doing his job. Alchemists are paranoid about their labs, but this place isn't where the real work is done. It's mostly so they can put on a good show."

Susanna gave me a quick tour before we headed to her lab.

"Everyone wants a basement office here because of the security measures," she said. "These labs are soundproof, with fire measures put in place for any accidents. They're top of the line. I was lucky to get a space here. That's Gerard Golovin's lab. Can you imagine? I'm on the same floor as the prime minister!"

Ignoring Susanna's fan-girl gushing, I glanced into the pristine lab full of state-of-the-art equipment. It seemed like a waste if it was mostly for show.

Before I could do any snooping, Susanna lead me to her lab. It was much more friendly, with a lived-in look despite all the machines. One section was walled off as a cubicle and here her bright personality shone through. The desk held her computer and office supplies. The cubicle walls were made of carpeted foam that allowed easy tacking up of photos. Susanna made good use of the space, covering every inch with snapshots of family or friends, old cartoons and odd alchemical designs that made no sense to me. A row of stuffed dolls sat on her cluttered desk—seven tiny witches with colorful hair under black hats.

She kept all her personal dirt inside the cubicle. The rest of the lab was pristine. On the counters, equipment was tucked neatly under cabinets. A steel worktable filled most of the space, and the base of a huge contraption sat on that.

The only decoration in the lab was a shelf high enough to be nearly out of reach that ran around three walls. Terra cotta gargoyle statues lined the shelf from one end to the other. These were the traditional squatting gargoyles with round faces, thick, wide mouths and heavy brows over deep-set eyes.

"You're making gargoyles?" I had a bad feeling about this.

"Not really. That magic is still lost."

Not to mention illegal.

Susanna glanced at the elephant in the room, the giant, lightning-filled glass ball suspended from the ceiling over the steel table. A burner was set to heat the glass from below. A second, smaller glass globe attached to the ball at an angle. All of it hooked into a computer by a fat wire. On the counter beside the device sat a jar of shiny black stones.

"It's a blazing alembic," she said. "Sort of. I modified it for my own purposes. Let's eat first, then I'll show you how it works."

I DEVOURED MY curry in five minutes because I hadn't eaten since noon. Susanna picked at hers, chatting while she ate.

"So are you and Henry Mason a thing? How does that work? You know, with him a gargoyle most of the time."

I choked on the water I'd been sipping.

"No! Not a thing." I hesitated. "Well, maybe. But what kind of thing, I don't know. Mason is…difficult."

"Aren't they all?" Susanna looked wistful.

"Does that mean you have a certain someone?" I glanced at the photos pinned to the cubicle, but didn't see any that looked romantic.

"I wish." Susanna wiped her mouth on a napkin. "No. I'm married to my work, as they say."

She rose and stepped over to the massive contraption hanging above the work table.

"The blazing alembic is a traditional alchemic device. Overly simplistic really, which is why modern alchemists tend to disregard it. But sometimes the classics work best. See here? I deposit the inert specimen into this globe, and it transforms matter into energy and back again."

I leaned in, fascinated.

"First, I heat the specimen over the ritualistic flame."

"Ritualistic? That's a Bunsen burner."

"Well, usually there's chanting involved." Susanna flexed her hands open and closed with nervous energy.

"Then I invoke the spirits to distill the matter, and, voilà! Energy is born. Then if I'm careful I can reverse it. Energy back into matter."

"So what exactly is your purpose?" I asked, not sure I really wanted to know.

"To create life." She grinned.

Of course. We all had our hobbies.

"No, I'm just kidding. No one can create life. I'm just creating energy. But with that energy, I should be able to animate one of these little statues. Sort of like a golem or a fetch. I've been successful a couple of times, but I can't get the animation to stick. Do you want to see it work?"

I wasn't sure that was a good idea, but Susanna was already lowering one of the clay gargoyles into the large glass ball. It hung suspended in a thick liquid, and I couldn't help thinking it looked like a baby in a womb. Susanna tinkered with a dial on the machine, and the burner flared up with a blue flame. She opened the jar of stones the size of peas and spilled a few onto the counter. Instantly, a squirmy kind of magic shivered across my skin, like a dozen spectral voices all nagging at the same time.

She chose one stone and gripped it between thumb and forefinger.

"This is how gargoyles were originally made, but the exact formula was lost during the industrial revolution. Or maybe the iron infestation dampened the magic. But Terra has released these magics from the core of the earth. So we might be able to bring back gargoyles or something like them." She had a pleased smile on her face. Then she dropped the stone into the alchemic womb with the gargoyle.

"Now what?" I asked, almost afraid of her answer.

"Well now, I chant." She had the grace to look embarrassed, but then she shrugged and sat on a wooden stool before the blazing alembic. She began to chant in a low voice. I couldn't make out the word she repeated over and over again, something like "Bah-way-mo," but I felt the spike in power immediately. Like most alchemists, Susanna was a natural lightning rod for magic. And the Penfield Building stood right over a major ley-line, which was probably why the alchemists bought the campus in the first place.

Magic glowed around her, building like a fog that only I could see. As the chanting continued, the magic thickened. Energy sizzled at her fingertips. Then, she laid her hands on the globe and screamed out her chant one last time. Magic burst from her in an electric blue arc, straight into the heart of the globe.

The stone exploded. The little gargoyle shivered and opened its mouth as if to cry or suckle. Its fisted hands flailed. Then it fell still and lifeless again.

Susanna slumped on her stool.

"Are you all right?" I laid a hand on her shoulder and she smiled tiredly.

"It takes a lot of juice, that's all."

I stared at the massive contraption of glass and tubes. Should I tell her it was completely irrelevant? That she was the catalyst that sparked the bit of life, not the blazing alembic?

Susanna recovered and jumped up to peer into the glass globe at the little gargoyle which was once again an inert terra cotta statue.

"Did you see him? Wasn't he beautiful?"

"Uh, yeah."

Susanna briskly shut down the flame, removed the gargoyle and dried him with a towel as gently as if he were a real baby.

"I can't seem to animate them for long, but I'm working on it."

"Why?" I couldn't help it. The question just burst from me.

Susanna held the gargoyle close, her expression confused.

"I don't mean to criticize your work. It's amazing. Really. But have you ever considered that just because you can do something, doesn't mean you should?"

Susanna frowned. Maybe that concept had never occurred to her.

"It's just a golem. A construct. I'm not hurting anyone with it. And besides, think of all the good we could do. The applications for science and technology!"

Nope. I didn't get it. But then I could sense the authentic life that Susanna had sparked in that gargoyle statue.

"Gargoyles were imbued with life by stealing the spirit of a fae. Doesn't that bother you?" I thought of Angus, with his off-kilter magic and Cyril, who may have jumped to his death because of this dissonance.

"But that's just it! My experiments don't use fae spirits, or any spirits at all, just pure magic drawn from the source, from Terra."

I glanced at the jar of pea-sized stones. I wasn't so sure of that.

"But it doesn't work," she said. "Not yet, anyway. The longest I've been able to animate one is just over four minutes. But at least Gerard was pleased with that result. He was really excited when he saw my demonstration."

Gerard Golovin. Somehow it always came back to the prime minister.

"He saw this?"

"Yeah, last year. That's when he offered me lab space here.

"Is he working on the same tech?" I knew the answer already. I'd seen Golovin's gencrew golems, and I was pretty sure they weren't powered by any ley-line. But I wanted to see how deep Susanna was in Golovin's schemes.

She shrugged. "Dunno. His office here is just for show. His main lab is on the island and has ridiculous security. A low-level tech like me would never get invited to it."

"But he was here? He saw your…" I waved at the gargoyles, "your set up."

"Yep. He came, he saw, he took my notes and patted me on the head like a good girl. Gods, if I wasn't so attracted to that guy, I'd hate him. If he figures it out before I do, he'll get all the credit despite the fact that I did all the legwork."

"If Gerard figures out how to make gargoyles, your credit will be the least of our worries."

"What do you mean?"

My stomach churned as I wondered how much I could tell her. I knew next to nothing about Susanna, but she seemed innocent, and I liked her. I didn't like many people.

"Golovin has already found a way to animate golems. Did you see his latest press conference when he showed off his new gencrew?"

Susanna's eyes widened. "But that's just an automaton. He promised me." Suddenly she wouldn't meet my eyes. "I mean when I asked him about it. He assured me the gencrew were simply mechanical."

"They're not."

She narrowed her eyes at me. "How can you be sure? Did you test them with a thaumagauge? That's the only way to be certain."

"Let's just say, I have a taste for magic. And Golovin's gencrew are not magically inert."

They also didn't use ley-line magic, I was sure of it.

I showed her the picture of Lorraine and Cyril.

"Do you know her?" I asked. Susanna pressed her lips together. I was losing her. She didn't like what I was saying, but I had to get her to listen.

"She was killed because of something she knew. Be careful. Don't trust Golovin. Don't tell anyone else about your experiments. In fact, you should stop this research right away. Before someone gets hurt."

Susanna crossed her arms. "You should leave now."

I nodded. I hadn't made a friend here tonight. But before I left, I held up one of the black stones.

"Just do me a favor and test one of these. I think you'll be surprised at what you find."

Angus waited in the shadows outside the Penfield Building. I handed him the stone I'd swiped on my way out.

"I know where Gerard learned to make golems. And I know where the missing fae went."

Angus held the stone in his closed hand and whistled. "That's a live one." He looked sad. "So it's true then. Those damned alchemists have rediscovered the magic of gargoyles."

I laid a hand over his. "We'll make them stop. I promise. But we have to tell Mason now."

"Aye. And it will break his heart."

20

very time I dreamed about a full moon, I cried. Sometimes tears flowed freely, leaving red streaks down my dream cheeks. Other times tears lodged in my chest, so tight around my heart that it could barely pump against the crush of painful memories. I'd been stuck in this dream many times before, on nights when my past lurked in the shallow layers of my subconscious.

Aaric died under a full moon. If I wanted to wake up, I knew I had to confront it. I forced myself to look at the deceitful glowing orb, half hidden by thickening clouds. The face in the moon turned into Aaric's with his wry smile that never quite reached his eyes. Aaric, my kissing cousin, my first love and only friend in those early days when Mom uprooted me as an awkward teen just coming into my powers and moved us, not just across the country, but to another world.

When Mom's illness became debilitating, Aaric came to bring her home to Asgard, where the famed Golden Apples would cure her. I was the bonus package he got to lug across continents to Bifrost, the rainbow bridge that connected our world to the realm of the Aesir.

But this dream wasn't about that time. This one was about the last time I saw Aaric. My last day in Asgard.

How many years ago now? Ten? More. Twelve years since he begged me to end his life. Of course I'd said no, denied him the one thing he wanted most of all. The one thing he wanted more than me.

But even as I begged him not to do it, my hands had not resisted. When had I ever resisted his touch? His fingers wrapped around mine, and those clasped the hilt of my blade pointed right at his heart. His touch was hot. A soft, sorrowful look filled his eyes. *He loves me enough to be sad. He loves me. He loves me…* His smile filled every surface of my mind. *He's shaking me… shaking and…*

"Kyra-lady, wakes up!"

A scream stuck in my throat as awareness slammed into me. I sat bolt upright in bed. Jacoby jumped back.

"What is it?" The lights flickered and something beeped in my kitchen. The timer on the stove? And what was that thumping noise?

"Stop that right now!" came Gita's raspy command. I jumped out of bed and ran for the living room, taking in the scene in an instant. The critters were all awake, rustling in their cages. Errol stood beside his bonsai tree. He held his walking twig high, and it sparked with crackling blue energy. Hunter peered over the rim of his tank, but when Gita shouted again, he dunked back into the water.

The patio door was open and cool night air blew through the room.

"Stop!" Gita stood over the dark form of Emil, who lay on the floor. He held my sword in one hand and drove it through his chest into the floorboards. *Thunk!* He pulled it out and drove it home again. *Thunk!*

The flickering lights were nauseating, and I felt like I was stumbling through a horror movie. I ignored Mr. Murray's irate banging from above.

"Gita! Take Errol into the kitchen and make him some tea," I said. "I'll deal with this."

Gita turned to me. Her face was streaked with tears, as if the midnight commotion had jolted her back to her rightful melancholy. She scooped up Errol and disappeared into the kitchen with Jacoby following.

Thunk! Thunk!

I pinched the bridge of my nose until the electricity stilled. The dim light from the window fell on Emil. His face was wet with tears, his chest soaked in blood.

Thunk!

"Stop that!" I grabbed the sword and wrenched it away from his blood-slick hands. "That won't work." I didn't tell him that the sword needed the touch of a Valkyrie to work its magic, or that I'd put it into stasis anyway. The less he knew about my magic, the better.

"Why?" he cried. "Why can't I just die?"

I sat down beside him. I wore only light shorts and a tank top to bed and the floor was sticky under my bare legs. Emil made a grab for the blade again. We wrestled, but he was weak from his wounds even though they were already healing. I tossed the sword across the floor, and it clattered against the wall.

"Why?" He looked like a little lost boy.

"Maybe you're not done yet."

He sniffled and laid his head on my knee. "What do you mean?"

"Maybe you have some purpose that you're not seeing. The gods will claim you when you're done."

"You believe that?"

I tried not to hesitate. I wasn't sure what I believed anymore. The gods I knew were selfish. It was usually better not to be noticed by them.

"I do."

He leaned on one elbow and wiped a hand across his nose, smearing blood across his face.

"But what purpose could the gods have for me. I'm a misfit. A freak."

I shrugged. "Misfits change the world."

He lay back in the puddle of his cooling blood. Under his torn shirt, his bones and muscles were already knitting together. But he'd be hungry from all that blood loss.

I couldn't send him back into the night like this. But I wouldn't leave him alone with my family either while I went out to get blood.

I untangled myself from his grip and went for my widget. At least that was still working. Errol had been getting better at reining in his magic, and the phones and lights had been working for several days. But tonight showed me that he couldn't stay here, not if every time he got upset, he almost blew a transformer.

I peeked at them in the kitchen. Gita was reading *Winnie the Pooh* to Errol and Jacoby by candle light. I could have kissed her.

I grabbed my widget and scrolled through my contacts. I almost called Gabe, but he was out on a date with Dutch again, and if they were patching things up, I didn't want to ruin it for him. I hesitated for a moment at Mason's number, then dialed Angus.

"Is everything okay?" he asked as a greeting.

"I have a bit of a situation here." I explained about Emil.

"You need me to bring blood?"

"Please. There's an all-night butcher in Abbott's Agora."

"I know the place. Hold tight. I'll be there in forty-five."

While I waited, I heated the small amount of pig's blood I kept on hand and brought it back to where Emil lay propped against my couch.

"Why does a nice girl like you have blood in her fridge?" Emil wrapped his shaking hands around the warm mug.

"Vampire slugs." I pointed to their terrarium across the room.

"Ugh. Disgusting creatures." He sipped the warm blood and grimaced. "I don't believe it, you know."

"Believe what?"

"That I can change the world. I don't even want to change it. All I want to do is live without people cursing me when I walk by. I want to smile and not have children scream when they see my fangs. I don't understand it. Trolls and goblins can walk the streets, and people barely glance at them. But not me." He bowed his head and his ridiculous curls fell into his eyes. In another age, he could have been a movie star with his boyish charm.

"The animosity towards the opji is deeply rooted." I laid a hand on his arm. The flesh was unpleasantly cool. "Old prejudices are hard to erase, and the attack this past spring brought all those old fears to the surface. It's not fair, I know."

He peered at me from under long lashes. A blood tear dripped down his cheek and he smiled.

"You're nice." His eyes flicked to the pulse at my neck.

"Drink your blood. There's more coming, but that will take the edge off."

"Why is that octopus staring at me?" He pointed at Hunter, who leaned halfway out of his tank, as if ready to launch himself at Emil.

"He's a pygmy kraken."

"There's a difference?"

I cringed. Hunter leaped, aiming right for Emil's face. I caught him, and he splatted around my arm. It was like catching a giant snot ball.

"Sorry about that." I dropped Hunter back in the tank. "He's very protective of me."

Emil glanced at Hunter, who now pressed all his tentacles to the glass. "You're lucky to have such good friends."

I found some old towels to mop up Emil's mess, then sat beside him. I wanted to be sure he drank all his blood. The critters were quiet again. Emil took my hand in his and I could still feel the tremors running through him.

To talk him off his existential cliff, I amused him with stories about my foster critters. We were onto the tale of how I tried to re-home Hunter with a nice dentist, but he kept escaping his tank and scaring the customers.

"The poor dentist developed a nervous tic," I said. "He couldn't sit in a chair or pour his coffee into a cup without checking them first. When Hunter disappeared for a week, a hygienist nearly had a nervous breakdown. That's when they asked me to take him back. He's been here ever since."

Hunter watched us from his tank as if he knew we were talking about him. Emil laughed. He stroked my wrist with his thumb. I felt that it was a gesture meant to soothe him more than a flirtation, so I let it be. His head drooped to rest on my shoulder.

And that's when Mason walked in.

I jumped up, not sure why I suddenly felt guilty. Mason narrowed his eyes and held up a canvas sack with two jars of blood inside. Emil rose and Mason handed him the bag.

"I think you should leave now," Mason said.

Emil sighed dramatically, bowed over my hand like a royal courtier and kissed it.

"Thank you, milady. I will not bother your sleep again." He smiled smugly at Mason and left.

I rounded on Mason. "You have no right to tell guests in my home to leave!" My raised voice caused a flurry of rustling in the cages. Hunter thrashed around his tank, spilling water on the floor.

"You're being reckless again." Mason's tone was calm, but he loomed over me, big, dark and menacing. Gita poked her head in from the kitchen, then ran to her closet and slammed the door. Jacoby came to take my hand in solidarity and snarled up at Mason.

"Jacoby, I can handle this. Why don't you take Errol outside to your house for the night?"

Jacoby shifted from foot to foot as if undecided. Then he sighed and left with Errol, slamming the door in protest.

In the sudden silence, Mason and I glared at each other.

"He's opji," Mason snapped. "They're all murderers. You were bitten by one, by the gods! You of all people should know how dangerous they are."

"Emil isn't like that."

"Why? Because he's cute and fluffy, like one of your damned rescues? Or are your feelings for him more personal?"

"How dare you?"

"Me? If you had a dick, I'd accuse you of thinking with it."

"And if you had a heart, I'd accuse you of being jealous."

We glared.

A stray beam of light caught the storm in his eyes. He grabbed my shoulders and pulled me in. Then he kissed me. For the barest second, I held back. His arms circled me like hands holding a butterfly. If I wanted to flee, he would let me. My fingers twined in his hair, and I sunk into the embrace. His grip tightened. My lips parted and met his, kiss for kiss. His tongue slipped inside me like a whisper of passion held in check, like he could lose himself in me if I opened the door.

I bit him.

He jerked back, tasting the blood on his lip.

"About time you gave in to that," I said.

His magic pulled at mine like a bow on a violin. He dabbed at his bleeding lip with a thumb.

"I suppose I deserved that."

A slow smile burned in his eyes. I could forgive him a lot for those eyes.

"I'm tired of your shit." I knocked his hand off my arm.

"My shit?" The word sounded odd coming off his tongue. Not that Mason didn't curse, but he usually did it in old French. My fist grabbed the front of his tailored shirt in a ridiculous show of confidence that I didn't really feel.

"Yes, your shit, Mr. Guardian. The shit that makes you look at me with longing one minute and push me away the next. At least Emil has the courage to take what he wants."

That stopped him. He stood back. His eyes were not those of an old man. They were neither hard nor angry. They were lost.

Leaning in, I held my lips against his ear. "You want me. And it scares the crap out of you." The intensity of my own desire frightened me too.

He shut me up with another kiss, this one hard and demanding. An animal groan escaped his throat.

I ground myself against his rock-hard erection. "Feel that? Part of you is still alive, old man."

I wanted to wrap my legs around him, to pull him down to the floor and…

Cold water splashed us and I jerked away from the embrace. Hunter squirted again, making it clear he didn't want to witness our mating ritual.

Mason laughed and leaned his forehead against mine. Water dripped down his face.

"I do want you," he said. "But when we make love, it won't be under the gaze of a dozen jealous creatures."

"We could go into the bedroom," I suggested. We looked through the door to see Kur asleep on my bed.

"You know, my place is very lonely," he said. "And I think I heard a thunder of dragons calling out in Dorion Park. Maybe Sunday night you could come over. I'll make you dinner and we can watch for the dragons."

"You can cook?"

He kissed the end of my nose and the feels went right through me.

"I can cook. I make a mean Bolognese."

"Sounds like a date."

"It does, doesn't it?"

21

Two days later, I sat in my office staring at my computer. I was supposed to be writing a blog post about my grubber encounter, but the screen remained blank, the cursor blinking with unfulfilled promise.

I couldn't stop thinking about Mason. We'd left things up in the air, and now I went over the argument in my head in minute detail, second guessing everything I'd said. I flip-flopped between mortification at being so forward and righteous anger at his behavior.

When a call came through on my widget, I answered it without checking the number.

The girl's voice was hysterical, so I didn't immediately recognize it. I held my widget away from my ear, then put it on speaker, so Gabe could hear too.

"The takers! They're here! Oh, God! It was right here, in the window!" Then came muffled sobbing and the sound of a slamming door.

Gabe watched the widget with raised eyebrows.

"Betsy? Is that you?"

"Yes!" Her voice came in a hiss.

"Where are you?"

"In the closet in my room," she whispered. "The takers came back! They took Maeve and now they've come back for me!"

"Stay on the line. I'm coming."

It was six o'clock in the evening, and Gabe had been preparing to leave for the day, but he said, "I'll drive."

I agreed. His little silver bullet would get there faster than my truck. As we pulled onto the road, I checked that Betsy was still on the line.

"I'm here." She sniffled. "Do you think it can get into my house? Don't they need to be invited, or something?" I didn't tell her that was an old myth about vampires.

"Just hold on tight," I said. "We'll be there soon." Then I grabbed Gabe's widget and dialed Hub. While it rang, I cycled through the list of detectives I still knew there.

"Hub dispatch," said a bored voice.

"Can I speak to Detective Kesik." I didn't think he would be receptive to my call, but I couldn't think of anyone else.

"What is it?" came the angry voice.

"This is Kyra Greene. We met at—"

"I know who you are."

I took a deep, calming breath. "Look, I'm heading to Rockland Road off of Talon Street. You know those takers who aren't kidnapping fae all over the city? Well, they're trying to kidnap a woman right now. You can either meet me there, or you can hear about it on the late news." I hung up.

Gabe whistled. "I love it when you use your executive voice."

"That guy just bugs me. I shouldn't let him."

Gabe barely slowed as we navigated around the mound of vegetation-covered rubble that was once a tunnel cutting through the city. No one bothered to clear it or rebuild because a major ley-line artery ran under it and the magic was unpredictable.

Ten minutes later we turned onto Rockland. It was dark and quiet. A single street lamp shone from the corner of Talon Street. But as we moved further into the residential area, the light faded.

"That's Betsy's." I pointed to the house with dark windows. "Drive by it slowly and park up the road."

Into the widget, I said, "Betsy, we're here. I'm going to hang up now so the noise doesn't spook anyone. Hub is on their way too. You just stay put, okay?"

I got a tiny "Okay" in return.

Gabe pulled up to the curb and left the engine running. His fancy car was quieter than a sleeping kitten and no one would hear it. But if we needed to get away fast…I hoped we wouldn't need to get away fast.

We stepped out of the car and I whispered, "I miss my sword."

The blade had passed its first separation test, and I had taken to leaving it in the umbrella stand. Gabe grinned and popped the trunk.

"Take your pick." He flicked open the locks on two large black cases to reveal an array of weapons.

I gave him the stink-eye. "What are you, some kind of superhero daylighting as an office assistant? Are you going to find a phone booth and change into tights?"

"Ha ha." Then he looked at me oddly. "What's a phone booth?"

"Never mind."

He reached for a knife and tucked it into the back of his jeans. "Cross bow or gun?"

"Seriously, what do you have all these for?"

"My family is…violent. These were my first toys."

"Is that why you work for me? Are you hiding?"

He flexed his broad shoulders and I realized how silly that question was. Gabe stood out in a crowd. He turned heads where ever he went. He'd have to go to another ward to hide.

"Not hiding. Just avoiding. So bullets or arrows?" He held up the gun in one hand and the crossbow in the other.

"I don't know. Depends on what we're dealing with. You take the gun. I'll take the crossbow."

We headed back towards Betsy's house, keeping to the shadows under the maples that lined the street. The air was still. Nothing moved, not even a leaf. Where the hell was Hub? Detective Kesik was difficult, but I'd expected better.

Gabe nudged me and pointed. He was going around the back of the house. I nodded and moved across the front yard to peer into the living room window. Nothing moved inside. I mounted two steps leading to the front door and tried the handle. Locked. I hoped that Betsy was still hidden.

The porch wrapped around the side of the house. Some boards looked rotten, and I avoided those as I crept to the far end and peered around the corner. A tall hedge blocked the view to the neighbor's and made the small path beside the house pitch black. I inched along, keeping close to the house, until I stood on the edge of the backyard. Ahead of me, a garden shed loomed out of the darkness.

My heart hammered in my chest. Something moved in the blackness beside the shed. A shadow against the other shadows. I sent out my keening, like a song on the wind, just a gentle nudge to taste the magic of whatever lurked there.

And what I tasted made me reel back.

No!

The shadow lumbered into the yard, heading for the patio door.

A hand gripped my shoulder, and I jumped, backing into Gabe.

"There's a gate on the other side," he whispered. "I can't get over it without being seen. Did you find anything?"

I pointed to the patio where the creature was bent to peer into the family room window. It was too big to be human, and it moved with blocky jerks. Just like the gencrew I'd met at the railroad excavation site.

"What is that?" Gabe asked. I cut him off with a finger to my lips. I had to be sure. I pushed out my keening again and tasted a familiar magic, like burned sugar.

It was Maeve.

Just then, she raised a fist and pounded on the window. Betsy screamed from inside. Gabe raised his gun to shoot, but I shoved his arm down and moved us both back into the shadows.

"Don't. That's Maeve, Betsy's sister."

"That thing?"

"It's a golem. The takers are snatching the fae to make golems."

"How did she get here?"

"I don't know. But we'll need help if we're to catch her alive." I looked toward the street. Still no sign of Hub. "Go call Angus or Mason. Get the Guardians here, but be quiet, so we don't spook her."

Gabe nodded and headed back toward the front yard to make his call. I poked my head around the house again. The golem drove a fist through the window, then broke away the rest of the glass. It groaned like a wraith as it tried to clamber inside.

Betsy was hysterical. I could hear her screaming and crying, and more crashing sounds as she threw things at the monster trying to break into her house. Why hadn't she just stayed in the closet? By now, lights were coming on in the neighbors' houses. Just great. I didn't need more spectators.

I had to do something, so I raised the crossbow and shot the golem in the butt.

"Hey! Over here!" I yelled.

The golem turned. In the light beside the patio door, I got a good look at its face. Except it had no face, just a general smudge of features—a slight indentation where there should be eyes, a small knob for the nose and a slash for a mouth—all dark red and glistening like wet, unfinished clay. The only distinguishing mark was the symbol cut into its forehead, that stylized "G" I was coming to know too well.

The mouth opened and a long, mournful wail came out. Then it lurched across the patio toward me.

Now what? I had nothing to trap it with. I glanced at the garden shed, then ran. Somehow, I had to lure the golem inside the shed and keep it there until backup arrived. I grabbed the door handle and pulled.

Locked. Damn the gods!

I turned to find the golem looming over me. It moaned.

My muscles had flashbacks to the time I fought a rock troll and lost. They seized on me and I stood frozen as the golem grabbed my arm and twisted. The tendons in my shoulder screamed. I hit it over the head with my crossbow, but it dragged me relentlessly toward the house.

A siren broke the stillness. Hub had finally arrived. The golem didn't react, but only continued hauling me toward the house.

Suddenly the backyard filled with piercing light as officers shone flashlights into the gloom.

"Don't move! We have you surrounded."

I dropped my crossbow. "I'm unarmed. Don't shoot."

The officer shone his flashlight across me and then swung it to shine right into the golem's face.

"What the hell is that?" said one cop.

"Don't shoot it!" I said, but I was too late. The cop panicked and let off a shot, hitting the golem in the shoulder. It finally let go of my arm. I stumbled back and fell. Pain lanced up my arm as I landed badly.

The cop kept firing, blasting the golem's chest, arms and legs, but still it shambled forward.

"No!" I screamed. It was just a girl! I tried to rise, pushing up with my one good arm.

A second cop came out of the shadows brandishing a long sword. He was a show-off, dancing around like a ballerina.

"Stop!" I shouted, scrambling to my feet. He cut off the golem's arms, then swiped at its leg, cutting deep into the ankle and nearly severing the foot.

The golem fell, and the cop raised the sword for the killing blow.

I jumped between them and held up my hands. "It's a girl! Just a girl! Someone turned her into a golem. We have to help her."

The cop checked his swing, but didn't lower his sword. He pointed it at my throat. Behind me, the golem moaned and struggled to sit up.

"You are interfering with Hub business," he said. "Stand down or I'll have you arrested.

I stood my ground. "You can't kill her! She's a citizen of Montreal."

"It's a monster."

We glared at each other, and I had choice words about who the real monster was.

"Hold!" came a stern voice. Detective Kesik stepped through the crowd that had gathered. I looked around. At least a dozen Hub officers stood with weapons ready. Kesik had taken me seriously after all. Several neighbors also watched. And Betsy stood by the patio door, guarded by an officer.

Kesik bent over Maeve, who had given up the struggle and lay on the grass moaning faintly.

"It's a golem?" he asked.

"Yes." Sort of. I didn't know how to put my suspicions into words. This creature was more than a golem but less than a gargoyle. It was some twisted hybrid of the two. At least Kesik was finally listening.

"There." Kesik pointed to the symbol on Maeve's forehead. "That's the only way to kill it."

Before I could react, the officer drove his blade through Maeve's forehead.

I screamed.

BETSY HAD STOPPED shaking. We sat on the front porch, and I'd wrapped her in a blanket. She took the news about Maeve's spirit being trapped in the golem as I expected, but her tears were exhausted now and we sat in silence, watching the Hub team carry the massive body away and pack it into a van.

My arm hurt and I cradled it in my lap, though I thought it was only sprained.

"She was just trying to come home," Betsy said in a small voice. I didn't agree or disagree. I didn't know enough about golems to understand Maeve's motivations. She could have been working on pure instinct, returning to a place that was familiar. Or the person who twisted her magic into the monstrous being could have sent her. One thing was certain; Maeve had been dead long before she made it home.

"I promise you I will find whoever did this," I said. Betsy just nodded and I felt like a phony. I couldn't save Maeve. I couldn't find her killer either. This wasn't my job. We had police and detectives for this stuff.

And it was obvious to me that Gerard Golovin was behind this. Maeve's golem was too similar to the gencrew. Hopefully, Kesik would figure that out when he examined the body.

One of Betsy's elderly neighbors arrived with a thermos of hot coffee.

"Why don't you come stay with me tonight?" she said to Betsy. I handed the girl off, thankful that there were still a few good people in this city.

"I'll go with them," Gabe said. He'd been sitting in the shadows at the end of the porch, and I'd forgotten he was there. "Make sure they get inside safe." He followed the two women across the road.

Rage burned through me. I found Detective Kesik talking to the techs who were scanning for magic residue and intercepted him as he left the yard.

"You knew about the takers," I snarled. "You knew, and you did nothing about them. And now you've killed an innocent girl."

Kesik paused, looked me up and down and took in my flared nostrils and accelerated breath.

"I killed a monster. There is no evidence that the golem was once human." He turned to leave, but I grabbed his arm.

"Your scans will prove it. And then what will you do? Hide the proof? Ignore it like you've ignored all the other missing fae?"

He frowned at my hand gripping his arm. "Remove your hand or I will have you arrested for assaulting an officer."

I hung on for another fraction of a minute. "We both know who is behind this. The question is, are you brave enough to bring him to justice?" I let him go, just as he yanked his arm away. He was expecting resistance, and I was childishly pleased when he stumbled backward.

Kesik left me fighting back tears of anger and sorrow. I surveyed the backyard. It was a mess of churned up grass. Broken glass littered the patio and the furniture was scattered. The Hub sirens were silent, but the flashing lights still announced to the world that we stood at a crime scene. Hub techs took pictures of everything as they made their report—a report that I suspected would be buried.

A young girl was dead because of political machinations. I wanted to scream and cry and stamp my feet at the unfairness of it.

Suddenly two Guardians landed in the grass. The gargoyles spread out, checking the perimeter of the yard. Then Mason was there, running up the driveway with Angus half hopping, half running behind him.

"Are you okay?" he asked.

"No." I sniffled. I really wasn't.

"Jesus Christ in a hand basket," Angus said from behind me. "What happened here?"

Mason's face was pinched in a frown as he surveyed the patio with the smashed window. I braced for another lecture about butting my nose in where it didn't belong. Instead, he opened his arms, and I flew into him as my sobs finally broke free.

GOLEM VS. GARGOYLE

(November 25, 2080)

No, we aren't doing a gladiator show where we pit golems against gargoyles. But I want to have a serious discussion about the distinction between the two. This is a topic close to my heart for many reasons, and something we should all be aware of. So here goes.

What is a gargoyle?

Gargoyles were first created in the Renaissance era by gifted alchemists who carved them from stone and gave them life through a complicated alchemical procedure. In a nutshell, the alchemist stole a fae spirit and stuck it in stone. For more about gargoyles, see the *Archives*.

What is a golem?

Golem is a generic term for any automaton animated through magic. Usually, this magic involves exhaustive rituals and rune work, often carved into the golem itself. Though golems need a strong power source (like a ley-line battery) for continued animation, the spell caster may initially spark the golem to "life" with a bit of their own magic, which enables a link between the two. Through this link, the spell caster can control the golem.

Golems generally don't have any capacity to think for themselves. They aren't sentient. The magic that animates them is purely mechanical, while a gargoyle takes on a spirit of its own once animated.

Breaking the spell will cause the golem to de-animate. Usually this can be done by destroying the activating rune tattooed onto the golem or destroying the fetch that acts as a magical link to the spell caster. Gargoyles are much harder to kill and often outlive their makers by generations.

Golems are neither good nor evil. They cannot be reasoned with. Their only purpose is to complete whatever task the spell caster set for them. If you get in their way, they will kill you. But in the end, they are tools of the spell caster that created them. Gargoyles are living beings, with hopes, dreams, and a spirit of their own. They can be good or they can be evil, just like the rest of us on this planet.

Golems tend to be faceless and haphazardly put together. I believe this is because of their limited use. They aren't made for a long life. A spell caster creates a golem for one purpose—whatever that may be. When done, the golem will be deactivated and returned to its natural elements. For this reason, they are often made of clay or other easily disposable material. The original gargoyles were works of art even before being animated. The care that went into their carving was part of the ritual of creating life. Each gargoyle I've met has been beautiful in his own way.

So what is the point of this discussion? Well, recently I came across a creature that seemed to be a hybrid gargoyle-golem. It looked like a golem—large and vaguely humanoid, like an impatient child put it together with clay. It even had a rune cut into its forehead. In fact, I've seen several of these creatures. Most were docile and acted like you would expect a golem to act. But one was… alive. That's the only way to describe it. It was sentient. And angry. It wore a rune on its head, but it was unclear to me if that rune was its animating force. I'm guessing that thaumagauge testing would prove it had an inner source of life-magic.

My biggest fear is that someone has found the lost knowledge to create gargoyles again. But then why do they need the rune work?

I'm sending this to you, my loyal peeps. Has anyone heard of such a thing?

COMMENTS (3)

Never seen one of these, but could the rune be a way to control the gargoyle?

alkeminator2000 (November 25, 2080)

> That's a great theory. Yes, it's quite possible that the spell caster was controlling the golem-gargoyle with the rune. The depravity of humankind never ceases to amaze me.
>
> *Valkyrie 367 (November 25, 2080)*

I am fascinated by gargoyles. I like your take on golems too. A hybrid would be really cool.

DaddysGirl (November 25, 2080)

The anger coming off Mason was palpable as I stumbled through the details of my encounter with the golem. Angus watched me intently, but I left out our theory about Gerard Golovin and his bag of tricks. For now.

When I got to the part about the cops stabbing the golem through the head, I stopped and closed my eyes, seeing the death again in bright detail. Mason caught me before I realized that I'd nearly fallen over. He turned to the Guardians who'd come with him.

"I'm taking Kyra home." He didn't let go as he spoke, and I sank into the feel of his arm around me. "Stay here and patrol. There may be more golems."

Angus nodded, but his eyes lingered on me, questioning. Was I going to tell Mason the whole truth? I nodded and he seemed satisfied.

"Aye, aye, bossman. Golems in this neighborhood will stick out like a sore throat. We'll find 'em."

I didn't think there would be more. Betsy was probably right. Maeve was trying to come home. Even if Golovin had other golems stashed away, they'd have no reason to come here.

Mason tucked me into the passenger seat of his car. My hands had stopped shaking, but I felt boneless, as if I might dissolve into a puddle.

"Gabe!" I suddenly remembered. "I should tell him I'm leaving."

Mason pointed to where Dutch and Gabe were already getting into Gabe's car.

"Dutch will take care of him. Now let me take care of you for once." Mason put the car in drive and zoomed around the Hub van with its flashing lights.

Traffic snarled on the backstreets leading away from Talon, which was always busy, night and day. Once we hit the old highway, the roads cleared. We drove westward in silence. Mason held my left hand in his right, his thumb circling mine, restlessly.

His car smelled new and the console was lit with dozens of gadgets.

"This is one of those driverless cars, isn't it? Why do you still drive it manually?" I asked, more to fill the empty space between us as we hurtled through the night.

He glanced at me and frowned. "Why wouldn't I?"

"Well, you like your tech so much. I thought you'd want the latest and greatest."

"Latest doesn't always mean greatest." He let go of my hand and gripped the steering wheel as if to emphasize his control over the metal beast. "Cars were meant to be driven, not to drive themselves."

I thought he was taking me home, but we didn't slow down as the exit to Morgan Road zipped by. I didn't complain. We had a lot to discuss and needed privacy—something that was in short supply at my place.

Mason slowed to tap his widget to the guard's at Gallop Bridge. The guard nodded and let us through without question. When he turned into Dorion Park, I opened my windows to let in the night air.

"Smell the trees," my Nana Greenleaf used to say, as if the magic of growing things could mend any hurt.

The house was dark as we pulled up. With its turrets, sweeping staircase and pillars holding up a balcony that overlooked the drive, the manor could have been the scene for a haunted house movie. But I sensed no ghosts here, only the pure magic of the forest with its myriad little lives.

Inside, Mason settled me on the couch before the hearth and lit a fire, even though the night wasn't chill. He left and returned with two glasses of red wine.

"Fortification," he said, then paused before handing me the glass. "Do you need something stronger? Whisky?"

I shook my head. "Wine is comfort food. Thanks." I sipped the velvety vintage while sorting my thoughts. Mason waited. He was perceptive enough to know that I hadn't told him the entire story. We also had two nasty fights and one hot kiss lingering between us. There was a lot of baggage to unpack. I started with business.

"Do you have any new leads on Cyril's murder?"

"Wait." Mason held up his hand. "I know we have a lot to talk about. This attack tonight. Cyril. But first I want to clear the air."

"Okay." I wasn't sure where he was going with this.

"You accused me of stringing you along. My 'shit,' as you put it. That wasn't my intention."

"And what was your intention?"

He looked me right in the eye. "To never fall in love to begin with."

I stared at him. He just put that out there. Right between us, like some shiny star full of sharp edges and sparkly allure.

"You know about my first wife. That didn't end well." He opened a wooden box on the coffee table and pulled out a small framed portrait.

"This was our daughter, Brigitte. She lived to be eighty-four. I nursed her through her last years." He paused, smiling at the image before handing it to me. I saw an older woman with blond hair braided in an intricate knot. She had Mason's eyes.

He took out another small portrait and handed it to me. "This was Amaya, my second wife." She was a beautiful dark-haired woman of Indian descent. "Of our eight children, three survived to adulthood. Those were good stats back then." He smiled sadly, and I wanted to hug him. Instead, I held the portraits of his dead family carefully. These were probably the only mementos he had of them.

"And this was my last wife, Jeanne. We were happy for a time." This portrait was a black-and-white photograph of a pretty woman with long straight hair, wearing a tie-dyed t-shirt and cut-off jeans. "She was barren, and I was okay with that. I didn't want to outlive any more children. But when she aged past me and realized that everyone would always wonder why that young man was with an older woman, she left me." He paused and stroked the side of the image with his thumb. "She died of cancer a few years later. I would have cared for her, but she didn't want a nursemaid."

I shut my eyes. It was so easy to forget that other people had histories. They had joys and traumas too. My pain and angst, my past relationships… they weren't unique. They were only mine. And these were Mason's. I felt honored that he shared them with me. Honored and a little ashamed that he felt the need to explain himself.

I tucked the precious images back in the box. "Why are you telling me this?"

"Because I want you to understand why I'm so bad at this relationship stuff. I've avoided it for over a hundred years."

"So why now?" Maybe I was fishing a bit, but maybe I needed to hear it again.

"Because you're easy to love." He leaned in and kissed me, soft and hesitant. Then he pulled back just enough so he could look into my eyes. "I tried not to, but you're brave and kind, and beautiful." His hand found the wisps of hair that had escaped from my braids at the base of my neck. "So here's my promise. I'm going to do better. Whatever's coming, we'll face it together. Agreed?"

I nodded, not trusting my voice.

"That means no more running into the night to fight monsters without me."

"Okay." It came out in a squeak. I sat back, cleared my throat and tried again. "I'll fight by your side, whatever is coming, but I can't promise not to face a few monsters alone. It's my job, after all." I thought about the knockers and the grubber. I wouldn't call Mason every time I had vermin bigger than a rat to contend with.

He considered me. This was an old-world man, probably used to submissive women who stayed home to care for the kids while he went out and did manly man things. I braced myself for a fight. I wouldn't give up my career. I was good at pest control. I understood fae monsters of all sizes and didn't even mind the blood and slime. If I was honest, I enjoyed it.

"Agreed," he finally said. "I wouldn't dream of interfering with your job. Not unless you asked. But this is different. Something bigger is happening in Montreal right now and I have a bad feeling it's all linked to that damned bloodstone."

"I think you're right. Even Cyril's murder."

He rubbed a hand across the nape of his neck. "You know something."

"Not really. Only that it's somehow tied to that body we found. Lorraine's."

Mason nodded. "Angus confirmed that they were close."

"I think that Lorraine saw something she wasn't supposed to and panicked. She went to Cyril for help, and they both died for it."

"Maybe. But that doesn't tell us what she saw."

"No. But I know what I saw."

I explained to him about visiting the GenPort site and the golems I found there masquerading as automatons.

"Are you sure they were golems?"

I considered this. The difference between an automaton and a golem was slight, but significant. Mason understood these shades of difference better than I did.

"I'm not sure of anything, but in the tunnel shaft, when I first encountered the gencrew—they call them gennys," I said with a wry smile, "its magic felt off. Kind of like Angus's magic." Mason frowned. This was a touchy subject and I went on carefully. "I couldn't prove it, but the gencrew just set my keening on edge, and tonight…" I fortified myself with a sip of wine. "Tonight I recognized the magic signature of the golem that attacked Betsy. It was her sister who went missing last week. I tasted her magic when I first went to investigate. It's…distinct."

"I don't understand." The crease between Mason's brows deepened as he frowned. "Someone kidnapped a girl from Talon and turned her into a golem? But who?"

"The takers. There have been a lot of disappearances. And the missing people have all been strong magic users. I haven't checked yet, but I suspect they were all elementals."

"Maeve too?"

"Yes. I was in her room. Her magic was all over it. She's…she *was* a fire elemental."

"Can you prove this?"

Not in a court of law, I thought, but I could prove it to Mason. "Do you still have that compass you brought with you to the Inbetween?"

"Yes." He rose and went over to the desk tucked into one corner of the large room, pulled out a couple of drawers and rummaged around until he found a small cloth pouch. Returning to the couch, he sat and dumped the compass into my hand. My keening hummed with the strident magic coming off it.

The compass looked like an old pocket watch, but with a digital read out.

"This device has two power sources." I looked at the compass with its wavering blue arrow. "One is a battery similar to a widget, fueled by ley-line electricity. You plug it in there?" I pointed to a socket on the side of the compass and Mason nodded. "But there's a second power source too. Faint. Like a barely glowing ember. I suspect most thaumagauges wouldn't even detect it."

My hand covered Mason's as he held onto the compass. The magic coming off the device felt oily and black. It flowed through his fingers right into mine. This was the worst part. I let the magic crawl through me, like a millipede with a thousand tiny barbed feet running across my soul. I filled myself with the magic, then I pushed it out of me with one big existential shove.

This was Valkyrie power. Old school. Sometimes, recently deceased souls could try to cling to life by latching onto the Valkyrie who came to set them free. It was a hazard of the trade, and part of my early training had been the art of expelling unwanted souls.

When I shoved, the magic exploded from me, and for a brief instant, it took the shape of a man—short and stocky with a low brow and a mouth pulled into a snarl of pure fury.

Mason's eyes widened. His mouth opened, but nothing came out. The spirit shrieked and raised a fist as if to strike at us. But without a mortal body, some ghosts can't keep their essence together. Even as his fist came toward me, he dissolved into mist.

Mason stared at the empty space for a long moment. Then he looked down at the compass. Its face was black and dead. I let my hand drop away from his and dug into the pouch at my waist for the small pillbox I had stored in there. Angus had made it out of the null material Joran used to subdue the dragons. I popped it open to show Mason the stone from Susanna's lab.

"If you take the compass apart, I suspect you'll find a tiny bead like this. Susanna Coulter has a jar full of them in her lab. They're like your bloodstone, only smaller. A tiny vessel that holds one spirit. I've been keeping this one as proof in case we need to bring it before the Triumvirate Council. But this is how they're making golems, and other gadgets, I guess."

Mason rose, still gripping the dead compass. He paced the room, his thoughts turned inward. Eventually, he stopped and I thought he'd come to a decision. But he whirled and threw the compass through the bay window that overlooked the garden.

The crash of breaking glass echoed through the house. A minute later, Dutch came running down the hall that led to the downstairs bedrooms. He wore only gray silk boxers and his hair was mussed. An also nearly-naked Gabe ran in behind him. They must have arrived just after us and hadn't wasted any time.

Both stopped when they saw Mason standing near the broken window.

"It's fine," Mason said. "No intruders. Just me throwing a temper tantrum."

Dutch stood up straight, somehow looking distinguished despite the lack of clothes. "Very good." He turned back to the bedroom. Gabe shot me one embarrassed glance, shrugging his bare shoulders and raising his eyebrows before following Dutch.

I went to the kitchen and rummaged in a closet until I found a broom and dustpan. Mason had gone outside, and he leaned over the low stone wall of the balcony. I swept up the glass, letting him come to terms with this betrayal.

Long ago, after sculpting Angus and imbuing him with the spirit of a dead fae, he'd vowed never to make another gargoyle. The process was cruel, and thankfully, the magic ritual for creating gargoyles had been lost. But now his alchemist brethren had taken the essence of gargoyle magic and corrupted it with an even older magic—the golem—to create a new creature, one that was bound as a slave to do their bidding.

I could only imagine the rage and disappointment coursing through him. I put aside the dustpan and went to stand beside him. We looked out over the vast dark expanse of Dorion Park.

Something huge roared in the distance and I shivered. Mason put his arm around me and snugged me up against him.

"This isn't quite the date I imagined," he said. The creature in the dark called out again. "But do you hear that? I'm sure it's dragons."

I listened to the calls. They were something halfway between a raptor's shrill shriek and a lion's roar.

"Do you think that's Ollie's thunder?" I asked.

"I don't know. It could be."

The calls grew louder and a shadow blotted out the bit of moonlight that fell on the patio. A dragon cawed as it flew over us. The beat of its massive wings whipped up the air, tossing leaves around the balcony. It flew so low, I could see the shimmer of its golden scales. In a heartbeat it was gone. Others followed, farther away. They were hunting in a pack.

"Amazing!" I'd been holding my breath.

Mason smiled and leaned in to kiss me. "Yes it is."

Another dark form fell on us from above. The dragon hit the balcony ungracefully, claws scrabbling on the flagstones until he righted himself.

He stood taller than me now, and his color had deepened to a rich royal blue. The fringe of baby feathers on his head was gone. So was the playfulness in his gaze. He looked fierce. And strong.

"Ollie?" I reached out a hand. He lunged for me. Mason yanked me away, but I stopped him. "Wait!" Ollie stood right before me, his snout breathing heavily into my face. He'd lost his round baby-curves and his snout had sharpened. He puffed out a breath and then ducked his head under my hand so I could scratch behind his ears.

Then he cawed once and launched back into the night.

Mason wiped the tears on my cheeks with his thumb. I hadn't even realized I was crying.

I had hoped for it, hoped that Ollie was growing strong and flying free with others of his kind.

"You made that happen," Mason said. "You saved those dragons."

"We did."

He nodded and his expression turned stern. "And we're going to fix this mess too. We'll make sure no more little sisters like Maeve go missing."

"Thank you." I tucked my head under his chin and he put his arm around me. We stood there, listening to the magnificent monsters in the night.

Waiting was never my strong suit. As I paced around my apartment, filling water bowls that didn't need filling and topping up kibble and fresh hay, I realized that I shouldn't have cleared my work schedule so soon.

Mason and I had agreed that we would break into Gerard's lab—the One-eyed God only knew how we would accomplish that. But it would happen tonight, so I postponed all my jobs to rest and get ready.

Only I couldn't rest. I filled Kur's ice bowl for the third time that day. So far, I'd plucked Hunter out of the coffee pot, the hamper and the bathroom sink. Clarence wore himself out after running around screaming, "Gobble! Gobble!" My critters could feel my agitation too. Finally, Gita snapped.

"Sit down already! You're pacing enough to wear a path in the floor."

"Fine." I turned to the coffeemaker for another cup, but Gita wagged a bony finger at me.

"No more coffee for you. I'll make tea. Something to relax you."

"No. I need to be awake tonight."

Gita squinted at me and crossed her arms. I sighed. "Fine. But nothing too strong." There was no use arguing with her. And I had time to nap. I glanced at the clock. It was barely past noon. Mason wouldn't be awake for another four hours at least. Thankfully, we were nearing winter—regardless of the bizarre heat wave—and the nights were long. We were going to need all the nighttime hours we could get.

I sat at the kitchen table and opened my computer to watch the news.

A live-feed showed yet another protest had turned violent at the site of the GenPort railroad excavations. I watched in horror as gennys pushed back peaceful protesters. How were the authorities allowing this? Hub had to know what the gennys really were. They still had Maeve's golem corpse. Surely, they could see the similarities to the gencrew automatons. They must know that something fishy was going on at the site.

Of course they knew. But Prime Minister Golovin had enough influence to shut down any inquiries. He couldn't shut down the protesters though. At least not without a very public use of force.

I watched protesters clash with security, and a sick feeling grew in my stomach. I'd had faith in the checks and balances of the triumvirate. Each faction was supposed to keep the others in line. But Gerard thought himself above the law.

The clock said 12:23 p.m., only eight minutes since the last time I checked. Gods, this day would drag on forever.

Had Mason been able to connect with Leighna's people? When I'd left him last night, he'd promised to contact the queen. We needed her on our side for this fight. If Gerard was really stealing fae and creating golems, we needed proof, but more importantly, we needed the authority to bring him to justice.

Gita plunked a mug of steaming tea in front of me. My knee bounced with jitters, but as soon as I tasted it, I could feel the calming brew go through me like a wave. Gita was a witch of the best kind. I sighed and took another sip.

Something tugged at my jeans. I looked down to find Errol climbing up my leg like a sherpa on a mountainside. I held out my hand to help, but he ignored it until he clambered onto the table. His gaze fixed on the scenes of violence streaming on my screen.

"It's horrible, isn't it?"

He said, "Grbltfzintth," but I felt his meaning projected right into my thoughts. Sadness at the way things were, but not resignation. Fire. Righteousness. The flame that burns down the old system and replaces it with something new.

"Errol, you're a radical!"

He grumbled and nodded. I wondered what violence he had witnessed, what wars he had lived through to give him such conviction.

Our world had seen enough war. The triumvirate had been set up to quell such conflicts. And yet, Gerard seemed hellbent on destroying the equilibrium. For what? For the fees he'd be able to charge people to use his new railway line? Granted, he was looking at a small fortune from passengers, not to mention what he could charge for cargo. Access to another ward would open up enormous trade opportunities. And there were those who argued that trade was always good. It brought wealth and progress.

But progress started the Flood Wars. Progress caused Terra to fight back. When the ley-lines burst, flooding the world in magic, Terra had decided that humans had progressed enough.

I flicked over to another news stream that showed an interview with a protester. A tall blond woman with fierce eyes looked straight into the camera and spoke with articulate conviction.

"Why do we need more? What are we missing that will improve our lives? Montreal Ward may not be a paradise, but we are protected from the worst of the magics that fill the Inbetween. And no one goes hungry here. Terra lets us produce enough to feed our population. But this railroad will bring growth and a whole new population. Will Terra let us feed them? No! We've already seen Her displeasure with the cave-in. And the spontaneous manifestations of magic that are popping up all over the city…"

Another protester shoved the woman aside. He held a sign that said, *Humans rule!* and screamed "Death to Terra!" into the camera. The image shook as one of the security guards tackled him, knocking the reporter aside. For a moment, I could hear screams and bangs while the camera showed only the cement street. Then it went black.

Errol and I stared at the black screen for several seconds before I shut the computer.

The clock read 12:28.

I turned to find Jacoby lurking in the doorway, clutching his new prized bear.

"Kyra-lady?" he asked shyly. "My bear feels bad. Cans you help him?"

Gently, I laid the bear on the table to inspect his wounds. He was an old toy, with patches of plush fur worn thin and several holes in the seams of his arms and legs.

I took out my sewing kit. "Is it okay if I patch him?"

Jacoby nodded, but looked nervous. I kept talking to distract him as I stitched a half-dozen tiny holes on the bear.

"What's your bear's name?"

"He haves a name?"

"I'm sure he does. He looks like Cyril or somebody loved him enough to give him a name."

Jacoby cocked his head and thought hard about this.

"Did someone loves you, to names you Kyra?"

"Yes, my mother." It occurred to me that I had no idea how dervishes reproduced. Did Jacoby have a family?

"How did you get your name?"

Jacoby played with the fringe around his left eye like he did when he was nervous.

"I likes cookies." He scuffed his foot across the floor.

"Cookies? You mean Papa Jacoby cookies?" That was the brand name for a soft molasses cookie that touted all-natural ingredients. They weren't around when I was a kid, but seemed to be a staple in school lunchboxes these days. I thought they were disgustingly sweet and preferred homemade.

"You named yourself after a cookie?"

He nodded.

"Well, I think that's a good name. I'm sure you'll come up with one for the bear." I finished sewing the last hole on the bear's leg and handed him back to Jacoby. The dervish hugged him and whirled.

"Hey!" I grabbed him and stopped him from spinning. "Bears get dizzy. So no spinning, okay?"

"K." He ran off with his treasure, then stopped and rushed back to me. "Dizzy! That a good name?"

"It sure is."

I took another sip of Gita's calming brew and then a deep breath. The clock read 12:42. I needed another distraction.

The mimosa plant sat on the sideboard beside the table. Gita had repotted it, and the fern-like leaves looked full and perky.

"Want to help me practice magic?" I asked Errol. He grunted and climbed into my hand. I grabbed the potted plant and headed out to the yard.

The weather had cooled, but not enough for November. The sky was brilliant blue and cloud free. It was hard to imagine that winter was only a few weeks away. I put Errol and the mimosa on the old picnic table, then went back inside for Bijou and Kur. I left the snail munching on the grass and whatever late season weeds he could find with Kur watching over him.

"Don't let him roam under the bushes," I said. Kur was usually a good babysitter, but I was glad when Jacoby popped out of his little house and sat down to supervise too.

The picnic table lurched as I sat on the bench. One more winter and it would be firewood. Errol sat with his back against the mimosa's pot, his face tilted to take in the sun. He opened one eye when I spoke.

"I'm going to try to touch one of those leaves with my keening."

He grumbled and settled back to sunbathing.

I could do this. I could touch the mimosa with my magic. Easy-peasy.

I reached. For a minute, I felt nothing. With all my anxiety over the news of protests and the golems, I had instinctively reinforced my psychic wards until they were as impenetrable as a fortress. I tried to relax, breathing in the sweet autumn air and exhaling until my wards eased.

I keened the tiny spark of life coming off the mimosa. It was bittersweet, like lemonade on a hot day. Next I focused on one frond—on one spike of one frond—willing my magic to touch it, but no matter how I pushed and strained, the leaf remained unmoved.

Then a tiny hand covered the knuckle of my index finger as I gripped the edge of the table. I looked down and Errol winked at me. He thumped the table with his walking twig and a tiny burst of magic flowed through me, not unlike the way I primed my sword. His magic tingled along my skin, under my skin, and…something opened in me. A dam I had long ago built burst, and I felt the well of a strange new magic within me. It filled my senses with the joy of growing things. Of loamy dirt and clean water. Air and sunshine. The wise rot of old dead things and the brisk hope of new life. If I had to give it a color, this new magic would be green.

It was energy in complete antithesis to my keening, and caused a sharp pain to stab through my head, like a knife dividing my brain. My keening was a passive magic. It felt. It sensed. It didn't reach. That's why I could never use it to touch the plant.

This new magic wanted to grab things. It wanted to paint the world in its light.

I reeled as nausea threatened to take me down, then the two warring magics seemed to come to an agreement inside me and the waters calmed.

I opened my eyes and reached for the mimosa again. All its fronds slammed shut like a dozen tiny umbrellas closing. I felt Errol's laughter in my mind.

Before I could react, my widget chimed with a new call, and I saw Dutch's number on the screen.

"Gabe isn't here," I said in greeting, still distracted by the mimosa. "He's gone on some errands."

"That's good because I called you, not him." Dutch's smooth voice was almost mocking.

"Oh! You have news from Leighna's people?"

"Yes. She's sending Merrow. Do you have room for all of us to meet there? We need a neutral spot and not public."

"Sure, I'll make room in the gym."

"Sun sets at 4:51. We'll be there by 6:30 to make sure the site is secure before Merrow arrives."

I glanced around my sparse backyard and to the bit of the parking lot I could see from this angle. Maybe I should reinforce the wards around the building?

"And Kyra?" Dutch's voice broke into my planning. "I won't be calling for Gabe anymore."

"What? Oh. That's too bad." I wanted to say more, but Dutch said goodbye and hung up.

I wondered why they'd broken up again. Gabe had seemed down that morning, but I'd just assumed he was tired.

His car pulled into the lot and he got out, carrying a bag of office supplies. I wanted to send him home without mentioning Dutch's call. He'd proven he was a warrior in the battle against the opji, and I would trust him with my family of rescues any day, but he didn't need to be part of this fight.

In the end, I left the choice up to him.

"You don't need to be involved," I said.

"As if I'd let you have all the fun." He smiled but I could see his heart wasn't in it. "I'll make some space in the gym."

I nodded and left him to it. Gita's tea was working its magic, and I felt the need to rest.

But sleep wouldn't come and I ended up staring at my window, watching the light shift from yellow to red to purple as the sun set.

24

e met in my gym, the part of my building that used to be a garage. I opened the large sliding doors to cool off the stuffy space. The night sky flashed with millions of stars, but no moon. As usual, the streetlight on the corner of my lot flickered, throwing lurid shadows around the yard.

Mason and Angus arrived first. Dutch drove, but after a brief nod at Gabe, he remained on watch outside the garage. Gabe looked like he wanted to follow him and only his pride was holding him back. Poor Gabe. I'd had my share of relationships that ended before they started. Maybe his feelings hadn't developed to the point of a broken heart, but it sure was a kick in the ego.

"It's hotter than hell's sweet kiss in here." Angus strolled into the garage. Mason followed, checking around the dumpster and the side of the building.

"You think someone is watching?" I asked.

"No. Maybe." The stiff line of his shoulders told me he was tense. "That was the point of holding the meeting here. Someone has been snooping in my office. I found a couple of bugs, but you're not on Gerard's radar, I don't think." He frowned. "We should close those doors, just in case."

I nodded and lowered the garage doors. The room suddenly seemed much smaller. I'd set up folding chairs and a card table. Gita brought ice tea. Jacoby had taken to wearing his teddy-bear backpack so that Errol could ride on the bear's head. The two of them now wandered around the gym, examining old cages and pet supplies I had stored here. Errol wore a silly grin on his face. I think he loved the company, and I wondered just how long he had been alone in that basement.

Leighna's advisor, Merrow, arrived by the side door. In her regular form, she was a dark-haired, gray-skinned woman of slight build who moved like a dancer or a gymnast. I'd seen her true fae form when she pulled Leighna from the ruins of the condo after the opji attack. That form was impressive—seven feet tall and covered in scales that looked like armored plates.

"Your upstairs neighbor is too nosy," she said. "I had to knock him out."

"You what?" I asked.

"Don't fret. It's a simple sleep spell. He'll wake up thinking he got the best night's rest ever."

I'd have to check on Mr. Murray later.

An older man sporting a military grade haircut and nondescript black clothes followed Merrow.

"This is Terry Sato," she introduced him to the rest of us. "Terry is here for Prime Minister Tremblay." Tremblay represented the human tribes of Montreal.

"I thought this meeting was a secret." Angus scratched his leafy beard. "How can we speak freely with a fae in the room and a human we don't know or trust?"

"You think we can trust the alchemists any more than the fae or the humans?" Mason asked.

Angus scowled.

"Gerard is up to something," Mason said. "We don't know who on Perrot Island is in on it. We need proof that his experiments are against the law and we need witnesses to that proof. Merrow and Terry are here to be those witnesses." If we were going to take down one of the reigning prime ministers, we'd need consensus among the rival parties.

"I'm not worried about her," Angus pointed to Merrow. "I've seen her ugly fae ass survive a falling building. But humans break too easily. I don't want to be blamed if he comes to harm."

"I will endeavor to keep myself whole." Terry Sato bowed.

"Queen Leighna wants to know what Gerard Golovin is scheming about," Merrow said. "But I need to be clear. I cannot take part in any illegal activity to obtain that proof. I can, however, follow along and report any findings to the parliament."

I looked at Terry who said, "Same. Minister Tremblay has asked for access to Perrot Island for years. The Alchemists always deny him. We would very much like to know what goes on in those labs and what Gerard is up to."

"Well then, it's time to grab the bull by the tail and look him in the eye." Angus rubbed his hands together.

Everyone settled on the rickety chairs around the card table.

"How do we even know that Gerard's lab is on Perrot Island? It could be anywhere," said Sato. Merrow cut him off with a wave of her hand and turned to me.

"First, tell me what crime you suspect Prime Minister Golovin is guilty of," she said.

"You first," I retorted, maybe a bit too harshly. Merrow gazed at me with a noncommittal expression. I pushed her. "There has to be a reason you and Leighna agreed to this. Why are you here?"

The room was silent while Merrow and I played chicken. I gave in first, but I turned to answer Sato's question.

"I've been to his office behind Abbott's Agora. It's too clean to be his real workspace. I suspect he keeps it only as a meeting place. But I found something interesting there."

I passed the pillbox across the table. Merrow raised an eyebrow when she saw it. I suspected her keening power was at least as good as mine, and she would feel the absent space in the natural web of magic left by the box. She reached for it and flipped open the latch.

Her eyes widened as she held the stone between her finger and thumb. "Abomination!"

"What is it?" Sato leaned in to get a better look. Without a thaumagauge, none of the others could sense the life-magic coming off the stone, except for Errol, who stood over the box, glowering. He held his walking twig like a weapon, ready to attack anything that might manifest from the stone.

"It's a bloodstone, freshly made. It holds the spirit of a person, probably fae," I said, then I addressed Merrow. "How many fae have gone missing in recent months?"

She pursed her lips as if trying to hold in the answer. "Many. Too many."

"What?" Sato turned to her. "Why haven't we heard about this? What's Hub doing about it?"

"They're looking into it. Quietly." Merrow's eyes flashed.

"Because you suspect someone high up the chain is responsible. Is that right? Maybe someone as high as a prime minister?" I asked.

Merrow nodded once and put the stone back in the box.

"I found a whole jar of these in an alchemist's office in Abbott's Agora. She got them from Gerard Golovin."

Sato paled. "So it's true then. I didn't want to believe."

"We must destroy those stones." Angus banged his knobby fist on the table.

"You can't!" Sato said. "If what you say is true, then those stones are the spirits of dead fae."

"Exactly," Mason said. "And the only way to set them free is to destroy the stones."

They argued the ethics for a few minutes while I watched Merrow work through the implications of the existence of a whole jar of bloodstones.

She turned to me. "Tell me again about this creature, you saw." Her quiet command broke through the argument and everyone else fell silent. "It wasn't really a golem, was it?"

"You should know. Didn't you see it?" I asked. Surely, Leighna's top advisor would have influence enough at Hub to poke her nose into any case she wanted.

"The body was cremated before we could examine it," she said tightly. "Just tell me what you know." Merrow had only two expressions: non-committal and angry. My questions were pushing her toward the latter.

"It wasn't a true golem. At least I don't think so." I told her about visiting Maeve's house after she disappeared and how the magic signature of the golem was too distinctive to miss.

"Someone kidnapped her and used her spirit to animate that thing."

"To what end?" Sato asked. "Are they building an army?"

"More like a workforce," Merrow said.

"I think so too," I said. "Gerard's new gencrew give off the same vibe. He'd have everyone think they're some fancy new technomancy, but I believe he's creating these golem-gargoyle hybrids to use as slave labor on his rail line."

"That won't stop the protesters," Sato said.

Mason stood and started pacing. "No, but it will limit the number of lives lost if there's another cave-in. And speed up the construction. He needs to get the work done before those protesters gain any real traction."

"So, he's been making these creatures from the souls of dead fae," Merrow said. She tapped her finger on the table. "Now we just need to prove it."

Mason attached a ring to a gleam and let it hang in the air. It projected a map of Montreal onto the table. He adjusted it through his widget, and the map zoomed in on Perrot Island, the alchemist stronghold.

Jacoby curled up at my feet and slept, but Errol was fascinated by the lines that wove through Perrot Island and Montreal. I'd lifted him to sit on the table and he traced lines on the map with his walking twig.

"What's he doing?" Merrow asked.

"Tracing ley-lines, I think." I got an image of pure bliss from Errol.

"How did he know that?" Mason asked.

"I don't know. He has a strong affinity for magic. I think that's why he affects the electricity so much."

Errol grew bored with the map and sat beside my glass of ice tea, dunking his dirty hat into it and sucking the tea off it like a teat. Ugh. I'd have to get a bodach-sized cup for him.

"Each of the alchemists have lab space on the island." Mason pointed to a group of buildings about ten kilometers outside the ward. "The Apex is here." He indicated the tower with the gemstone that funneled ley-line power into the ward. "Gerard's lab takes up this entire building. If he's got any illegal experiments going on, they would be there."

"And where is your lab?" I asked. Mason pointed to a smaller building on the western edge of the island.

"I keep only a small office here. My main lab is at my home."

"But we can meet at your office and deploy from there."

"Yes. Security won't be an issue until we get to Gerard's lab. I'll be sending you all street views of the site."

"So you're going to what? Break into his offices and steal his lab notes?" Merrow's eyes narrowed.

"Yes," Mason said.

"And how will you get past the security? There's bound to be surveillance cameras and electronic locks."

"If only we knew someone who could disrupt electrical currents." Mason grinned and looked pointedly at Errol, who was sucking on the tip of his tea-soaked hat.

"Okay." I took a deep breath. We were really going to do this. "Tell me your plan."

Ten minutes later, we all sat back digesting Mason's words. It wouldn't be easy. Security on Perrot Island was ridiculously tight. Mason's credentials would get us into Gerard's building, and Errol would have to disable the locks from there. I could think of a dozen ways this could go wrong. And there was no guarantee we would find hard proof that Gerard was breaking the law.

A commotion from outside had us all turning toward the side door. Merrow's fae guard stepped through, pushing Susanna in front of him.

"This one was spying outside."

"I was not!" Susanna jerked her arm out of his grip. "I came to talk to Kyra and I saw she had visitors. I didn't want to interrupt."

"She shouldn't see us together!" Sato stood up as if ready to fight. "We'll have to detain her until after."

"After what?" Susanna asked. "Until after you break into my boss's lab?" She grinned, but her face was flushed. "So maybe I overheard a little before this thug stopped me. But what if I tell you that I'm the only way you'll get inside that lab?"

The room was silent, except for a grumbled oath from Errol. Susanna seemed cloaked in a cloud of strange energy. It was a stew of contrasting magics, and I was trying to parse it when she pointed at the map of Perrot Island. "And you're on the wrong track. Gerard's real lab isn't on Perrot Island. But I can take you to it."

"Why should we trust you?" Angus said.

Susanna tossed a small bag on the table, then crossed her arms and hugged herself. "Because I brought that as goodwill."

The bag held part of her cache of bloodstones. Merrow jumped back from the table. She could also feel the jagged mix of magic coming off the stones.

Sato opened the sack and frowned. "Are these all…" He couldn't finish that thought.

"Souls," Angus snarled. "Call 'em what they are. They're stolen souls."

"I swear I didn't know that when he gave them to me." Susanna hugged herself even tighter. She looked lost, like her center of gravity had shifted and she couldn't find her footing. I felt sorry for her.

"Be clear," Merrow said. "Who gave those to you?"

"Gerard." Susanna's answer came in a small voice. "Prime Minister Golovin."

25

abe wanted to come. I'm not ashamed to say that I played the guilt card with him.

"If something happens to me, I need to know someone will do right by these guys." I swept my arm around the room to encompass all my rescues.

"So you want me to babysit." Gabe folded his arms across his chest and glowered. He had a good glower. His dark brown eyes really went for it.

"I want you to promise me that you'll find homes for everyone, if I don't come back." I had no illusions about our escapade that night. Even with Leighna's intervention, I could still end up in jail. Or worse. If Golovin found us poking around his lab, and he was guilty of the crimes we suspected, he wouldn't let us get away to tell the story.

I sighed and laid my hand on Gabe's arm.

"Look. A small party is better for this kind of thing. Angus is staying back too. We're going in, getting the proof we need and getting out. But I'll focus a lot better if I know you're here taking care of things."

Gabe wasn't done with his glowering, but he nodded once. Gita slipped her hand in his.

"I'll take care of him tonight. You go play detective. We'll play scrabble." She patted his hand.

"Check her sleeves for spare tiles," I said. "She cheats." Gita snorted and pretended to be affronted, but she didn't deny it.

"I comes with you, right?" Jacoby tugged on my shirt.

I knelt to look him in the eye. "Only if you think you can handle it. This will be dangerous."

He considered it for a moment then nodded.

"Good. You have a very important job." I handed him the backpack he'd been using to cart around Errol. "Once we get inside, you need to make sure Errol gets away safely. You bring him right back here. Gabe and Gita will be waiting for you."

Jacoby nodded, but his eyes were wide and scared.

"Good. We're heading out," I said. Gabe only nodded again. Gita sniffled and waved us away. There would be no goodbyes tonight.

I grabbed my sword from the umbrella stand as I left and walked the few blocks to Abbott's Agora so I wouldn't have to park the truck nearby. The others had gone ahead to scout. Susanna went with them because Sato wouldn't let her out of his sight. Jacoby hopped along with Errol riding on the stuffed bear's head. They were an odd sight, and I was glad that few people were in the market as we passed through it.

The old school buildings loomed up like mountains in the moonless night. Mason and Angus waited across the street, watching the Penfield building from the shadows of an old, boarded up high school.

"Anyone go in or out?" I asked as we approached.

"Just Susanna," Angus said. "She went inside to make sure we'd be alone. Sato went with her."

"Where's Merrow?"

Angus pointed back toward the market. "Talking on her widget last time I saw her. She'd better get here soon or we're going in without her."

"Hey," Mason nudged me. "I'm glad you brought your sword."

"I felt naked without it." As soon as the words left my mouth, I couldn't help but picture myself naked. With Mason. The startled look on his face made me wonder if the same idea passed through his mind too.

"I mean, I just couldn't leave it."

Cue the awkward silence.

"I'm going to walk the perimeter," Angus mumbled. "I'll take the dervish."

"I stays with Kyra-lady!" Jacoby protested, but Angus grabbed him by the shoulder and hauled him away.

"Not too subtle, is he?" I said.

Mason tugged me deeper into the shadows of an old oak tree until my back pressed against the rough bark.

He kissed me, hard—hands gripping my hips as if he was afraid to let them go. After a moment, he stopped and pulled me into a hug. I reveled in the feel of his hard body pressed against mine from head all the way down to thighs. My nose found the hollow under his chin, and I breathed him in.

His breath tickled my ear, and he said, "I've been wanting to do that all day. While I was stone, I had time to think about what you said. And when this is over…"

I pressed a finger to his lips. "Don't jinx it."

"Right." He kissed my finger, and I slipped it inside his mouth. The heat of his tongue on the sensitive pad of my finger almost undid me.

"If you schoolchildren are finished necking in the woods, can we get on with this?" Merrow's voice was sharp and pitched so it didn't carry.

Mason grinned. "Yes, ma'am. We're coming."

I fought down the urge to giggle.

Mason stole one last kiss. "I still wish you hadn't put your sword into stasis. Never know when you're going to need that kind of power."

"It's sharp enough to cut off heads. That will have to do."

"Do you at least have your null bracelet?"

I patted my pocket. I wouldn't put it on unless I had to. It protected me from magic overload, but it also stopped me from using my magic. I didn't know what we were walking into, and I wanted to be ready for anything.

"I just want you to be safe." Mason's arm closed around me again, and he whispered into my ear. "I wish you were far away from this mess."

I pushed him back so I could look him in the eye. "Well, I'd rather be here with you."

He nodded and we emerged from the shadows to face Merrow and Sato. Angus returned with Jacoby, who seemed overly excited.

"He's jumping at every leaf blown by the wind." Angus scratched his beard and considered the dervish. "You sure it's a good idea to bring him?"

"We need Errol to get inside, and Jacoby to get him out fast. As soon as the security is broken, he's out of there. I'll make sure."

Angus nodded. "Well, I'll be waiting right over there for him." He headed to the old oak, and within a moment, his brambly hair and beard camouflaged him against the tree.

The door to Penfield building opened and Susanna poked her head out.

"Come on!" She beckoned, but Merrow made us pause.

"I want to be clear. Sato and I are here as witnesses only."

"We got it," Mason said, not hiding his derision. "You won't get your hands bloody, but won't stop us from bloodying ours."

Merrow pursed her lips like she would argue, but then nodded.

"Come on!" Susanna hissed again. Her eyes darted up and down the lane that ran around the building. Terra had long ago reclaimed the running track and football field behind the old gymnasium. They were now nothing but weeds. But the market filled the front acreage of the campus, and unwanted witnesses could come from that way at any time.

"I told Hakim that I was giving you a demonstration in my lab. It's not unusual, even in the evening, so we're clear." Susanna held the door open and we all filed in.

"Not good enough," Merrow said. She strode forward to face the guard who sat behind his small desk and tapped him on the head.

"Hey!" he said before his eyes rolled to white and his head lolled against the wall.

"What did you do?" Susanna touched Hakim's cheek, but he didn't wake.

"Just a sleep spell." Merrow said. "He'll wake in a few hours feeling refreshed but not remembering us at all." I marveled at this level of accuracy in Merrow's spell casting.

"We just need to do something about these cameras." Merrow continued. "There can be no record that we were here."

"Errol, can you disable the cameras from here?"

The bodach grumbled.

"He said no, but he'll scramble the signal so all they'll get is static," I said. The lights flickered as Errol pushed out his magic.

Sato turned to me with a frown. "You understood him?"

"Sort of. Not his words. It's more like he can speak right into my head."

"Interesting."

I didn't like the way Sato studied my bodach, and I decided to keep an eye on him.

"I want to see your lab first," Merrow said. "You have more of those bloodstone abominations?"

"Yes. This way." Susanna led us to the stairwell and down one floor to her basement lab. "I locked them away after you told me what they really are." She glanced at me, smiling shyly as if I could forgive her crimes. I was thinking about it. I wanted to believe that Susanna's crimes were due to ignorance.

She opened a cabinet with a key and took out a glass jar filled with the black stones.

"So many!" Merrow hissed.

"Gerard was pleased with my progress to, you know, make the gargoyles," Susanna said, "and he insisted these would take my work to the next level. I don't know where he got them from. Or even if he knows what they are."

"He knows." Mason's tone was flat and hard. He stood by the blazing alembic and turned in a slow circle to take in the whole lab with the shelf full of terra cotta gargoyles.

"You stupid, arrogant…" He cut off his words but his eyes flashed. "You have no idea what kind of power you're playing with."

Susanna smiled mildly. "But I guess you do. Rumor says you made a few gargoyles in your time. That stink of arrogance you smell is coming off of yourself. If you think that no one can replicate your design…"

"Can and should are different concepts. Look them up." Mason's hands tightened on the edge of the table, and I thought he was ready to break something.

"Whatever." Susanna looked shaken but she wasn't backing down. "Maybe those beads are what you say they are, but that doesn't mean my research is a total wash. When this is done, I'll find another way to create life."

Mason spoke through a clenched jaw. "When this is over, I'm going to dismantle your lab and get you barred from ever practicing alchemy again."

Even in the dim light, I could see all the color drain from Susanna's face. Time to take things down a notch.

"Let's just see Gerard's lab and get out of here," I said. We moved off down the hall and I grabbed Mason's arm, holding him back.

"What the hell are you doing? We need her!"

"She's making gargoyles," he hissed.

"You knew that already."

"I didn't really believe it, but when I saw her set up…she could actually pull it off. I won't let that happen." His expression was grim.

"I agree. But let's play nice until we get the evidence against Gerard. I don't want to spook her."

"Fine."

We stopped outside the small lab that I'd seen on my first visit.

"You told me this is only a front, that Gerard's real lab was somewhere else," I said.

"It is. But we go through here." Susanna led us through the pristine workspace that Gerard used to greet officials to a door at the far end. She unlocked it with a key from her belt, and it opened inward to darkness. The smell of damp earth rose from the opening. She flicked on a switch and revealed stairs leading downward.

We followed again. The walls were rough cement pocked with holes. The wooden stairs creaked as we descended to another hallway. Jacoby clung to my pant leg as we stood at the bottom of the staircase, staring into the gloom.

Susanna flicked another switch and a bare bulb lit the tunnel.

"This leads to one of the old dormitories," she said.

"Are there more of these?" I asked, fascinated. Why had I never heard of these tunnels?

Susanna shook her head. "There used to be tunnels under all the buildings. Students used them to get to class during the winter so they wouldn't have to go out in the snow. And for other after-hours pursuits. They called it booty-call lane." She smiled.

"When the sports complex was built, they destroyed most of the tunnel system. This is the only one left. There was an exit that came out near the old arena that way." She pointed to the left. "But the outside door is rusted shut. We're going that way." She pointed down the longer hall to the right. "To Stewart Hall."

"But that's all boarded up. There's nothing there," I said.

"Is that right?" Susanna turned and headed down the tunnel.

Stewart Hall was a crumbling old building at the east end of the market. Not even squatters lived there anymore, not since the stories of ghost spiders started circulating. Apparently, the spiders were as big as cats, but only those with an affinity for magic could see them. I'd checked it out some years ago and found nothing. The alchemists bought the building and said they would restore it, but then left it boarded up and vacant. At the time, I'd wondered if the stories were a setup to keep people away from Stewart Hall.

The tunnel cut straight through to another door at the far end. This one looked serviceable, with a rusted railing and six steps of broken concrete leading up to it, but we turned off before that, down another short tunnel that led to more doors. These were once painted blue and now were crisscrossed with scars of rust and locked with a padlock.

"This is as far as I can take you. I don't have a key," Susanna said, pointing to the lock. "And on the other side, there is another door with a security pad. You'll have to get through it somehow."

"We'll manage," I said. "Thank you for this." Susanna smiled and backed away, but didn't leave. I turned to Mason.

"Can you break the lock?"

He nodded. I felt the shift in his magic as he turned one fisted hand to stone. Then he bashed the lock. Its rusted hasp gave way. The door swung open on silent hinges. On the other side, the tunnel changed dramatically. Gone were the pockmarked cement walls with streaks of rust and water damage. The floor and walls gleamed white under a track of bright overhead lights that ran all the way to another set of doors about twenty meters in.

These had no apparent handle or locking mechanism. To the left of the doors was a keypad and scanner.

"Errol, can you disable this?" I asked.

"And the camera." Mason pointed to an opaque window above the door.

"Right. The camera too."

Jacoby stepped forward. Errol stood on the bear's head and stretched towards the digital panel. He wasn't quite tall enough to reach, but he didn't need to touch it. He pointed his walking twig, and I keened the magic zap from its end. The panel went dark.

"Mfglbt."

I got an image of a computer recording device in my head.

"I think he says that he needs to disable the camera from inside."

The doors hadn't opened. I looked to Mason, who shrugged and took a heavy knife from his belt to pry the doors open. He worked at it for several minutes until a crack appeared. I waited for an alarm to sound, but apparently Errol had done his job.

Merrow and Sato hung back. She signaled to me.

"I will hide us with glamor now." She moved closer to Sato. "Remember, we are here only to observe. If you find trouble on the other side of those doors, we can't help you."

Won't help us, I thought but only nodded. Susanna hadn't taken off yet, and she watched from a short distance away as Mason worked at the doors. When he pried them open a bit, we each grabbed one side and dragged the panels wide. Jacoby helped on my side, then ducked through before I could stop him.

We stepped into an underground lab filled with high-tech alchemy machines. Another kind of blazing alembic filled the center of the room. Instead of a globe, wires were attached to a tall glass tube, big enough to hold a human. In the corners stood several dead-eyed golems. Like the others, they looked only vaguely humanoid.

Even if I couldn't see Merrow beneath her glamor, I could always sense her. I turned to face her. "Do you see those? That's the GenPort logo on their foreheads. What more evidence do you need?"

Merrow refused to break cover and remained silent.

Mason frowned as he examined the blazing alembic. "This is very similar to how we made gargoyles, back in the day."

I moved closer to examine one of the creatures. Its blank face only hinted at features. Shadows hid the sightless indentations where eyes should be. Were these the empty shells waiting to be imbued with life? I reached out with my keening, and felt...

The golem's head jerked up.

"Mason!" I screamed. Too late. Powerful arms shot out and grabbed my shoulders, lifting me inches off the ground. I fought, kicking out, but my feet hit the golem with little impact. It locked my arms against my sides, restricting my breath. I stopped struggling.

The room fell quiet. Golems restrained Mason, Jacoby and Susanna. Two more blocked the way out, and behind them a third, inner door slid shut. The golems stood unmoving as if now that they had caught the intruders, they were waiting for their next instructions.

"Jacoby! Get out now!" My yell was more of a wheeze as the golem squeezed the breath out of me.

Jacoby ported away but hit the wall. He tried again, rebounding off the far wall. Then he panicked, shrieking and bouncing around the room as he tried to port away and couldn't.

"Stop!" I wheezed. The room was protected by a ward.

I shifted in the golem's grasp as I found more air.

"Jacoby! Stop!" The dervish hit the wall one more time and fell to the ground, panting. Smoke rose from his ears.

Not good.

"It's okay, come here." I said in a soothing voice. Jacoby stared at the golem behind me with wide eyes. "Look at me." I forced his gaze to mine. "That's right. Just look right at me. Everything's going to be fine."

Right about then, the clapping started.

A tall, gaunt man stepped from the small room off the far end of the lab. If I'd expected anyone, it was Gerard Golovin, but I didn't recognize this man. He had a wide mouth over a weak chin. Graying brown hair swooped back from his prominent forehead, and his dark eyes glittered with something between glee and insanity.

"Well, that was entertaining." He continued to clap, encouraging an invisible audience. "Thank you for bringing me such wonderfully magic creatures." He stepped over to Jacoby and smiled down at him.

"You're welcome," Susanna said. I gaped as the golem released her, and she stepped away. "I told you she'd come. She's got a hero complex, you know." She turned to me and smiled her angelic smile. "This is for Joran."

26

Susanna sauntered over to the door, passing freely between the two golem guards before turning back to me. Her pretty, cherubic face took on a new, hard demeanor.

"You're not the hero anymore, Kyra. It's all about perspective. Gerard is a great man. He's the hero in this story now."

"Clearly being a hero isn't something you've ever worried about." I glared back. How could I have been so stupid to fall for her innocent girl act?

Susanna held a hand over her heart. "You crush me. I thought we were friends. No worries. We're all five-by-five. See ya!"

She turned to leave, then stopped. "Oh, Pierre, there are two more of them lurking behind a glamor somewhere. Watch your back." She pressed the panel beside the door. It slid open and then shut behind her.

Pierre! I glanced at Mason, still locked in the golem's grip. His face was a portrait of fury. Pierre had conspired with his ex-wife to murder his child. Pierre had hunted him for years, and now he'd found him.

The room fell silent except for a clicking sound from the massive machine as Pierre fiddled with a dial.

Mason broke the silence. "Are you working for Gerard Golovin?" He pitched his voice low and deadly.

Pierre turned, his expression dark. "I don't work for anyone. Golovin and I have an arrangement. I make him a few gargoyles," he waved at the golems, "and he gets me this."

He turned to the machine with the tall tube. For the first time, I noticed that a long wire connected it to a metal plate with a twelve-inch arm sticking straight up in the air. On the end of that was a clamp that pinched Mason's bloodstone.

"It's strange and annoying that I could make all those tiny bloodstones for Gerard, so he could create his ugly golems, but I never found the trick to breaking this one. It is truly an extraordinary thing." He caressed the bloodstone like it was a precious gem.

"You'll never break it," Mason said. "I've tried a hundred different ways to destroy it, even knowing that I might set Polina free, but I couldn't. And you're only half the alchemist I am."

"That might have been true once." Pierre smiled coldly. "But you gave up real alchemy after you made your precious Angus. I have been honing my craft ever since."

"Don't you get it?" Mason shook his head in disgust. "Polina cursed you just as surely as she did me. How long have you been trying to free her? Three hundred years? You should be dust in the ground, my old friend. Only her curse and your obsession are keeping you alive. It's not natural. And if you do break the bloodstone, she'll toss you like garbage as soon as she's free."

Pierre crossed the room in three long strides and punched Mason in the stomach. With the golem still gripping his arms, Mason couldn't even double over. He simply went limp as all the air rushed out of him.

"I've wanted to do that ever since you took my darling Polina from me." Pierre grinned like a kid facing a pile of birthday presents. "Now do shut up, while I finally free her."

Mason sucked in air, then found his feet again.

"You should kill me now, Pierre. The only chance you'll have is while I'm restrained. And it won't last. Once I'm free, I'll come after you and I won't stop this time."

What was he doing? Trash talking his way into a quick death? But Pierre just smiled a cold reptilian smile.

"I would never take Polina's vengeance from her. She has great plans for you. She whispers them to me at night." His eyes were full of mania as he gazed at the bloodstone, locked into the vise on the machine. "She comes to me and tells me all sorts of things. I feel her inside me."

He was completely bonkers.

"She knew you would come. Knew you wouldn't stay away. But you," he came to stand in front of me. "I heard about you from Joran. Do you remember him? He was my son. And you killed him."

"Your son?" It was such a disconnect that the rest of his words were momentarily lost to me.

Pierre smirked. "I created him but not in a lab." He giggled. "Though I suppose I could have done that too. No, I found him on the street, him and his sister. A couple of starving kids, running from abusive parents. I took them in and gave them everything they wanted. But I also molded them to my purpose. So you see, I made them as much as Mason made his son, Angus."

Angus? I was having trouble following Pierre's mad ramblings because my attention was on the golem that held me in its vise grip. I tried to work myself loose, but the more I struggled, the tighter it held on until I thought the pinch of its fingers would break my arms.

Pierre continued to prattle. "You can understand that I was rather put out when I learned of Joran's death." He hovered over me, his eyes drawn to my sword. "But at least it brought me to you and the final piece of the puzzle."

"It won't work." I croaked out the words. "Barton Kemp couldn't get my sword to break the bloodstone and neither will you."

He glared at me, his nose almost close enough to touch mine.

"Don't worry, I don't need you. Unlike that simpleton, Kemp, I understand how Valkyrie blades work. And without a willing Valkyrie, they are useless. But I've been watching you. It seems you bring other assets to the table." He looked at Jacoby and smiled. "I would have plucked this little guy off the street. It would have been much simpler, but he kept disappearing. Can't do that now, can you?"

I struggled in the golem's grip and kicked out. Pierre sidestepped me and reached for Jacoby.

"No!" I yelled as Jacoby squeaked and ported away, leaving only his teddy-bear backpack in Pierre's grip with Errol still clinging to the bear's head.

Jacoby continued to ricochet around the room.

"Hello, what's this." Pierre peered down at Errol. The bodach jabbed him in the cheek with his twig. A zap of galvanic magic stung Pierre. His face went red and he snarled. "You'll do."

He stomped over to the machine, opened the glass tube, dropped Errol inside and slammed the door. At three inches high, Errol looked lost in the giant tube. He ran around the edge, prodding the glass with his stick, until Pierre hit a switch and blue energy sizzled through the glass perimeter.

Errol toppled. His tiny body arched as the machine pumped massive amounts of magic into him. He screamed inside my head. The glass tube glowed and hummed loud enough that I could barely hear Pierre's constant babble over it.

I fought against the golem's restraints, until my arms were bruised and my breath came in heaves. Across the room, Mason fought too.

Where the hell was Merrow? Was she really going to stick to her "witness only" plan while Errol was being murdered?

Pierre studied the bloodstone with a fierce grin. The machine zapped Errol at five-second intervals. Each time, his body convulsed. Jacoby cried and bounced futilely against the walls.

I had exhausted my struggle, and I looked around the lab for a weapon. Anything. I spotted a row of grow lights with potted plants under them and reached for them with my magic—no plan, no thought other than distracting Pierre. I strained to thrust my magic outward. Nothing. I pushed again. This time, my magic lashed out, and the plants exploded. Their container shattered, showering the room in glass. I gasped as a sharp pain lanced through my head. The room turned black for a moment. When I recovered, I felt blood dribble from my nose. The plant stand lay in a mangled heap of vines, dirt and glass.

So much for my green magic.

Pierre continued to fiddle with the connection from the tube to the bloodstone. Something was wrong. His machine wasn't working. He cranked a dial and magic zapped Errol again. Harder.

Errol's screamed tore through my mind, leaving the edges of my psyche ragged.

Jacoby screamed too, then ported right inside the tube with Errol. He hugged the bodach against his chest.

No! I couldn't lose them both!

Pierre cranked the machine again. The magic zapped Jacoby. He yelped and danced like he stood on a hot plate.

Then he started to spin.

I screamed at him to get out, but he was already too far gone.

"Ah, that's more like it!" Pierre shouted above the noise. "Has anyone ever seen a dervish go nova? It's a beautiful thing! Apart from breaking our bloodstone, the chemical reaction will be quite stunning." He grinned proudly.

Jacoby spun faster. Smoked poured from his ears. I could no longer see Errol, lost in Jacoby's fur as the dervish hugged him. Around the bloodstone, a ball of blue energy formed. I locked my personal wards down tight, knowing what was coming.

Jacoby spun. Faster. Tiny spikes of blue magic jabbed him, urging him on. His feet no longer touched the ground. A whirlwind of smoky magic lifted him. His eyes rolled to white, and his head fell back. Fire flared around his feet and legs. Flames filled the glass tube until Jacoby was lost inside. A moment of silence, then... BOOM!

What happened next took seconds—fractions of a second, maybe—but it felt like forever.

Glass exploded, tearing through counters, machines and skin. The lights went out as debris smashed the bulbs. In the darkness, something hit my golem. It lurched, giving me a precious second to free my arm and draw my sword. I slashed off its other arm and planted my foot in the middle of its chest, kicking it against the wall.

Security lights came on, teasing the smoky room with an eerie blue light. My keening sensed the ghosts before I saw them. The blue ball of energy around the bloodstone splintered into human forms. Dozens of them. Hundreds. Thousands. They blew through the lab, shrieking in fury for being imprisoned or in glee for finally being free. They flew around my head as I crouched on the broken glass. Even with my tight wards, they buffeted me with so much magic that the edges of my vision darkened. I could only think how glad I was that my sword was silent.

The ghosts continued their caterwauling for another minute, then blew through the walls and disappeared.

The broken track lights sparked. I coughed through the smoke and rose, looking for the others. Merrow was gone or still hidden in glamor. I couldn't see Errol. Jacoby was dead or unconscious in the wreckage of Pierre's machine. Pierre lay unmoving beside him.

A woman stood naked in the middle of the room. Large dark eyes surveyed the wreckage and landed on Mason who was slowly rising.

"Hello, husband."

27

She wasn't a ghost. That was my first thought. She looked like an angel, with red gold hair flowing down her pink body. Her pink, very solid body. She looked at the broken glass around her feet and made a little moue with her lips.

"Pierre!" Her voice whipped out, and Pierre sat up with a jerk. Blood leaked from a wound on his head. "Get me some clothes and shoes."

Pierre rose on unsteady feet and went to a row of cupboards at the back of the room, pulled out a bundle and returned. He handed her a green silk robe and a pair of sandals. He wore a stupid grin on his face.

"Polina, my love!" He tried to kiss her, but Polina thumped him on the chest with the flat of her hand. Her fingers crackled with magic. Pierre flew backward and landed hard against the broken machine.

Polina put on the clothes and smoothed her hair as if she had just stepped from the bath.

"That's better."

I sat among the glass and debris, trying to quell the nausea rising in me from that blast of magic. I needed to get to Jacoby. I rose onto my knees, wobbled and tried to stand.

"Kyra! Behind you!" Mason yelled. He lunged, knocking me aside just as the one-handed golem's fist whooshed through the empty air where my head had been. Mason and I tumbled across the floor, landing with me on top, gazing down at his bloody, bruised face.

"Isn't that sweet," Polina's voice dripped with sarcasm. The golem lunged for us again, but Polina shot out a hand and made a crushing motion with her fist. The golem's head exploded, and it crumpled to the ground, inches from my face.

Polina continued as if she hadn't been interrupted. "Always the knight in shining armor, aren't you, husband? Saving little girls and gargoyles and every goddamned soul you come across, except for me. Your wife!"

I stared at the clumps of red clay that had been the golem's head. By the One-eyed God! What kind of magic did she possess to destroy with a mere thought?

"Are you okay?" Mason whispered.

I tried to focus on his face. His lip was bleeding. His eyes were dark and angry.

"It was…there were ghosts. So many ghosts. Did they all come from the bloodstone?"

"Yes," he said through clenched teeth.

My head pounded. Mason rolled me to the side and helped me sit up. We faced Polina who watched our little interaction with a sneer marring her perfect face.

"You always were a fool for love, Henry." She turned toward Pierre, who had pushed himself up again and now hovered behind her with blood dripping into his eyes from a gash on his forehead.

"Polina, I did what you asked," Pierre said. "My daughter waits outside to take you from here. Your granddaughter, of a sort. She carries your blood. I kept the line alive just as you asked. Tell me what more I can do."

Pierre trembled with joy or anticipation or a perverse combination of the two. I liked him better when he was just a mad scientist. This new sycophantic Pierre was pathetic. Polina seemed to agree.

"Do shut up." Her hand shot out, and my stomach roiled as magic hit Pierre. His mouth disappeared. It just vanished, leaving only a smooth expanse of skin from nose to chin. His eyes bulged. He tried to scream but only managed a muffled hum. He tore at his face with his nails, scoring it with red lines, before falling to his knees.

"Whoops! I guess I'm out of practice." Polina laughed. It was a girlish sound. She waved her hand again, restoring Pierre's face, but he was broken. Tears cut through the blood on his cheeks, and his eyes had gone blank and glassy.

Mason stood and faced his ex-wife. "You've been gone a long time, Polina. You won't find it so easy to do as you please now."

She flexed her neck side to side and rolled her shoulders as if testing her body.

"Really? Because I feel good. Strong. You left me in that damned prison for how long? Hundreds of years, at least. But I had company. Did you see all those souls that escaped with me? Weren't they delicious? Another hundred years and I could have consumed them all." She rubbed her stomach like a child anticipating a sweet treat.

Mason's right arm turned to stone, and he raised it to strike, but Pierre suddenly came out of his stupor and tackled him. They tumbled to the ground like a couple of brawling boys.

Polina smiled, stepped delicately over the broken glass and out the door.

"Kyra! Don't let her get away!" Mason's cry was garbled as Pierre's hands closed around his throat.

I glanced at Jacoby, lying inert among the remains of the machine, then at the door where Polina had disappeared. I followed her.

The explosion had knocked out the lights in the tunnel, leaving only the glare from the lab. I ran into darkness and stopped at the fork. To the right, lay the long, dark path back to Susanna's lab, but a faint glow—a paler blue against the blackness—told me the door was open to the right.

I dashed up the stairs and came out behind the old Stewart Hall. A blast of pure magic smashed me against the metal door and I fell, gasping for breath as the wind was knocked from my lungs.

"Does he love you?" Polina stood ten feet away. The moon graced her, and she seemed to glow like an angel of death. I braced for another blast of magic. Instead, she stepped on my fingers and twisted her foot to grind them into the cement. I screamed, then used the pain to fuel rage. With my good hand, I yanked her by the ankle. My angle was bad, and I couldn't drop her, but she staggered to regain her balance. Pain lanced through my broken fingers as I clenched them around a fistful of rock and sand and flung it at her face.

"*Putain!*" she screamed, reverting to old French in her rage.

I barely stood on shaking legs while she wiped her eyes. I had no strength left…bleeding from several cuts…my left hand useless…my wards shredded. Even in this sorry state, I couldn't shake my Aunt Dana's teachings.

Never lie down in defeat. You are Valkyrie. Act like one!

I dove at Polina and tackled her around the waist. A breath of air rushed out of her as we hit the brick wall. For a moment, I could do nothing but hang on. I punched her in the gut. It was feeble and inconsequential, but I raised my fist for another strike…

…and found myself flat on my back, staring at the stars. My limbs twitched with the remains of her magic strike. Then Polina loomed over me again.

I desperately wanted my null bracelet but couldn't move even the few inches to pull it from my pocket.

"You didn't answer my question, little whore. Does he love you?" Her face twisted in rage. Magic lashed around her in a furious cloud, making her hair billow on invisible currents. Deep creases etched a line from her mouth to nose, and her skin seemed to sag. She'd expended a lot of magic, and it was wearing on her.

I couldn't speak through the pain. I could only hope to outlast her. But then she smoothed down her hair and stepped away. The swirling magic quieted. "Of course he does. Henry always was a hopeless romantic."

How easily she tucked away her immense power. But I could still feel it coiling around her as she readied for another strike. I scrambled away, hugging my broken fingers to my chest.

Polina yelped as a figure leapt from the shadows and tackled her.

"How dare you!" Polina screamed after a brief scuffle. The figure flew, landing at my feet in a broken heap. Brown eyes stared up at me with fury.

Emil.

What was he doing here? I didn't care. I had never been so happy to see a vampire in my life. He rose and twisted a broken arm back into place, then stood between me and Polina.

"I will tear out your throat and drain you dry, witch." Emil showed his impressive fangs.

Polina looked around Emil and smiled at me. "Oh, this will be fun. Does Henry know you have another admirer?"

A car pulled up, and Susanna poked her head through the driver-side window. "Grandmother! We have to hurry!"

Polina spun. "Never call me that!"

Susanna looked stung. "Yes, Gran—I mean, yes, mistress. But we have to go." Sirens wailed in the distance. Hub was finally coming to investigate the explosion.

Polina glanced back at me with a smirk. "This is better anyway. Give Henry a big kiss for me, won't you? And tell him that we will catch up on old times soon."

She blew me a kiss. Emil lunged for her, but I held him back. She was too powerful.

Polina walked over to the car. "Such an interesting carriage. I think I'm going to enjoy this new world." She fiddled with the door for a moment, then got in, and they drove away.

I turned to Emil. "Can you wait here for Hub? Tell them to go down the stairs and turn right."

Emil nodded. "Go."

I ran back into the darkness and skidded to a stop inside the lab. Pierre and Mason were at a stand-off. Pierre had found a shard of glass and he held it like a knife, even though blood dripped from his hand. He was panting. Mason's shirt was slashed in several places, and blood matted it to his side. His left arm was still stone, and he swung it like a boxer, connecting with Pierre's jaw, then smashing down on his skull.

Pierre crumpled to the ground and didn't get up. A pool of blood spread out from his head.

We stood staring at his body for several long seconds. The only sound was Mason's breathing. It was wet and ragged, as if he'd punctured a lung.

"Get down on your knees! Hands on your heads!" A voice shouted from the doorway. Hub officers in tactical gear swarmed into the lab, their flashlights piercing the gloom like white blades.

"I said get down!" The voice shouted again and I knelt. Rough hands cuffed mine and jerked me upright. My broken fingers lashed me with pain and I nearly fainted. Mason was already cuffed beside me.

An officer knelt beside Pierre. "He's dead."

The lead officer jerked me backward. "I'm arresting you for murder and destruction of property—"

"Stop! Release these prisoners." Merrow chose that moment to drop her glamor. Sato stood beside her, looking shaken.

Merrow approached and the officers raised their guns. She held out her widget and said, "I am Queen Leighna's personal assistant, here by her orders. Check my credentials." The cop took her widget, scanned the ID and handed it back to her. "I can attest that this man was killed in self defense only." She pointed to Pierre's body. "He is the criminal here, not those two."

As the officer uncuffed me, I was happy with her intervention, but not enough to forgive the fact that she didn't step in sooner. In her true form, she could have stopped Pierre before…

Jacoby!

I ran to his side. Errol had crawled out from under him and sat leaning against the dervish with a dazed look on his face.

"Mrthbtgh." I couldn't understand him and got nothing through his mind-speak. He tried again and I shook my head. He laid his head on Jacoby's arm and tears soaked his long beard.

Jacoby lay like a limp rag. Even the fringe of gray fur around his eyes drooped. And he was still. Too perfectly still.

No! He couldn't be dead! Not Jacoby, the rascal who was so full of mischief…so full of life.

I reached for him with my keening, and felt the swell of his lungs expanding, so slowly it was barely perceptible. I dug deeper for his magic. It was there, but dim like a shuttered lantern. He was alive.

"Hey, buddy." I smoothed the fur back from his face. It was surprisingly soft. "You were very brave. You took care of Errol, just like I asked." My voice broke. I couldn't stop the tears. They couldn't take Jacoby from me. Not again. Damn Pierre and Gerard and their schemes! Damn Joran and Susanna for acting as their pawns. And damn Polina for fueling their obsessions. They'd taken Alvin and Theo, and now I could lose Jacoby.

I laid my broken hand on his frail chest. Errol stood on shaky legs and gripped my little finger. I felt another hand close over my shoulder. We stood like that—Errol, Mason and I—waiting for Jacoby to open his eyes.

ub detained us for a full day, not exactly in jail, but not free to leave either. From the small interrogation room, I watched the sun come up through a dirty window. Mason was being held in a separate room. I hoped the sunrise had come fast enough to heal his wounds, but none of the officers who came into my room would update me on his condition.

And no one mentioned Emil. Maybe he got away before Hub could detain him.

Some time after sunrise, a medic came in to treat my cuts and set my broken fingers. Detective Kesik arrived as the medic was leaving. He brought me coffee and a muffin that had known better days. He leaned a hip on the table in front of me and said nothing for nearly a minute, hoping to unnerve me. But I was too tired for games. I sipped the tepid coffee and ignored the muffin.

When he realized that his intimidation wasn't working, he sat across from me and pinned me with his gaze. "Tell me again how you ended up in the private lab of the prime minister with a dead man and contraband bloodstones."

"Now, you see, it's all about perspective. You chose all the wrong highlights. Why not ask how we managed to save the ward from a mad alchemist hell-bent on exploiting the dead souls of fae?"

Kesik leaned back, unsmiling.

"I haven't known you long, Miss Greene, but it seems like every time we meet, there's a dead body involved."

"See? Wrong perspective again. Every time we meet, I'm helping you solve a case. In fact, we handed you this one on a silver platter, complete with unbiased witnesses. Where is Merrow, anyway?"

"Gone." He finally smiled. "Back to the Queen, leaving you in my tender care."

I huffed out a breath. I really didn't like this guy, and my edges were frayed. "I have nothing more to say to you."

"Oh, you will." Kesik thumped the table with the flat of his hand and left. He tried to talk to me several more times during the day. I made one futile attempt to leave. And though Kesik insisted I wasn't under arrest—yet—there were guards outside my door.

In truth, I didn't try very hard. Mason was locked up in another room, waiting out the sun, and I wouldn't leave without him.

Before Hub had dragged me downtown, I'd called Gabe. Without question, and despite the late hour, he'd come to collect Jacoby and Errol. At least I knew they were safe at home. The best way I could help them now would be to stop Gerard Golovin from executing whatever master plan he had in the works.

For that, I needed to wait for Merrow.

I slept on and off with my head on the table, each time waking to look at the sun's position through the window, since Kesik had taken my widget. A junior officer brought me food in the afternoon. I picked at it. And when the sun set, I paced the small room until the door opened again and Merrow entered.

"Leighna wants to see you now," she said.

"Finally. I'll just go home and change first."

"No time. Golovin will be there too, and she won't be able to hold him for long."

Terrific. Merrow looked fresh and put together, like she hadn't spent the night in an exploding lab and then a day in a stuffy interrogation room. My clothes reeked of smoke, and I had little sweaters on my teeth. I didn't even want to look at my hair.

The guards were gone from outside my room, and I ran down the hall without being stopped. At least I had a fresh shirt in my Hub locker. I splashed water on my face and raked a brush through my hair before braiding it again. A quick look in the mirror told me I looked a little better than a fresh corpse. It would have to do.

I drove to the Winter Court with Mason and Angus.

Mason looked tired. The sunrise had mended his wounds, but did nothing for his state of mind.

"How's Jacoby?" he asked.

"No change." I'd called Gabe as soon as the Hub agents had given me back my widget. Jacoby was home now, but still unconscious. If it were anyone else besides the queen requesting my presence, I would have skipped out to be home by his side.

"What about him?" I jerked a thumb to the backseat where Angus sat lost in his own thoughts, staring out the window at the night.

Mason made a noncommittal shrug. "That jar of bloodstones upset him."

I could understand that. With those stones, Golovin had the potential to create dozens of gargoyles—beings like Angus who would live forever trapped in a body that was not their own and enslaved to GenPort.

Mason put the car on auto-drive—something that told me just how tired he was—and leaned his head against the seat.

"You know, I've been dreading this day for centuries. But in a way, I'm glad it's come. Polina might be free, but at least now I can stop her. Not just detain her. I'm going to end this."

"*We* will end it," I said.

He squeezed my hand. "Thank you. I know what this mess has already cost you."

I thought of Jacoby, of Alvin and Theo, of Gita and Errol, all lost or hurt by events spun out of control. Events that started when Joran first came to town.

"I've been trying to work out something. Susanna is his sister, you know. Joran's I mean. They have the same look. And Susanna called Polina 'Grandmother' too."

"Oh, I bet she loved that."

I laughed. "Not so much."

"Polina hates anything that reminds her of her mortality, even her own daughter."

"I can work with that." One day we would face her again and I'd need all the ammunition I could get. "Do you think she'll kill Susanna too?"

"Not yet. With Pierre dead, she needs to find her way in this strange world.

But as soon as Susanna outlives her usefulness, Polina will use her for some dark rite. That's how she thinks. People are tools to her."

We arrived at the Winter Court. There were only a few other cars in the lot at this time of night. Merrow parked beside us and we all headed toward the front entrance. Mason held me back until the others were out of earshot.

"I want you to know that as soon as this meeting is over, I'm leaving for France."

"What? France?" My mind frantically calculated the dangers of a journey that could only be taken by boat. "That will take months! Why?"

"Polina will want Pierre's body. She's been attached to him through some dark spell for centuries. I won't let her have it. Hub is already cremating him, and I'll take his ashes back to France."

He wouldn't look me in the eye. There was more to this reckless journey. I crossed my arms and scowled. I was tired of my people being in constant danger. And as unlikely as it seemed, Mason was definitely one of my people now.

"You realize that one in five vessels never makes it across the Atlantic."

He nodded. Since the Flood Wars, the ocean had been reclaimed by magical beasts, much like the Inbetween.

"Even so, a round trip should only take a couple of months, if I can find what I'm looking for quickly."

"And what exactly is that?"

"The only thing that has a chance of defeating Polina." He looked away, as if not wanting to commit to more. I frowned.

"And in the meantime? What if she makes a play before you return?"

He shook his head. "She's weak. She'll go into hiding and build her strength."

"I could barely fight her last night! We need to stop her now."

"I can't!" His voice was anguished. "Don't you understand? I'm not strong enough to defeat her. I never was."

"But this…this thing you're bringing back from France is?"

"Maybe. It's a long shot, but the only one we've got."

"I could go with you." I hated the smallness of my voice in that moment, but I felt like we were on the brink of something. Something bigger growing between us, and now he was leaving.

"It's too dangerous." He held up a hand when I began to protest. "And you're needed here. Tell me you'd really leave Jacoby now?"

I ground my teeth. He was right. I couldn't leave. Not for a months-long journey.

He cupped my cheek, sneaking his fingers around to the back of my neck so he could pull me closer.

"When I come back, we'll sort this out." His eyes searched mine. I willed back tears and nodded.

"Whatever this is."

"Whatever this is," he agreed. His kiss was light, a simple promise of more, then Angus called out, "Are you two planning to keep the queen waiting much longer? 'Cuz I've got to piss as it is."

Mason bumped his forehead against mine and grinned. "Time to face the firing squad."

Leighna and Gerard Golovin waited for us in the council chambers. The queen sat in her usual chair in front of the odd wall with the moving wallpaper. It looked like frost on glass that continually grew and morphed in a kaleidoscope pattern. Before her, a metal box sat on the coffee table. My keening picked up the null space around it. The box was a safe for a magical artifact.

Sato and Prime Minister Tremblay sat in chairs opposite Leighna while Golovin paced the room, stopping when we entered.

"Finally," he said. "Now will you tell us what this nonsense is all about. I have a gala to attend at the museum tonight. I'm already late." He was dressed in a black suit that shimmered with a damask pattern. It was a fashionable style that made my eyes hurt as much as Leighna's wallpaper. Every time I saw Gerard Golovin, two words came to mind: slick and dangerous, like the oil spills I remembered in my youth that devastated entire ecosystems.

"Prime Minister Golovin, sit down there, and we can proceed." Leighna pointed to the only empty chair in the room.

Gerard raised an eyebrow at her formality, then decided to be ornery and stood at the end of the table with his hands clasped behind him. Maybe he thought he looked tough and military that way, but the flashy suit ruined the effect.

"Does this have anything to do with the explosion at Abbott's Agora last night?" Gerard asked.

"Yes, it does," Merrow said.

"I hope you caught the criminals responsible." Gerard's eyes rested on me, then Mason.

"We were more concerned with the illicit experiments going on in your lab," Leighna said. "You know, the secret one in the old Stewart Hall. Your associate, Pierre Garnier, was making gargoyles for you, wasn't he? The Black Hat Act prohibits the creation of life, in any form."

A muscle twitched on Gerard's cheek, and he took too long to answer. He was deciding which was the worst of his crimes and didn't deny the existence of the second lab. "You have no proof that I was involved in any of that. I let Garnier use my lab. So what? I did an old friend a favor. I had no idea that he was into illicit magic."

"Actually, we have ample proof. Several witnesses in fact." Leighna pointed at Mason and me. "And at this moment, Hub forces are raiding your GenPort site and confiscating your gencrew. And not the Hub officers that you've been paying off. I made sure to send in fae and human advisors too." She smiled coldly.

"Now, I'm giving you one chance to come clean. We all know those gencrew are not automatons, or golems or whatever you want to call them. They're gargoyles, animated by the souls of fae citizens stolen right off the streets of this ward."

"I had no idea what Garnier was doing. And you can't prove otherwise." Gerard's face reddened. "I'll see you crucified in the media for this, Leighna. Your approval ratings are already at an all-time low after your brother's attempted coup last year. This will finally take you down."

Leighna leaned forward and opened the box on the table. Magic brushed against my wards as she revealed the bloodstones. "No, Gerard. It's your turn to step down. These were found in your lab. Your personal lab."

"A bunch of rocks? That's your proof?" Gerard scoffed.

"I think you know these are no ordinary rocks. Anyone with a bit of keening or a good thaumagauge can sense the magic coming off them. These are bloodstones. Each one holds a soul you stole. Someone your takers killed for this purpose."

"You can't prove I had anything to do with it!" His voice rose, flirting with the edges of hysteria.

Merrow stood and faced him. "I was there, Gerard. So was Sato. We heard Pierre Garnier confess before he died. Along with Henry Mason and the Valkyrie, we have witnesses from all three parties and one independent. And by morning, we'll have your gencrew in custody. That's enough to sway any judge."

Gerard swung his gaze around the room, finding no allies in this group. Then a switch flicked in his head and his expression went from defensive to offensive. He clenched both fists at his sides.

"You are fools. The gods are fickle. Terra will take as easily as she gives. Have you all forgotten the Flood Wars already? Need I remind you how Terra shut down entire governments by flooding the land with magic? An effective way to kill a society so reliant on technology. And what about us? What do we rely on? Magic. It fuels your city, runs your cars and heats your homes. Magic given to us by Terra. What happens when she takes it all away? We'll need an alternate source of energy. That, ladies and gentlemen, is our future." He pointed to the bowl of bloodstones.

Prime Minister Tremblay rose and jabbed a finger at Gerard. "Terra won't take away magic as long as we live within our means. As long as arrogant fools like you stop trying to expand our footprint."

Tremblay had been against the GenPort expansion from the beginning.

"And how long do you think Montreal can continue to thrive under Terra's restraints?" continued Gerard, exasperated with our stupidity. "We can't grow any further and expect to feed our population because some angry god is always ready to take back any new land we clear for crops. We can't dig for fossil fuels anymore. We can't expand off this island at all. Terra is nothing but a big mother hen, who's so concerned with keeping her nest safe, she's going to smother her chicks. And you're the fools who will let her." He was panting now. He held out his hands. "So are you going to arrest me or not? I have a gala to get to."

Leighna rose. She looked at Prime Minister Tremblay, who nodded. Then she turned to Gerard.

"I think we can all agree that arresting one of Montreal's prime ministers will cause civil unrest that we can ill afford right now."

Gerard looked smug, but Leighna wasn't finished. "But you will step down as prime minister and leader of the Alchemist Party immediately. I don't care what excuse you use, but make it believable. Your gencrew have already been taken into custody. They will be destroyed along with the bloodstones. You will be forbidden access to Perrot Island, Abbott's Agora and any other alchemy property. I can't stop you from building your damned railroad since parliament has already passed funding for it. But know that we will be watching you, and if I even hear a rumor of impropriety on that construction site again, I will shut you down and deal with parliament later."

Gerard glowered at her, but just nodded. He strode to the door, stopping in front of Mason.

"Looks like you'll finally get what you've always wanted—control of the alchemists. Just remember, it's only yours because a better man had to step away."

Mason's face was impassive as Gerard stormed out.

"Though I don't agree with his last assessment," Leighna said, "I do hope you will consider running for prime minister."

Mason shook his head. "I'm sorry, I can't do that. As long as my curse stands, I would be an ineffective leader."

Leighna nodded. "Fair enough."

"But please, tell me what has been done about Polina," Mason said. "Has Hub found her? Did she try to leave the city?"

Merrow stepped forward to answer. "Hub has not been looking for her. You forget that I was witness to events last night. From my perspective, the lady Polina is a victim in this as much as the rest of us. More perhaps."

"So that's it?" I said. "You're just going to let her go? She tried to kill her own child."

"Of that, we have only your word. And even if it's true, I'm quite sure that we can't prosecute a three-hundred-year-old crime." She turned to Mason. "And you should be grateful for that, since by your own admission, Mr. Mason, you are the one who imprisoned her in that stone."

"So they win," Mason said. "Gerard goes free and Polina too. She's quite mad, you know. She won't just disappear. And she has no skills to assimilate into our world. It's not like she'll get a job as a waitress and raise a family."

"Then perhaps we should be trying to help her instead of hunting her." Merrow glared at Mason, and he glared back. Then his shoulders sagged just a fraction. He shook his head.

"Fine." He headed for the door. "You do what you have to do, and I'll do what I have to do."

Leighna, Merrow and Tremblay were already ignoring us as they made plans to fill the void on the council with a new alchemist leader. Mason stopped at the door to meet my eye.

I love you, I mouthed the words silently. From across the room, Mason gave me a small smile, and my heart seized. I should have told him sooner. I should have told him the night he opened up to me and showed me his family. Now it was too late. France was a long way off.

He said a silent *goodbye*. Then he was gone.

Gita created a shrine for Jacoby. He lay on a cushion of folded blankets on the ottoman in my living room, his bear backpack tucked under his arm. Each morning she replaced the garlands of fresh flowers and herbs that surrounded his unresponsive body. Errol kept vigil at his side, watching the slow rise and fall of Jacoby's chest with a grim expression.

I kept telling myself that some small ember of life still burned in Jacoby, and he would wake up soon. Every day that passed made it harder to keep believing.

Gita and Gabe conspired to let me rest. Gabe postponed all my jobs to give my hand time to heal. Gita fed the critters so I could sleep in. Even Hunter behaved. They were trying to take care of me the only way they knew how. But nothing would mend my heart until Jacoby woke.

Despite their efforts, I didn't sleep well. Something about the whole encounter with Pierre, Polina and Susanna nagged at me. And Friday morning, three days after the explosion in the lab, certain knowledge woke me like a spike in my gut.

Still in my pajamas, I hurried to the living room and fired up my computer. It was old and took a few minutes to boot. I could hear Gabe talking on his widget through the office door, assuring customers that I would return to work soon.

Gita brought me a steaming cup of coffee just as my computer blinked on.

"You should not be working today," she said. Her face was a mess of tears. Nearly losing Jacoby had finally jarred her back to her normal banshee mindset.

"I'm not working. I just need to check something." I called up my blog and scanned the comments on posts going back a year. Where was it?

"There!" I stared at the post I'd written last spring about the shushers. Someone named Daddysgirl had made the five-by-five reference. It was an expression made famous by a character on *Buffy the Vampire Slayer,* a show that was old even when I was a teen. It was such an odd saying that it had stuck with me.

And Susanna had said the same thing as she left the lab that night.

I stared at the screen, unbelieving. Not wanting to believe. Then I frantically scrolled through my posts. Daddysgirl had commented on every one of them going back to…

Going back to my original post about gargoyles when I'd first met Mason. Dear gods.

"This is my fault." Even to my ears, my voice sounded hollow and tinny.

"What's this?" Gabe said as he came into the living room. I swiveled the screen so he could see.

"Susanna is Daddysgirl. She's been stalking me online for two years. I'm the reason they came for the bloodstone in the first place! I'm the reason that Jacoby is gone!"

"Hey, hey!" Gabe knelt by my side and pushed the computer away. I covered my face in my shaking hands. It was all my fault.

"Look at me." He pulled my hands away, careful not to rattle the bandaged one. I looked into his sweet face, with eyes darkened by worry. "First off, Jacoby isn't gone. We'll find a way to wake him."

"You don't understand! Susanna is Joran's sister. She's been here for at least two years, learning about Mason, and I led her right to him."

Gabe scowled. "That doesn't mean—"

"But it does! Look. The first time she posted was when I wrote about the Guardians. That's what brought Joran to Montreal. I did that! And now Cyril is dead and Jacoby is…" I choked off a sob. Gabe gathered me in like a small child with a big hurt.

He patted my back for a moment, then forced me to sit up. He wiped my tears with the cuff of his sleeve then tipped my chin up so I looked him right in the eye.

"Listen to me. You are not responsible for the evil that other people do. Your blog helps people to help animals. Every day, I get messages asking about one critter or another. Some days I spend more time fielding those emails than actual work calls. You created a community from a fractured world, and you should be proud of it."

I sniffled and nodded, wanting to believe, but I wondered if Mason would agree. I was responsible for all the problems in the last year, and for the death of one of his Guardians. If I were him, I'd never speak to me again.

"It will turn out all right," Gabe said. "You'll see. But you might want to get dressed. There's a sheepish looking vampire waiting in the office to see you."

Emil lounged in my chair with man-spreading legs. He leaned his elbows on his knees and hung his head as if contemplating the linoleum.

"Were you following me Friday night? Is that why you were waiting outside Stewart Hall?" I crossed my arms and leaned against the door frame. His curls and innocent charm wouldn't fool me. I'd made that mistake with Susanna.

"Yes." He spread his hands wide. "But only to apologize for my bad behavior when I..."

He couldn't seem to find the words, so I supplied them. "When you broke into my home, stole my sword, and spilled your blood all over my floor?"

Emil shook his head and rose. "I'm sorry. I shouldn't have come." Before he made it to the door, I stopped him.

"No, I'm sorry." I rubbed my tired eyes. "You helped me, probably saved my life. And I appreciate it. Really."

Emil hesitated, ready to leave, then nodded.

"I don't think that woman—she is a witch?"

I nodded.

"I don't think she wanted to kill you. Not yet, anyway."

"Yeah, I got that feeling too." Polina had other plans. Or maybe, despite her impressive display of magic, her power was rusty. Before she'd run off, she'd seemed weary. But now, thanks to Susanna's intervention, she'd have the chance to regroup and re-energize. I really didn't want to meet her when she was at full strength.

"Can I offer you some coffee? Or blood? I think I have some left."

"No. I just came to apologize properly. I am trying to control the blood lust." His eyes sparked with gold for a moment. "But it's not easy. I'm thinking of traveling the Inbetween for a while."

"That's not a good idea. The opji hunt outside the ward. They won't take kindly to another vampire in their territory."

He shrugged.

"I have a better idea." I rifled through the drawer of my desk and found the spell that Leighna had given me. I handed it to Emil, and he held it delicately, like he'd never seen real paper before.

"What's this?"

"A spell that Queen Leighna gave me to put my sword into stasis. It may take some practice, but I think it would work for your blood lust too."

He read the ingredients and instructions with a frown.

"But I have no magic to enact spells."

I tapped his chest, feeling the magic course through him.

"Of course you do. You just have to learn to tap into it."

He looked down at my hand, his expression sad.

"Could you teach me?"

"No. But I happen to know a bodach who is a great teacher." And Errol could use the distraction.

"Then I will learn." He smiled and his face regained his boyish charm.

Once he controlled that pesky blood lust, he was going to be a lady killer, but not in the literal sense.

I thought of Leighna's warning.

"One last thing. If you decide to use the spell, a kiss will break it."

Emil ran a thumb down the side of my face. "Well, it's a good thing then, I have no one to kiss."

Dear Reader,

You probably know that authors love reviews, but do you know why? Reviews are important because they help other readers know what to expect from the book, they let me know how my books are received by readers, and they help booksellers decide which books to show to new readers.

If you enjoyed this book I would be grateful for your honest review. It can be as short as you like. Even a few positive words will go a long way. And I'll try to make it as painless as possible. Use this link to find the review site of your choice. kimmcdougall.com/review-dervishes-don-t-dance.

And thank you for joining me on Kyra's adventure!

Kim McDougall

Want to find out more about Kyra's world?

Learn more about the Valkyrie Bestiary series at KimMcDougall.com including deleted scenes and more series fun.

Or join Kim McDougall's reader group to get the latest release updates and a free eBook at KimMcDougall.com/contact.

Poke around at Kyra's blog at ValkyrieBestiary.com

Other places you can follow Kim McDougall: Amazon, BookBub, Goodreads, Facebook, Twitter, or Instagram.

WHAT TO READ NEXT

Critter wrangler rule #7: Some monsters just have to die.

Someone is plotting to put all gargoyles in jail…or six feet in the ground.

For decades gargoyles have patrolled the night in Montreal Ward. They are dubbed Guardians by the humans and fae who live on the fringes of society, those who survive in neighborhoods the police don't care about. But when a Guardian is accused of murder, their reputation blackens.

Mason promised to return from France with the one weapon capable of killing the formidable witch who was reborn from the bloodstone, but no one has heard from him in months. Now Polina gathers forces. Without Mason or the Guardians, Kyra has no backup as she tries to solve a murder and face off against new and terrifying monsters…all while caring for her growing menagerie of extraordinary critters.

A new adventure in the Inbetween, where magic is the only rule of law. Hell Hounds Don't Heel is the third book in the Valkyrie Bestiary Series.

Hell Hounds Don't Heel is the third book in the Valkyrie Bestiary Series, and is now available in eBook, audiobook, paperback and hard cover.

Find it at https://kimmcdougall.com/hell-hounds-don-t-heel

About the Author

If Kim McDougall could have one magical superpower, it would be to talk to animals. Or maybe to shift into animal form. Definitely, fantastical critters and magic often feature in her stories. So until she can change into a griffin and fly away, she writes dark paranormal action and romance tales, from her home in Central Ontario. Visit Kim online at www.KimMcDougall.com